PRAISE FOR
KINGDOM COME
AND
TIM GREEN

"Green keeps the suspense building and the reader continually off guard." —*Chicago Tribune*

"Green's fans will enjoy his latest action-packed crime caper." —**HarrietKlausner.wwwi.com**

"Green is a craftsman of the written word." —*Winston-Salem Journal*

"A bravura thriller with brass knuckles." —**EDGEBoston.com**

"Green keeps the pages turning." —*Booklist*

"A helluva good ride." —**Who-dunnit.com**

"Green is a master scene-setter." —**NELSON DEMILLE, author of *Wild Fire***

"Green has a great ear for dialogue [and he] writes with admirable economy." —*Kirkus Reviews*

Money from the bank starts to flow.

ALSO BY TIM GREEN

Fiction

Nonfiction

TIM GREEN

KINGDOM COME

WARNER BOOKS

NEW YORK   BOSTON

Copyright © 2006 by Tim Green
Excerpt from *American Outrage* copyright © 2007 Tim Green

Cover design by Flag
Cover photograph © Stockbyte / Picture Quest

Warner Books
Hachette Book Group USA
1271 Avenue of the Americas
New York, NY 10020
Visit our Web site at www.HachetteBookGroupUSA.com

Printed in the United States of America

Originally published in hardcover by Warner Books
First Paperback Printing: March 2007

10 9 8 7 6 5 4 3 2 1

For Illyssa, because,
All days are nights to see till I see thee,
And nights bright days when dreams do show thee me.
—SHAKESPEARE (SONNET 43)

ACKNOWLEDGMENTS

With each book I write, there are many people who help with essential steps along the way, and I would like to thank them.

Esther Newberg, the world's greatest agent and my dear friend, for her wisdom. Ace Atkins, my dependable, brilliant, and talented friend, for his careful reading and fantastic ideas. Jamie Raab, my publisher and editor, who polished this story with unmatched insight and creativity. And the women who worked with her, Frances Jalet-Miller and Kristen Weber, as well as all my friends at Warner Books: Larry Kirshbaum, who's no longer with the company but who, along with Rick Wolff, gave me my chance; Maureen Egen; Chris Barba and the best sales team in the world; Emi Battaglia; Karen Torres; Martha Otis; Paul Kirschner; Flag Tonuzi; Jim Spivey; Mari Okuda; Fred Chase; and Tina Andreadis, who we'll all miss.

My parents, Dick and Judy Green, who taught me to

read and to love books and who spent many hours scouring this manuscript so that it shines.

A special thanks to former FBI agent John Gamel, who helped me navigate the inner workings of the FBI and kindly took my calls at all hours of the day.

AUTHOR'S NOTE

This is a work of fiction. My good friends Mike Allen, Tim McCarthy, Bucky Lainhart, Darlene Baker, and Scott Congel inspired me as I was creating the characters called Mike Allen; Tim McCarthy; Darlene Baker; Bucky, his wife, Judy, and their son, Russel; and the Scott King character and his wife, Emily. But all of the other characters, including in particular James King, are completely fictitious and the product of my imagination. Scott Congel's real father, Bob Congel, is in fact a close personal friend who has treated me and my family like part of his, with great kindness and generosity. He is no closer to the James King character than I am to Thane Coder. So any resemblance of these characters to real persons, living or dead, is coincidental. In addition, some real locations and actual events are mentioned, but they, too, are used fictitiously.

Stars, hide your fires:
Let not light see my black and deep desires:
The eye wink at the hand; yet let that be
Which the eye fears, when it is done, to see.
—MACBETH: ACT 1, SCENE 4, LINES 50–53

1

Most people would have done what I did," I say.

"That's an interesting statement," the shrink says. "Most people wouldn't kill a man who was like a father to them."

"He wasn't my father."

"I said 'like' a father."

I nod, because that was true.

"I guess, when you think about it," I say, "he gave me things my father never did. But he also took things away. Money. My wife. My child. Things no father would take from his son."

"What do you mean he took them?" the shrink asks. "That's not what really happened, is it? He didn't take your wife."

"Okay. He moved the pieces on the board in a way that they were taken from me. It's all the same."

"And he deserved to die for that? The others too?"

"I don't know if any of them deserved it," I say. "But it happened, and it would have happened that way to most people. All I wanted was to get ahead, to have my wife, my family."

"Do you really think so, Thane?" he says, looking at his note-book. "That most people would have done what you did?"

"I thought you shrinks are supposed to ask about my mother. What's all this father stuff?"

"You didn't kill your mother-figure," he says in his deep rumble of a voice.

"Or my wife."

He raises an eyebrow. "Why do you mention her? Did she deserve what happened?"

I look away and sigh. "In a way. Maybe. I dream about it. Her."

"Freud said dreams are wishes," he says. "Look. Let's just start from the beginning. How about you tell me the story?"

"So you can write a book?" I ask.

"So I can help."

"You think I need help?" I say. "I'm a shell. A couple of weeks and I'm out of here. This is just going through the motions. I'll walk out of here and I won't even be Thane Coder anymore. Mike Jenkins. That's the name they're giv-ing me. They've got me a job in a metal shop. Fifteen dol-lars an hour and a little two-bedroom box outside Boze-man. You ever been to Montana?"

"You're still a person," he says. "You still need to cope."

Over the past six years, I've seen other guys like this. Other shrinks with dreams of helping those beyond help, or who didn't have what it takes to have an officeful of books and leather furniture. They never really help. They just dredge up the muck that's better off left at the bot-tom. But there's something about the idea of finally being free that makes me giddy enough to want to talk, even about this.

"How far back?" I ask with a sigh.

"What about the storm?" he says, tapping his pen. "Tell me about that. From what I've seen in your file, that seems to push a button."

On the other side of the brick and bars, I hear the sound of the scum spilling out into the yard below. Hooting in the cold air. Their words drift skyward in smoky puffs. The noise of their obscene banter is muffled by the dirty window of the small square room. I look out and see the wall. At its crest the empty eye of the tower stares down. A guard bent over a book. His rifle nowhere in sight.

I think about Jessica, my wife. Pretty dark hair. Sexy in a girlish way. She was a sweet girl. That's how I'd describe her, what she was, even after everything. Even though I blame her.

How sick.

How could a prison head doctor understand that?

"I never thought I could kill anyone," I say, then I sigh again because I know I'm going to tell him, even though it won't do either of us any good.

"I don't mean in a rage, or in self-defense, or in a war. I mean killing someone to get what you want. That wasn't me. But even the best of us has that bad side. I'm not saying I was the best, but I wasn't the worst either. I think I was about where most people are. It was the situation."

He's taking notes now, the blue Bic rolling across the yellow paper. One fat finger is constricted by a college ring with an orange stone. The gold inscriptions are flattened and worn. I'm used to the shrinks writing when I talk, but not this way, in big looping letters that list to one side.

"What?" he says.

"Nothing. I loved my wife. Jessica. I loved the men too. The ones I killed. You believe that? But love, hate. Sometimes they're close, right?"

The shrink smiles like I just figured out that the world is round. He grabs his college ring and gives it a twist.

"And, I wanted the money. Real money. Yeah, I know. I had millions coming to me. But the more money you have, the more you want. You own a mansion on the beach in Tortola, you want a private plane to get there. Then your neighbor takes you out on his yacht and you think how nice that'd be. Maybe a chopper to get there quicker. It never ends. Trust me, when I started out, I thought if I could make a hundred thousand dollars a year with a mortgage-free house I'd have everything I ever needed. That was before Jessica, though."

"You blame that on her, then?" he asks. "This greed."

"I grew up where you didn't try to pass things off on other people," I say. "But you listen, then you figure out how much of it was me and how much her. You'll get it."

I take a deep breath and say: "Six years ago, but it doesn't seem that long. It was a bad night."

"In what way?"

"In the way that after that, it was all downhill," I say. "The weather too, this cold rain and wet snow that fell straight down. The sky was black."

2

I WAS SHIVERING. SLUSH PLASTERED the hair to my head in ropes. Melted snow dripped off my nose into my mouth. I wiped it with the tip of my finger and smelled the dead animal smell of the batting gloves on my hands. My black windbreaker rubbed quietly against my jeans while the rubber boots that came up almost to my knees squeaked softly.

My truck waited out on the road, outside the boundaries of the ten-thousand-acre hunting preserve, far enough away so that no one would see me come or go. It was a two-and-a-half-mile walk to the lodge. I call it a lodge, but that doesn't give you the real picture.

The place was as big as the man who created it. A monster laid out nearly three hundred feet end to end. Something out of Disney World. Out of scale. Logs as thick as manholes and longer than telephone poles stacked three stories high. The roof, two-inch-thick rough-cut cedar planks, towered above. The main chimney stood fifty feet tall. The foundation boulders were the size of small cars.

Inside there was fifty thousand square feet of space

with beds for forty people. European antiques, ancient firearms, Remington bronze casts, mounted animal heads, and century-old paintings filled every open space. There was a movie theater, a hot tub room, a catering kitchen, an elevator, and a wine cellar with catacombs like an English castle.

I walked to the bridge and stood where you could see the house across the half-mile-wide man-made lake while a bizarre flash of lightning brightened the sky. There was no thunder, only silence so strong that it hummed in my ears. In that blink of light, I saw a truck left outside next to the dark brown lodge. It looked like a Matchbox toy next to the building. Through the falling slush, a dull yellow glow leaked from the upper windows.

The lodge had been built on a peninsula and I had to go another mile, around the back end of the lake and into the woods guarding the main entrance with only the sound of my squeaking boots to keep me company. A circular cobblestone drive led upward to the main entrance and then back down past a small apple orchard and to an underground parking garage. I trudged up, my boots slapping in the slush, then descended a hidden set of wrought iron stairs that led to a lower level beneath the elevated drive. The space was dank with the smell of wet stone.

The double doors—like all the doors in the lodge—were salvaged from an eleventh-century Persian fortress. They were arched, bound and studded in bronze with bolts and hinges meant to keep invaders out. But this was upstate New York, a rural place where people left the keys in their cars and their front doors unlocked. The security system at the lodge was to protect against stealth, not force. Every entrance electronically monitored by Eye Pass.

Family members and a handful of close friends—
I was considered something in between—all had their
retina patterns programmed in the system. I punched the
button and put my eye to the small opening, staring into
the green light until there was a small sharp beep.

The lock clicked and the light on the keypad went
from red to green. One muted rumble of thunder rolled
overhead as I slipped inside.

When I shut the door, I could hear the blood pulsing
in my temples. Water dripped off me onto the stone floor.
On the wall I saw my picture, among all the photos from
hunts over the years. I was posed between James King
and his son Scott. Ben was there too, the four of us with
shotguns, a black Lab, and big smiles, a double row of
broken mallards beneath our waders.

Past the picture wall were racks of camouflage hunting clothes. Jackets, pants, and hats. A wall full of boots.
Blaze orange for deer season. Leafy green for turkey.
Pale yellow striped with brown cattails for duck. Ahead
stood three mounted wolves fighting a moose. Another
mount showed a bear doing battle with a bull elk.

A yellow light spilled out from the hot tub room. The
sound of the churning water made my stomach queasy.
I eased my way close enough so I could peer through
the bars in the ancient doors. Plush ruby red towels and
steam curling up from the bubbling cobblestone pool,
but no one in the tub. I slipped inside and checked the
showers.

Empty.

I steadied myself against the rough granite wall and
breathed the warm damp air. When the pounding in my
head subsided, I headed for the family hunting lockers, looking for the one with "Scott" painted on a wood

placard along with a birch tree and a wolverine. I knew the combination. Why wouldn't I? Scott and I had been good friends since college. He taught me to hunt.

The door clicked and swung open. The light went on. The bone-handled knife was on a shelf. Scott traded a pair of jeans for the razor-sharp blade with a Mozambican poacher while he was on a safari. I unsheathed it, eased the door shut, and crept up the back stairs and then through the kitchen and all the way to the third level.

I tiptoed down the wide hallway under the gaze of all those dead animals. The door to the master suite was locked, but I knew how to open it from when Scott and I would sneak girls out to the lodge and take turns as to who got to sleep with their date on the big bed with the coyote pelt comforter. College days long past.

I worked carefully, stopping every few seconds to listen for sounds from within. But then I was in there with the stuffed ducks, the stone fireplace, and the leather furniture. The big cherry bed rested diagonally in the middle of the room with that comforter thrown over the footboard. I looked down at the man who did more to shape my life than my own father.

Silence.

James slept on his back. I blinked and moved my face close to his to be sure it was him even though I knew. It was the first time I'd ever seen the man with his eyes closed and his mouth open wide beneath that round red nose. His brow was lined from years of high stakes, but his thick jowls were slack. The corners of his eyes were creased with sleep and age and tufts of his white mane showed thin and graying against the snowy pillow.

My heart beat fast and hard and my throat felt like it was going to close. My eyes moved off his face. His red and white striped pajamas were held closed by pearly white buttons.

I concentrated on the second button from the top while I raised the long blade and a feather pillow from the bed. I forced myself to focus on the stabbing motion of the knife, not murder. Just punching the blade through a pajama top the way you'd stab a piece of rotten fruit with a pencil when you were a kid.

A carnival of thoughts washed through my head. Everything I'd have if I did it. Everything I'd lose if I didn't. It all pointed to Johnny G, the union boss, and the deal he cut, not with me, but with Jessica. If we helped get rid of James, and made it look like his own son had done the deed, then I would control King Corp. I could cut a deal with the union, use their men and their contractors to build Garden State Center.

They'd get their money, I'd get the power of running things, and Jessica and I would get kickbacks. Cash. We agreed to do it, and once you cut a deal with this union, there was no going back. It was my life, or James's. When I got to that realization and it still wasn't enough, I thought of Teague, my infant son. I thought of his shiny white coffin, the size of a small tool chest, and I just did it. I plunged that knife and smothered his rage with the pillow at the same time.

James King jerked back and forth under my full weight, but only for half a minute and that surprised me. I guess I expected something more from a man who had moved so many other men's lives like chess pieces. I took the pillow away slowly. But the bone-handled knife was buried to its hilt and the dark scarlet stain had already spread beyond the pajamas and onto the sheets.

3

I SAID SCOTT TAUGHT ME TO HUNT, but it was the times with James that taught me how to kill. Two weeks before he died, we were out with a banker, Bart Swinson. I didn't usually get into the financing aspect, but Bart was a big college football fan who actually remembered my glory days at Syracuse. James thought it would be a good thing to have me around.

The early light was weak, but I could see the smoke of James's breath in the damp dawn air. James adjusted his gun barrel. I knew he was nudging the red dot of his laser-sight just a bit to where the aorta joined the heart. That was the perfect shot.

He inhaled deep and caressed the trigger. It was his if he wanted it, but instead, he relaxed his finger and without moving anything else, nudged an elbow into the banker's ribs. Bart inhaled sharply and swung his .300 Ruger in a broad arc that startled the deer. I bit the inside of my cheek and blinked at the sound of the shot. The deer tumbled, but then jumped up and started to run.

"Missed," James said.

"No," Swinson said. "It went down."

"Missed the kill shot," I said.

We were decked out in new Cabela's camouflage jackets, pants, and hats, sitting in padded chairs lined up along the south opening of a European game stand. A twelve-by-twelve-foot tower of stone, twenty feet high with a cedar shake roof and a propane heater. The tower stood in the middle of a clover field that was flanked on either side by wooded slopes. It was early in the season for killing deer, but Cascade was a ten-thousand-acre preserve surrounded by a high fence that let us operate under a different set of rules.

We descended the tower's stairs and went to the spot in the field where the deer had been. A spray of crimson blood was spattered across the clover. James knelt down and picked a blade. He held it up in the early dawn light and sniffed it.

"Gut shot," he said.

I pursed my lips and shook my head.

"What?" Bart said.

"Bad way to go," I said.

"I thought these things took them down," Bart said, hefting his nickel-plated .300.

"Got to hit them right," James said, patting him on the back. "Don't worry, we'll find it."

"You sure?" Bart said. He was from New York City and it was his first deer.

"Want me to call Bucky?" I asked.

"No," James said to me. "He's showing those marine biologists from Harvard his spawning program. They can't figure out how he does it."

"The guy who built the lodge?" Bart asked. "The guy I met last night who takes care of the place?"

"He's the best hunter I've ever seen," James said. "Russia. South America. Africa. No one better."

"I thought he was a builder."

"He's everything," I said, walking in the direction the deer had run and kneeling down to pick my own cloverleaf.

We went up a hillside and through a thick stand of saplings shot through with brambles. By the time we reached the top of the ridge, Bart had to stop, hands on his knees to catch his breath. In front of us was a field, bisected by massive power lines.

James broke out of the trees and stood over the banker, patting his back. The sun wasn't up yet, but the sky was blue. I knew by the look on James's face that he wanted me to push on, so I started off, keeping my eyes on the blood trail, but listening to James.

"Thane's got a plan," he said to Bart. "We should be able to get our steel in by the end of the week."

"You cut a deal with the unions?" Bart said, his eyes wide.

"No," James said, "we're going around them, or over them, I guess. Thane got his hands on some Sikorskys. We're airlifting in the steel."

"Well . . . that's—"

"Great news, right?" I said, stopping so they could catch up, then continuing on the trail.

"Listen," James said, patting the banker hard on the back, "I get the feeling your people were ready to call in the outstanding loans we already have. I know they didn't believe a project this big could really happen. But this will put us officially 'under construction.' That'll lock in our tenants. My son Scott's got signed leases with Home Depot, JC Penney, Lord & Taylor, BJ's, Circuit City, Costco, and Target. Stores that have never even been on the same site before."

"The biggest project ever," I said. "Every banker from London to Singapore will be camping outside our door."

We had reached the other edge of the field and looked down into a gloomy tree-filled ravine. I put up my hand.

"Shhh."

I crouched down and grabbed Bart by the collar, pulling him behind a thick oak tree. The loamy scent of dirt and dead leaves filled the air.

"He's right there," James said in a whisper. "Get your gun up."

Bart fumbled with the .300, bringing it to his shoulder. His arms were shaking.

"Where?" he said in a hiss, looking over the top of his scope.

James peeked around the edge of the tree.

"Just this side of the stream," he whispered. "Next to that big black stump."

Bart nodded and aimed his rifle.

"Safety off," James said, flicking the gun's safety off for him.

Bart nodded again. James raised his own gun, aiming it. I saw him pull the trigger almost the instant Bart shot. The deer went over like a duck in a shooting gallery. James dropped his gun to his side and Bart jumped up, whooping and hugging us, slapping high-fives.

"God damn," Bart said. "I did it."

We half walked, half slid down into the bottom of the ravine. James took out his hunting knife and slit open the animal's belly. Bart lost some color and looked away.

"Nice one," James said. "Big day for you, Bart. First kill and a huge new deal with King Corp."

"Deal?"

"We thought we'd give you a chance to do the deal," James said. "You're our biggest bank relationship."

James cut the deer's throat and spilled the guts out onto the ground. He sliced off a wedge of the liver and held it up to Bart.

"First deer," he said. "You gotta eat the liver."

"Two billion dollars at one hundred over LIBOR," I said, gripping the banker's bony shoulder through the jacket. LIBOR was the lending rate set by the London banks between themselves. One hundred points over that was merely one percent.

Bart looked from the scarlet meat to James and made a laughing sound.

"I can't do that."

James shrugged and, dangling the meat, said, "Then you're out. You gotta do this though."

"That's what they do?" Bart said, blinking at him. "Really?"

"Everyone."

Bart took it from him and nibbled at it, wincing.

"The whole thing," I said, slapping his back. "Come on."

Bart put it in his mouth and swallowed, choking, but keeping it down. James and I laughed.

"Come on," James said, "you don't get the deal, but you got the buck. This'll look great over your fireplace."

James grabbed one of the deer's hind legs. I grabbed the other and we started dragging it to the top of the ravine, sticks snapping beneath our boots. Bart stood there watching.

"We can do a deal," Bart said, scrambling to catch up and helping himself up by grasping the trunks of small trees.

"No, you're out," James said, looking back.

We were at the top of the ridge now and breathing hard. James looked out over the open field at the orange glow in the eastern sky and inhaled deeply.

"You know what I love?" James said, nudging the carcass with his boot. "Bucky's boys will clean this up, butcher it like they do at the grocery store, and it'll show up on the table in a week or so with a good bottle of Meritage."

"Why am I out?" Bart asked.

James looked off at the sky again, then back at Bart and said, "Because I gave you a chance and you don't want it. The Bank of Switzerland will take it and be glad."

James shook Bart's hand.

"Congratulations," he said. "Bucky will be along to get you. Let him know if you want it mounted. He's got a great taxidermist."

James turned and started to walk away across the field, leaving us.

"James," Bart said, raising his voice. "I can't do one hundred over LIBOR. No one can. Two fifty I can do, maybe."

James kept walking.

"It's the biggest retail development in the world," I said. "It's thirty minutes from New York City and it's ours. It's happening."

"You guys are overextended," Bart said, his voice as clear as a bell, directing it at James's back. "Everyone knows that too. This thing's gone on for three years. You've leveraged every project you own. This preserve, even. There are other banks you owe. If your loans get called, King Corp could go under. You can't demand one hundred over LIBOR from that position."

"We'll find out when he gets back to the lodge," I said.

"James, you don't just do deals like this," Bart said, yelling to him.

"When he capitalizes this deal," I said, my voice low, but carrying clearly in the quiet dawn, "the rest of our projects will drop like fruit. If you're out, you know what he'll do to you. He'll spend the next six months refinancing every project your bank owns and your bonus will look like a dishwasher's paycheck."

"One hundred is insane, James," Bart yelled. "I could be a laughingstock."

James was across the field now, and he ducked into the woods.

All of a sudden, Bart took off running after him. I jogged along, chuckling. Sticks snapped under his feet as he chased James down into the wooded ravine.

When he caught up, he said, "Jesus, how am I going to look?"

"Like you beat everyone else to the punch," James said, smiling, reaching up the hill, and holding out his hand. "Now you go wait for Bucky with the deer and we'll meet you. Come on, Thane."

"But you're not calling UBS, right?"

"We have a deal, don't we?"

Bart nodded.

James set off through the woods at a pace that left me breathing hard, taking long strides until we came to the bridge. Across the water, rising out of the mist, the lodge lay sleeping like a giant.

"Look at that," James said. He put his hand on my shoulder and gave me a brief squeeze. "Family. At the end of the day, that's what it's about."

4

"What about your family?" the shrink asks in a voice too quiet for a man his size.

"Blue-collar. My dad was a whip-your-ass-with-the-belt guy until my older brother died. Drunk driving with his friends. After that, my old man's hair turned white. He barely talked.

"My mom dropped out too. She'd sit in this old La-Z-Boy rocker, eyes glued to the tube or a romance novel. Meals pretty much came from a can or they didn't come at all."

"It's hard for any of us to think of parents as just people," he says.

"I remember when I got a scholarship at Syracuse to play football," I say. "They gave me some spending cash—the school, I mean—and I got my mom one of those reclining chairs that gives you a massage that she used to beg my dad for. She never even sat in it. That's where she stacked her books."

"You said a scholarship," he says in a hushed tone. "That's a big deal where I come from."

I twist up my lips, nod, and say, "I was a second-team

All-America middle linebacker, drafted in the sixth round by the Giants. The American dream. Right. Four days into camp I tore up my rotator cuff. That was it. Big deal."

"And you felt, how?"

"Like a loser."

"You went further than a lot of people."

"After I met Jessica, I did. The development business was like checkers to her. She could show you how to move a piece and there you'd be, staring at a triple jump. Not like Machiavellian tactics, just little maneuvers that changed the balance.

"They all loved her. Bankers. Tenants. She had this easy-going way, looking people in the eye, listening to their stories, laughing at their jokes, and really laughing, having fun, everybody liking her and me too by extension. Anytime there was a big deal to get done, if I could get that guy and his wife together with me and Jessica, it was in the bag.

"She was on top of things, office politics, the deals being done, and we'd strategize together about how to get ahead. And she was nice about it. It didn't seem like some campaign strategy. She didn't nag me. We were partners and she always made me feel like I was in the lead, like I finally found the way I could climb to the top and that she was just there to carry my water bottle."

"A wife can be a big asset," he says.

"I think she wanted me to do well because of how she grew up," I say. "Her father died and left them with a bunch of debts, and they lost their house and lived in a tenant trailer on a dairy farm. Right next to the barn. She, her mom, and her older brother all worked it for some old guy who wanted to get into her pants. He paid them crap. They ate a lot of ketchup sandwiches and wore three layers of clothes to try to stay warm in the winter.

"But she got out," I say. "Academic scholarship, then me."

"You met at school?" he asks.

"No, I was already working for James and she was going to Hunter College in New York City. I was there on business, I finished this deal, and took a walk in Central Park. One of those warm spring days. That Literary Walk where they have the American elms, you been there?"

He shakes his head no, and says, "I took my kids to that zoo a couple years ago. The penguins."

"Yeah. So, she was sitting there by the Shakespeare statue, studying biology. This weird picture of a beetle with a stalk of some disgusting plant busting through its shell.

"You ever hear of a nematode? It's some fungus-dispersing worm that infects the beetle's brain and takes over. The beetle crawls up into the treetops, above the jungle, then it kills the beetle and sprouts so its spores get spread by the wind."

The shrink makes a kind of unpleasant face.

"I thought, man, this girl is too pretty to be that smart. Glossy black hair. Little upturned nose. Big brown eyes. The kind that can look inside you. People always thought she was a lot younger than she was.

"She was wearing this khaki skirt and a black tank top. Very nice. We ended up at one of those outdoor cafés on Columbus Avenue. She was on the outs with some rich boyfriend. Life is timing, right?"

"And then you two had a family," he says.

"A broken one," I say.

He raises his eyebrows and waits.

"The worst thing that can happen," I say, staring into his dark eyes, willing him to feel just a touch of the agony. I feel the gears in my mind slipping, everything spinning, heating up, smoking. Going nowhere.

"We had a baby," I say. "He died."

I shake my head and let it hang down.

"When we found out she was pregnant, we painted his room. Just the two of us, drinking a little wine, spattering each other with paint. Laughing until we cried. These cool green mountains and a night sky with the moon rising. All the stars on the ceiling."

I shake my head and go silent.

"You want to tell me what happened?"

"No," I say, and the word comes out louder than I meant it to.

He sits and waits.

"After we were together awhile, she came back upstate," I say. "She did everything for me. Cooked. Massaged my back. Let me go out with my buddies. Never calling all the time and harping like some wives. I was crazy about her. I would have . . ."

"What?"

"I was going to say 'killed for her,'" I say with a stupid smile, shaking my head.

"And you did," he says.

"It was the union," I say.

"How so?"

5

I WATCHED ONE OF OUR THREE BIG Sikorsky helicopters lift off in a cloud of dust, its blades pounding the air. Under its belly hung a bundle of steel girders. It rose slowly over the high fence and then tilted toward the woods beyond. On the far side of the job site, we found an abandoned factory with a railroad spur, a line of track off the main railroad, where we could ship and stockpile our steel.

On the other side of the site, just off the interstate, the union had a picket line that the trucks wouldn't go through. The union wanted a payoff. Cash. Big money. And, for King Corp to use union construction labor at high rates. Men getting paid sometimes without even showing up. James never played that game, because, if you could beat the union, go around their picket lines, you could put the millions they normally skimmed into your own pocket.

We needed to get the steel on-site to start construction, big I-beams, tall as telephone poles. Once the steel is up, a project is considered a go. You can get financing. Money from the bank starts to flow.

Ben Evans, my college roommate, teammate, and best friend, pulled up to the picket line that morning with a convoy of thirty trucks carrying steel. A decoy, while I got the real stuff flown in from the opposite direction. We both had partnership interests in the project, so beating the union put money into our pockets too.

Around ten a.m., two guys in a Buick showed up at the gates of the old factory, but we had two state troopers sitting there in a patrol car. At eleven, the troopers let Milo Peterman past. Milo was a King Corp partner in the Garden State project. James brought Milo in because he knew everybody in northern New Jersey. Connected. Not in a mob sort of way, but legitimate political connections. A guy who could get all the permits you need to do a job that big.

He was a sloppy-looking man, even in a suit, with thin greasy hair, big black plastic glasses, and a belly stretching his white dress shirt, bulging from his dark suit. Milo heaved himself out of his BMW and stamped toward me with his hand on the flap of hair covering his head to keep it in place as a Sikorsky hammered by overhead.

"What the fuck are you doing?" he said. His forehead was crunched tight and his dark eyebrows made a steep V.

"Getting the steel in," I said, wondering why he was acting so crazy.

"Why the fuck didn't I know?" he said, spittle flying from his lips.

"James said not to bother you," I said. "That you had enough going on."

Milo clenched his hands and turned this way and that, looking at the piles of steel, the railroad tracks, and one of the big helicopters as a crew in hard hats tethered up another bundle of steel.

"Fuck me," Milo said, and when he turned back my way, his face had fallen. He looked right through me and I saw that his eyes were wet.

"Fuck me," he said again, this time a pitiful squeak.

I watched him stagger off and climb into his car. He pulled away fast, with his tires kicking up stones and making a little dust cloud of its own. I shrugged and got back to work.

Around four, I got into my Escalade and drove over to the front entrance to the job site. The only thing left of the picket line were three rusty oil drums on the roadside. Two overflowed with garbage. The third was still smoldering from the union's fire, and I could smell the stench of burnt plastic as I rolled down my window to tell the security guard to unlock the gates. A ten-foot chain-link fence topped by a roll of razor wire surrounded the two-hundred-acre site.

Ben was inside, wearing a hard hat and jeans.

He saw me and opened his arms. We hugged each other, laughing and slapping each other on the back.

"You should've seen Johnny's face," Ben said. His bony cheeks were red beneath his rectangular glasses. His eyes were bottle blue. "I thought he was going to pop a vein in his neck."

"No such luck."

"Almost done," he said, raising his voice as an empty helicopter took off for a final load.

"Good timing," I said. "Look at that."

Thick dark clouds were churning toward us from the west. A chilly wind whipped up the dust and grit.

While we inventoried the steel, the sun disappeared

behind the clouds, darkening the sky. Rain started spitting down on us, but we waited until our crews were done
before we got into my truck and headed for the gate.
The security guard's eyes popped out of his head and he
wrung his hands together in a washing motion. He signaled us frantically to stop and walked over to the Escalade after we drove through.

"There were some guys around here asking about
you," he said. "I thought you should know. One of them
had this thing on his lip. They were telling me you guys
had some kids and I was like, well that's none of my
business or yours, but they just stood there smiling at me
for a while before they got into this black Suburban and
drove off."

I told him not to worry, thanked him, and rolled up
the window. The first rumble of thunder echoed across
the sky.

"What do you want to do?" I asked Ben

"What can we do?"

"Yeah," I said, taking my foot off the brake. "It's their
bullshit scare tactics, like those baseball bats."

"I hope so," Ben said.

He was looking straight ahead at the rainy gray road,
worried. He had good reason.

6

I FELT LIKE I WAS RUNNING from something, like I'd just pulled a teenage prank. We took the parkway north to Route 17, winding our way through the Catskill Mountains, heading home. Lightning flashed and you could see the mist rising from the trees. The news was on the radio, but the clatter of the rain on the windshield was so loud I had to turn it up.

There was a breaking story in Monticello. A man named Milo Peterman had been found shot three times in the head. Police were calling it a mob-related hit.

"Pull over," Ben said, grabbing for the door handle, his face pale.

I veered off the road, lurching to a stop. Ben leaned out and vomited. Then shut the door and wiped his lips on the back of his sleeve. He was already drenched. His straight blond hair was matted to the sides of his head and the tips of his bangs touched the rectangular glasses. He kept his eyes straight ahead and told me in a quiet voice to go.

I checked the rearview mirror, gripped the wheel, and pulled back out onto the rain-slicked road. Milo had a fishing cabin in Monticello. He grilled hamburgers one night for Ben and me on the deck overlooking some trout stream. The only thing he had to drink were wine coolers. We rode in silence until I couldn't stand it and said, "Last time I saw you that wet was that night on New Year's in Palm Beach."

That made him smile. We'd been college roommates, teammates too, on the football team. Ben's family had a place in Palm Beach. I'd never been south of Binghamton and he took me down there for the holidays our freshman year.

"Those women were so sad," he said, referring to that night, closing a local bar, both of us three sheets to the wind, hormones running wild.

"They weren't bad-looking."

"For three a.m.," he said. "They must have been in their forties."

We went home with them, a big place on the beach. I was with one of them in the master bedroom when we heard Ben fall into the pool. He was so drunk, I actually jumped off the balcony into the pool to save him.

We grinned back and forth at each other until the memory faded.

"Milo," Ben said, shaking his head. "Shit."

"Never trust a guy who drinks wine coolers."

"It's not funny."

"I didn't say it was."

"He had to have something going with the union on the side," Ben said. "Yeah, he got the permits, but I bet he's the one who kept that union two steps ahead of us. Every move we made, they knew. It took us a year to get that site prepped."

"He showed up at the factory," I said, glancing over at Ben.

"Why the hell didn't you tell me?"

"Didn't think anything of it, really. It was weird. He was upset, but he was an odd duck. I thought he was just pissed because he liked to have his hands in everything."

"That's my point," Ben said. "We didn't tell him about the Sikorskys."

"So when we flew the steel over their heads today," I said, "they figured Milo double-crossed them."

"Honestly," Ben said, "I don't give a shit about Milo and his Presidential Rolex and his greasy hair. I care about them showing up and talking about our kids. Jesus."

"Your kids are in Palo Alto," I said, sorry when I did. Ben's wife had taken off with them a year ago.

"Who talks like that though," he said. "About someone's kids."

"Someone trying to scare you," I said, talking braver than I felt. I thought of Tommy and Jessica at home. My foot pressed a little harder on the gas.

"That Johnny," Ben said. "They call him boss, but he doesn't run the whole union, right?"

"Pension fund treasurer or some crap," I say. "James said he's pretty high up in the Buffalino Family."

"Yeah. James also said we didn't have to worry," Ben said.

That's when I saw the lights coming at us from behind. I sped up even more, checking the mirror.

"What are you doing?" Ben asked. He looked behind us. "Shit."

The lights kept coming. The red arm on the speedometer crept up over eighty and my hands were sweaty on the wheel. I could barely see through the pounding rain.

The lights were close. A black Suburban. The shape of two heads behind the windshield. I thought about Milo. Dead.

They came right up our ass and bumped me. My heart felt like it was going to bust out of my ribs, and I grabbed the wheel so hard I couldn't feel my hands. My foot went to the brake, but I had this idea that I should punch the accelerator.

Ben braced his hands on the dash.

We shot ahead and I felt that electric thrill of running down an open field with a ball tucked under my arm. My truck had a big engine and it could fly. I took the next bend and felt the wheels going, but eased up just enough to keep us from a wipeout.

"Shit, slow down," Ben said, yelling above the sound of the rain.

I didn't. I punched it again. I could barely see the road in the dark rain, but they were right behind me. I focused on the white line at the far edge of the headlight beam. My hands sweated as I held tight.

"God damn," Ben yelled.

I didn't even respond. Then we hit this long straight stretch and soon the truck was even with us. I took a quick look and saw the pale moon of a face looking over at me. Union goons I didn't recognize, but that's who they had to be. I knew what they were going to do the instant before it came.

They slammed into me and I fought to stay on the road. My foot went back to the brake, and I was all of a sudden burning to kill them. I slammed my Escalade right back into them and punched the gas again, driving them toward the shoulder. Ben was screaming at me. I was just reacting.

When their truck hit the guardrail, it sprang back at us and both vehicles swung toward the other side of the road. I was just getting it straight when my right wheel hit the beginning of another rail and we were airborne.

I don't know how many times we flipped. That's a blur. But I heard the crash and felt the airbag blow up in my face. I was upside down and I felt this warm trickle of blood running down my cheek and tickling my hairline. We were both coughing from that powdery crap in the airbags.

The stink of hot rubber and gasoline was everywhere and I was afraid I'd throw up and choke on it hanging there. Somewhere above us I heard the sound of a vehicle door slamming shut. There was the glow of headlights and I could make out a steep bank that led up to the road. I couldn't see who, but someone was splashing through puddles, coming toward us.

The beam of a flashlight bounced around. I froze with my mouth clamped tight. The storm was whipping itself against the underside of my truck and thunder rumbled through the hills. The flashlight was on me and I winced in its glare. I pulled my hand free from the airbag, shielding my eyes.

Whoever was holding the flashlight had a gun in their other hand.

7

It wasn't the guys who ran us off the road," I say. "They must have kept going. It was witches from the FBI."

"Witches?" the shrink asks.

"That's a habit from Jessica. You didn't use the B word around her."

"A nasty woman you'd call a bitch," he says, puckering those fat lips. "Witches. That's something more."

"I guess they were more. Like part of it all."

"What? A conspiracy?"

"I don't know. Maybe destiny," I say. "You believe in that? Like it's a script and we just read the lines?"

He looks down at his hands.

Without looking up, he says, "Do you think you know what their lines were?"

"Of course. Look around."

I gaze around the empty room. Fluorescent lightbulbs shine down. One flickers like a dying insect. Blue paint, surplus, a color no one wants, covers the walls.

"You get to think a lot in here," I say.

"Tell me about them, the witches."

"They were following us," I say. "Me and Ben. After Milo,

I guess they figured we'd either be the next targets or the next ones to go on the take. Either way, we were close to the action and that's where they wanted to be."

I sat in the backseat of the car with Ben. They took us to a diner up the road in a little place called Roscoe. We were both wet. I was bloody from a gash in my neck.

One of them was a redhead. Pale skin. No makeup. Green eyes, though, the deep emerald kind, and actually kind of pretty. The other had this frizzy nest of gray hair pulled back as tight as it would go, leaving a wild bunch of it resting on her back like a squirrel's tail. She was wiry and muscular like a man. She had gray eyes, and even though her skin had this yellow cast to it, you could tell she was too young to have all that gray in her hair. Young or not, she had the angry look of a woman who'd felt some hard knocks and maybe that's what the gray was all about.

The diner's booths were empty. Dinner hour was long gone. The only sign of life was a bleached-blond waitress in a white apron whose eyes went wide at the sight of us.

"Are you folks all right?" the waitress said, stretching her neck to look at my cut and touching my arm.

"Just wet and dirty," the frizzy-haired agent said, showing her badge. "Do you have a phone I could use?"

"Only place on earth where your cell phone won't work," the waitress said, proud.

She motioned toward the back. Ben told me he'd call a car service and followed too. I could see the redhead was spattered with mud, her wet clothes clinging to her skin. She swept a strand of straight red hair out of her eye and introduced herself as Agent Lee. We sat down in a booth.

Outside the storm carried on. Flashing. Rumbling. Teeming rain.

The other one with the frizzy gray hair came out, sat down with a huff, and said, "Forty minutes for the troopers."

The waitress filled the coffee cups in front of us, studying our dripping and bedraggled clothes. Agent Lee asked me if I wanted anything and I ordered coffee.

Ben came back and said, "I got a Town Car. They said thirty minutes."

"Faster than the troopers," the agent with the frizzy hair said. "High rollers."

Agent Lee said, "Agent Rooks and I are with an Organized Crime task force. We think we can help you. We were at Milo Peterman's earlier today."

"We heard about him getting killed on the news," I said, picking up a spoon and turning it over.

"Milo was seen eight months ago with Johnny G at a strip club in Newark," Agent Lee said. "These people don't just kill someone and walk away, there's too much money in a project like yours. They'll try to contact one of you. Getting run off the road like that is kind of like a calling card."

"Welcome to the neighborhood," Agent Rooks said.

"They almost killed us," Ben said.

Agent Lee looked at him without speaking for a moment until she said, "We'd like the two of you to let us know if they try to contact you. Especially Johnny G."

"I thought you said *you* wanted to help *us*," I said.

"We can help each other," Agent Lee said.

"You should talk to James King," I said, swallowing some coffee.

"I read that article about James King in the *New York*

Times," Agent Lee said softly. She slid two of her cards across the table at us. "About the autonomy he gives his top people. I'm guessing that you're exactly who we should be talking to."

"If anyone besides James is calling shots, it'd probably be Scott, his son," I said. "Maybe you should talk to him."

Agent Lee shrugged, but kept her eyes locked on me. "Call it a hunch. We can help you, Mr. Coder. We've been watching John Garret for over a year."

"That didn't help Milo, did it?" I said.

"Maybe he was part of the problem," Agent Rooks said. "You ever hear of learning from other people's mistakes? You help us, we help you. We just pulled your ass out of a burning wreck, so you're up, right?"

"How are we helping?" Ben asked, his eyes sharp behind the rims of his wire glasses.

"We call people like yourselves Cooperating Witnesses," Agent Lee said.

I snorted.

"A wiretap?" Ben said.

Agent Lee let her head tilt to the side.

"We're businessmen," I said, getting up from the table. "Straight up. Milo wasn't. Here's a deal for you, you do your job and we'll do ours."

Agent Lee cleared her throat and Agent Rooks said, "You weren't so straight up when you claimed that Mercedes convertible your wife drives as a business expense, were you?"

I kept my face blank.

"My wife works for my corporation," I said. "You can talk to my accountant."

"Your accountant put that pool in?" Agent Rooks said,

a crooked smile on her face. "The one with the stepping-stones and all that granite?"

"I paid for that," I said, swallowing some bile.

"You wrote a check for ten thousand dollars," Rooks said, her teeth showing as yellow as her skin. "That was a hundred-and-fifty-thousand-dollar custom pool. And it's funny, isn't it? That the same company got the contract for that King Corp hotel in Toronto."

My stomach tightened and I felt Ben's eyes on me. Jessica had been hounding me for that pool and when I had a chance to steer the hotel concrete work to which-ever contractor I wanted, I hadn't been able to resist the massive discount one of them offered me for my own pool.

"Are we under arrest or something?" I asked, shoving my hands in my pockets.

"Mr. Coder, relax," Agent Lee said, shooting her partner a glance.

"Not yet," Rooks said, ignoring the look and grinning up at me.

I looked from one of them to the other, smiled, and said, "You're wet."

"The state police will want a statement," Agent Lee said.

"Tell them to call my lawyer," I said.

Ben slid out of the booth without looking at them, which lifted my spirits. Then, from the corner of my eye, I saw him glance at me before slipping one of the agent's cards off the table and into his pocket. I never imagined Ben would do something like that to me, and it cut me, deep.

8

"Why?" the shrink asks.

"We were like brothers," I say. "That love-hate thing. Those witches were out to get me. He knew that. He heard them. So I let them build me a pool, cheap. Is that any reason to turn on a friend? Because you want nice things?"

"Because you wanted them, or her?" he asks.

"Of course she wanted nice things," I say. "Every woman wants nice things. Imagine growing up with that cow shit smell and flies running across your face on a summer night; you'd want them even more."

"But you? You wanted them too, right?"

"Who doesn't? We had these plans for this twenty-thousand-square-foot house, right next to the one we had. A ten-acre lot on the lake. What's that look for?"

He shrugs and says, "You're talking to a guy who grew up with one bathroom for seven people."

"Well, Doctor," I say, "you wouldn't like going back to one bathroom any more than me. The more you have, the more you want.

"That's just how it is. Me. Her. You. Everyone. Five years

before this crap I had partnerships in four other King Corp projects besides Garden State, I had three, four million dollars' worth of equity. My problem was that when the stock market started its free fall in 2000, I bought into it.

"I rode it up in the late nineties, yeah, but then I rode it down. Hard. The worse it got, the more I bought. Then I started buying on margin."

"Like doubling down at black jack," he says, nodding his head.

My hands are sweating and I tuck them between the chair and my legs.

"Yeah."

"But your luck changed."

"No. I hit bottom and got bailed out."

"By?"

"James."

I watch for the lids of his eyes to raise. They don't and I say, "You don't seem surprised."

"Lots of times," he says, nodding, "the folks we have the hardest time with are the ones who saved our ass. He gave you the money?"

"With strings. Accelerated payouts. Basically he bought back my ownership interest in the projects. Turned out to be a hell of a deal for him. Tripled his money. Like he needed it. When all was said and done my equity was zero. I had three car payments, a three-million-dollar home with a monster mortgage, a six-figure American Express bill, and a wife itching to build a castle.

"Garden State Center was the light at the end of the tunnel. The biggest shopping mall on earth. Fifty movie theaters. Twelve department stores. Seven hundred shops. Two hotels. Bigger than the Mall of America. Ben and I were the construction partners. Two percent each. The windfall payout on the financing would be two hundred million easy. Four million in my pocket. Tax-free.

"That wasn't even so much compared to what a lot of people made with James. Like Milo? His take on the windfall payout was supposed to be twenty million."

"But everything has a price," he says.

"Yeah," I say. "James snapped and we jumped. If you had deals to do, you didn't worry about anniversary dinners or soccer games or Christmas or cutting a vacation short.

"I can't even count all the ball games I missed. The concerts. Birthday parties. But I still had it better than Ben. That's the good thing about a wife who wants things.

"His wife nagged him nonstop, wore those Birkenstocks and bell-bottom jeans. Granola girl. Philosophy major. Finally she took the two kids and ran off to Palo Alto with some English professor. Ben always came in second.

"Even the way everyone gave me the credit for airlifting the steel over the picket line and busting the union. It was really Ben's idea. I think people remembered me because I was the one who had my picture in the paper with those big Sikorsky helicopters, and I was the one who stood up to Johnny G when he came ranting and raving up to the gate where we were staging the steel. Maybe that's why Ben took that FBI agent's card, decided enough was enough with his best friend always getting the cream."

"So you got the credit for making the project happen?"

"Most people gave me credit. Not the one that counted, though."

"You mean James?"

"That world is like a shark tank. You act and you react. You eat or you get eaten. That's what he taught me and that's what I did."

"Even if it meant taking a life?"

"In a way."

"James never did that, though," he says, "use union tactics. Murder."

"Not a bullet to the brain," I say, "but he'd destroy people. You'd either win or lose with him. It was absolute."

"What about win-win?"

"Exactly. There was no win-win with James. That's what I learned."

"With you?"

"With everybody," I say. "High stakes. High risk. It was like the day after we broke the union picket line."

"Go back to that," he says. "You were on your way home after they ran you off the road."

9

By the time i got home to Skaneateles, Jessica and Tommy were asleep. I checked all the doors to make sure they were locked, then I set the alarm and took my shotgun out of the closet and slid it under the bed with a box of birdshot. When I got into bed, Jessica moaned and rolled the other way. I lay there for a long time, listening. I don't know when I finally fell asleep.

I know it was barely light when she shook me awake.

"What's this?" she said. "What happened?"

I sat up and looked at the pillowcase, stained with blood.

"I cut my neck," I said, reaching for the wound.

I told her the story about breaking the picket line and getting run off the road. I told her about Milo.

"My God," she said.

We crept quietly downstairs, careful not to wake Tommy, and she made a pot of coffee. We sat at our kitchen table looking out over the lake. The sky began to burn deep red in the east.

"The FBI was there," I said. "They said the union's just trying to scare us."

Jessica nodded and said, "You've got to get some security people down there."

"We've got guys at the site."

"Not rent-a-cops," she said. "Bodyguards. Tell James."

"He's been battling these guys his whole life," I said. "He won't go for it."

"Don't be like your father, Thane," she said, looking away from me and getting up. "I'll make you some eggs."

"What's my father got to do with this?" I asked.

"You think that chemical company respected *him*? They paid him what? Ten, twenty thousand dollars a year to wade around in that poison muck with a shovel?" she said, wiping a wisp of hair from her eye with the back of her wrist, her cheeks flushed. "Those who ignore history are doomed to repeat it."

"I make that in a month. You should know. It goes out that fast."

"You don't want your son in decent clothes? You only have one," she said.

Both of us froze, thinking the same thing, Teague. Even after a decade, a wound so raw you couldn't breathe on it without flinching.

"It's called market value," she added quickly, scampering away from the subject, me letting her. "You're the one risking your life, *he's* the one making billions."

"I'm a partner in this," I said, wanting to assuage her, make it better. Move on. I *had* learned from her. I wouldn't have gotten all those partnerships if I hadn't.

My cell phone rang. James. I listened and said I'd be there and hung up.

"He beckons?" she said, her eyes intent on the toast she was buttering.

"We're meeting at Cascade," I said, going over to her and putting my arms around her waist. "A big announcement."

"Like what?" she asked, setting down the butter knife.

"Someone has to get Milo's share," I said.

"Not his wife?"

I shook my head. "King Corp partnerships never vest until financing goes through. Milo bought it two weeks too soon."

"You got the steel in there," she said, turning to me, putting her arm around my neck.

"Twenty million," I said. "You could build your house."

I couldn't resist. She'd been working with the architect for two years on the plans. Three stories. Marble pillars. Another granite pool. Five-car garage. Miles of glass to enjoy the view. It would take a colossal windfall to afford. Her eyes strayed from me to the vacant lot on the waterfront bluff adjacent to our own back lawn.

"We could."

"Wives are invited to dinner. Seven o'clock. Eva will be there. So."

Eva was James's wife. Jessica gripped my shoulders and said, "I knew you'd do it. All along, I knew. You just needed a push."

"I'd like to give you a push," I said.

I put my hands on her narrow waist. She looked up with her crooked smile and touched my cheek with the back of her nails.

"You can," she said.

I looked at my watch. I knew better. I'd seen James cut a forty-two-year-old lawyer out of a partnership for being late to a lunch meeting. Late at King Corp was inexcusable.

"Tonight," I said.

"I wouldn't miss it."

I ran upstairs, put on khakis and a plaid shirt with a collar that covered my wound. Going to the lodge wasn't like going to our offices in Syracuse, where everyone wore a jacket and tie. With James, you never knew. You were just as apt to find yourself talking business in a fishing boat or a duck blind as the conference room.

I gobbled down my breakfast, kissed Jessica hard, then got into the Mercedes convertible and headed out. Ben was already waiting in the conference room at the lodge. He was tilted back in a chair and stared out the window where the water shimmered in the sunlight, his eyes half closed.

"Fucked-up night last night, huh?" I said, guessing at his thoughts.

He spun his head around and said, "You cleaned up nice."

"I guess we both look pretty damn good next to Milo."

We stared at each other before Scott King came in and broke the uncomfortable moment.

Scott was big and burly with sandy hair that was thinning fast. He was built like a bear with the heart and stamina of a draft horse, but could slip through the woods like an Iroquois. I got up and smacked my hand into his, answering his force with my own vise grip. We slapped each other's back in a brief hug. Then Ben got up and did the same thing. The three of us had been friends since the day we reported to football camp our freshman year at college.

We trained together and we partied together. Vacations. Summer break. There wasn't a week that went by when the three of us weren't hanging out. It was like that for all four years. When I got drafted, I thought we'd never be like that again.

Then I blew out my shoulder at the Giants' training camp. You want to talk about depressed? It was dark. The team sent me packing, and I was actually living back at my parents' house wondering what the hell I was going to do when Scott and Ben showed up at the door. They took me to Coleman's, where we all got drunk and Scott announced that I was going to work for his dad. It was a done deal. He'd already done the same thing for Ben. The plan was that the three of us would earn our stripes and then build our own empire together.

While we were with his dad, Scott went down to Florida to work with an old partner of James's for about ten years before coming back to join King Corp and reuniting the old team. And, even though it wasn't the same, and even though we never did go out on our own, you don't go through all that together without staying friends.

"Big announcement, huh?" Scott said. He grabbed a can of Diet Coke from the sideboard and cracked it open. He sat down and swung his feet up on the table in a way only James's son could do.

Ben and I looked at each other, then him.

"Change the company forever," Scott said, taking a sip and looking over the top of his can. "So he says. Don't worry. Word is that all three of us are going to be happy."

I looked at him, wondering how that could be possible.

"Where is my dad, anyway?" he said.

"Where's my Beretta?"

When we heard that voice—not just the voice, but the tone of it—we all jumped up like choirboys caught drinking the sacramental wine. We were grown men, all three of us.

10

You said your father was a 'whip-your-ass-with-a-belt' guy. Is that what James made you feel like?"

"He was tough, but he wasn't going to throw a punch at me or anything."

"I'm not talking about that. I'm talking about that choir-boy thing, how he made you feel."

I put my hands on the edge of the battered wooden table and I lean toward him.

"You hear this," I say, "and then you tell me how I felt."

I was glad he was looking at Scott instead of me. James was about six feet tall, not as thick as Scott, but solid, with a full head of white hair, long and swept off his forehead. His back was straight and he stood in the doorway with that mischievous glint in his eye. That glint could mean he was royally pissed off or that he was just having fun.

"What do you mean?" Scott said.

"I thought we'd shoot some ducks," James said. "But someone took the Beretta out of my locker."

Scott's face got red and he said, "Maybe Bucky put it in mine by mistake."

"That must be what happened," James said, "because I know you wouldn't have taken it and used it and not put it back. I'll have to get on Buck."

Of course, when we walked downstairs, Bucky was right there laying out shotguns and boxes of shells on the workbench in the gun room. Scott made a detour and came back with a gleaming twelve gauge over-and-under. It was engraved with the swirling silver lines of a duck hunting scene. The thing looked like it belonged in a museum, and Scott used his sleeve to wipe some dried mud off the walnut stock.

"Yeah, it was there," he said, laying it in front of his father on the bench and glancing at Bucky.

"Bucky, do you think you could put this away in the right place?" James said.

Bucky was more than just a hunting guide, although he was the best at that I ever saw. He was more too, than the guy who ran the entire hunting preserve and oversaw the construction of the lodge. He was a man whose opinion was valued by other men, whatever their station, whatever their education. I've seen him make PhDs blush and tycoons clamp their mouths shut tight. And it wasn't unusual at all for James to call him into a high-powered partner meeting to ask his advice about a complex issue.

He was the guy you'd want to be close to if there was ever a nuclear war or something like that. Bucky would be the one to figure out how to survive. He had a drooping brush broom mustache and a barrel chest. His eyes were dark, red-rimmed, and so serious they were almost sad as he looked from the gun to Scott, then at James.

"Thought I did," he said, putting on his country-boy

manner the way you or I would put on a hat, "but I forgot to put beans in the coffee machine this morning too. Hot water with my eggs."

James slapped him on the back and smiled, then said, "Get these guys some gear."

I took a lightweight cattail camouflage suit off the rack—2X—then found some size thirteen boots on the wall of cubbyholes where pairs of the things were stored from the floor to the ceiling. While we were dressing, I gave Ben a grin and thought about the card he'd taken from the FBI. In a boardroom, my man was an ace, but you could tell by the expression on his face—like he ate a bad piece of fish or something—that he never got into the killing. It didn't matter if it was ducks or rabbits or boar or deer. When something died, Ben always looked the other way.

Bucky passed out the guns and we walked outside. His blue Suburban was parked right there under the bridge to the main entrance above. Bucky drove us out to the swamps, and Russel, one of his sons, quickly butted out a cigarette. Russel was a baby-faced, thicker version of Bucky, but not as tall. Bucky scowled at him and as we unloaded I heard him mutter something about what kind of a fool would smoke when you know it's going to kill you.

Russel looked at Bucky from under the bill of his cap with big drooping eyes, ignoring the comment the way the sons of tough fathers learn to do, and he ran us over to a small cattail island in a flat-bottomed boat. The blind was like a miniature baseball dugout whose roof and outside walls were plastered with dead cattails. James stood in one end of the blind with Scott next to him, then me, and finally, Ben on the end.

The sky was clear and blue, too nice a day for duck hunting, but these ducks were farm-raised and conditioned to fly right past us on their way back to the old barn where they lived and were fed. It's called a "flighted hunt."

The decoys bobbed on the water in front of us, and Russel stayed outside the blind, blowing tentatively on his call and hunched his wide shoulders down over a black Lab that whined and shivered in anticipation. James talked to Bucky on the radio, and a minute later a flight of ducks appeared over the trees to the south and swept right toward us, a big green-headed mallard in the lead, quacking happily in answer to Russel's call.

We shot flight after flight until our gun barrels were hot and the Lab was gasping for breath over a mound of broken ducks. Even Ben blasted his gun off a few times, but I never saw a bird fall from his shot and we kidded him about that.

"That's it, James."

It was Bucky's voice crackling over the radio.

"That's it?" James said, his thick eyebrows disappearing under the bill of his camo hat. "Any more back at the barn?"

"Sure."

"Okay. Get some."

We all sat down on the wooden bench that was tucked into the back of our narrow blind. The water in front of us was dark like oil and, where it wasn't broken up by patches of cattail islands that were brown and dead, it glittered with sunshine. I looked out at one of the decoys that was turning little circles in the breeze and saw that its pale gray back was speckled with blood.

"Milo was a duck hunter," James said, looking out over the water.

I felt a charge go through me and my breath go short. Out of the corner of my eye I could see Ben's glasses shifting my way, looking down at James.

"He'd always jump up and start shooting before anyone else could get a shot in," James said. "Remember that? Can you really trust a guy like that? He was great with the town boards though, and the EPA. He got that site ready, but he got in too deep down there. Obviously."

Behind us on the old trolley bed we could hear Bucky's truck racing past on his way back from the duck barn.

"Anyway," James said, "I'm saving the big announcement for tonight. I want all our families there because it affects everyone.

"All three of you are going to be happy," he said, and my heart seemed to swell up against the inside of my ribs.

"You should be anyway. But I wanted to get this thing with Milo out of the way. You've all done things to help this project, but that's your jobs. And, in all honesty, one of you was more critical in putting this financing into place than the other two . . ."

In the distance, there was the sound of quacking ducks. James picked up his gun and stood and we all did the same. Getting Milo's percentage in this deal would wipe out all my financial worries. Pay off my mortgage. My credit cards. Have real money that could only grow bigger and bigger. I could spend without thinking, and stop worrying about what Jessica spent. She could build that house. She could start tomorrow. Even half of Milo's share would put me back in the driver's seat.

Russel started calling to the flight of ducks, but they veered off before coming in.

"Hold the damn dog still," James said, leaning forward so he could scowl down at Russel.

Russel sat down hard on the dog and blew like hell, his cheeks puffed out like red balloons, pointing his call after the flight. One lone duck peeled off and circled back toward us, coming in.

"Thane, you take it," James said.

I realized that I was holding my breath. It was a green head, a big mallard. He gave a quack and cupped his wings. His feet came down like landing gear and he kind of floated there, wobbling a bit in the current, sailing in. A sweetheart shot.

I fired once. Twice. Three times fast. The duck veered and a few feathers floated down, but he started flapping like mad and quacking his ass off, and away he went, disappearing over the wooded ridge beyond the swamp.

"So," James said, sitting back down and keeping his eyes out on the swamp. "I'm giving Milo's equity to Scott."

11

"And that made you feel what?" the shrink asks.

"Truth?"

"That's why I'm here."

"At that moment I felt like jamming that twelve gauge right in his face and pulling the trigger."

"But the gun wasn't loaded."

"What do you mean? How do you know?" I ask.

"My granddaddy was a hunter," he says, leaning back and folding his hands over his belly. "Three shots in a duck gun. Federal law. You said you took all three."

I tucked my lower lip under my front teeth.

"So you really couldn't have," he says.

"You ever go down into a basement and see something out of the corner of your eye?"

He says yes.

"So maybe it was like that. Something dark that flashes on the edge of your brain. It doesn't mean anything. It's there, then it's gone."

"But, eventually, you did do it."

"But that was the closest I came to wanting to and I couldn't, so it's almost like it didn't count."

"Okay, so let's say you really didn't want to," he says. "So, how come you did?"

"I told you. It was the situation. I really didn't have a choice."

"I think we all have a choice. I know you don't like it, but that's where I'm heading here. You wanna cope with things on the outside? You gotta own up to the deed. All the way."

"You know what I remember?"

"What?"

"The goddamn look on their faces. The two of them. Like him getting Milo's share was obvious. Like it was totally fair."

I heard Ben exhale and when I turned to look at him, he was pretending to be interested in that line of trees where my wounded duck had gone. And he pissed me off too, because instead of gritting his teeth or breathing heavy through his nose, he wore this little knowing smile on his face. I wanted to punch him in the mouth, but James was talking to me.

"We just closed a deal that puts a lot of money in everyone's pocket and you don't look happy," James said.

I turned and saw him looking at me, staring. I should have said something right then. Jessica would have ripped him. But, in a pinch like this, despite all the years of her coaching, despite working my ass off to be the big tough football player, I turned into the thing I was always afraid I'd become. My father.

"No," I said, "I am."

"Good," James said, looking at his watch. "I've got a four o'clock call."

We piled out of the blind and into the boat. Russel

brought us back, an unlit cigarette hanging from his mouth and his thick hands controlling both the dog and the motor. As we drove away in Bucky's Suburban I saw him cup his hands and lean over a flame. While Bucky drove us to the lodge, James quizzed us on the construction schedule. We sat in the back with Ben jammed in between me and Scott.

"I've got to be honest, James," I said. "I'm a little worried about these union guys. I was thinking maybe we hire some security people. For the site. For us too, maybe."

"All talk," James said, swatting his hand at air. He leaned across Bucky and pointed out the driver's-side window at the dead trees rising up from the water. "They're like bees, the union people. You don't bother them, they don't bother you. If that's what happened to Milo, it's because he stirred them up. I like those wood duck boxes, Buck. Let's put in some more."

"But someone ran us off the road," Ben said.

James turned around and looked at him, smiling.

"What, some old lady? A crazy kid?"

"We think some of Johnny G's guys," Ben said.

Scott leaned forward and looked at Ben with narrow eyes.

"Did they catch them?" he asked.

Ben shook his head.

"How do you know it was Johnny G?" James asked.

"It was a black Suburban," Ben said. "They came right at us in that storm."

James nodded, but turned his attention back to the curving road up ahead and said, "If I reacted every time one of these people looked at me funny, I'd still be digging basements."

"Maybe just some extra guys at the site," I said.

"Call the police," James said. "That's how we handle it. I set a precedent with these people a long time ago. We don't cut deals and we don't run scared."

"The FBI's been watching Johnny G," Ben said.

"Good," James said. "Get them involved."

"They are," Ben said. "They want *our* help."

Bucky pulled the Suburban to a stop in front of the lodge.

"Okay," James said, hopping out. "Do that. I'll see you guys at dinner."

Scott hopped out too, and Bucky. The three of them disappeared into the lodge.

"You want to throw a line in the water before dark?" I said. It was my turn to smile.

"Jesus," Ben said, looking at the door they'd gone through and shaking his head.

"The man just stole twenty million dollars right out from under us and you think he's going to hire body-guards?" I said.

We got some gear and a boat and headed out onto the water. Down past the bridge, around a bend, there was a cove where these dead trees, bleached and broken, poked up out of the black water. The bass loved it in there and as soon as I cut the motor, I tied on a lure and tossed out my line.

Ben stood up and rigged a popper of his own. He wound up and whipped his lure hard across the main body of water into another clump of dead trees.

"Watch that thing," I said, flinching.

A kingfisher chattered past and the croak of a nearby frog made the silence bigger. A locust buzzed and a small breeze rippled the water. Ben reeled in his lure without stopping until it bumped up into the boat.

"You've got to snap it a few times," I said, showing him with a few flicks of my wrist. "Then let it lay. Like it's wounded. That's when they'll hit it."

"I don't see you catching anything," he said, knitting his blond eyebrows and winding up again.

This time, when he whipped his arm, the drag screeched. I saw a bright light and felt a bolt of current flash between my lip and my brain. Ben's face lost its color and his mouth made a big O as he reached for me. I felt the cold metal of the second treble hook rattling against the plastic belly of the lure as they bumped against my chin.

"Holy shit, Thane, I'm sorry. Holy shit."

I dropped my pole and felt for the lure that was hooked through my bottom lip.

"Pliers," I said. "In the tackle box."

Blood dribbled off my chin. Ben's hands shook as he dug through the box. Most pliers have cutters on the base. All you do is cut the barb off and the hook passes right back through without making a mess.

"There aren't any," he said in a high voice. "Just this."

In his hand was a buck knife in a leather case. I shook my head and held out my hand.

"Holy shit," Ben said.

I opened the knife, handed it back to Ben, and rolled my lip over the top of my thumb.

"Cut it," I said.

"I can't."

"In about two minutes this fucker is going to hurt

a hundred times worse than it already does. Cut down through my fucking lip and hurry up."

All that I said speaking from the back of my throat and without the use of my lips, but Ben got the idea anyway. He eased the blade toward my mouth. I gripped his wrist to help steady him. His forehead glowed with sweat. I could feel the edge of the blade along my lip. When he slit it open, I saw stars and lost my breath. I dropped his wrist. The lure clattered on the bottom of the boat and I roared in pain, clutching my face.

"Jesus. I am so sorry."

"Fuck!" I screamed, sitting down hard. My howl echoed off the far hill and back out across the water. "Fuck you, Ben, and fuck them."

I wiped my eyes on my sleeve and my blood pattered into the bottom of the boat. I grabbed the tackle box and ripped some gauze pads out of the little first aid kit, clamping them on my lip.

Nasty, right?

Well, that was nothing.

When we got back to the lodge, I went straight to the bar and wrapped a bundle of ice in a paper towel for my lip. I knocked off two quick glasses of scotch, and one of the serving girls walked by and told me Jessica was here. I checked the room list and went upstairs. The rooms had names like Railroad, Hunting, and Iroquois. They were decorated that way. We were in the Fishing Room. Jessica's Louis Vuitton overnight bag was on the bed, but she was nowhere in sight. Back downstairs, Steven, the chef, told me he saw her go past in a bathing suit and a robe so he figured she was on her way to the hot tub room.

I jogged down the spiral stairs to the lower level. One of the monastery doors to the hot tub room was open and steam curled up toward the thick log beams in the ceiling. I could smell the chemicals over the musky scent of wood, leather, and animal fur from the mounted moose. My lip throbbed. When I opened the door, I heard Jessica's laugh above the bubbling tub, but couldn't see anything through the hot wet cloud. There were some dim yellow wall sconces and a couple of lights glowing under the roiling water, but otherwise it had the dark close feel of an animal den.

When I stepped to the edge of the enormous cobblestone tub, that's when I saw her, sitting in the back corner. Yes, she had a robe wrapped around her bathing suit and just her feet were in the water. But on the other side of the tub, with his hairy arms up on the sides, a cup of beer in one hand, head back, and laughing along with her so hard I could see the fillings, was Scott.

And I'll tell you the truth. Then, at that moment, it was no fleeting dark thing. It was like a glob of concrete in my gut and everything was red.

12

"WHAT'S SO FUNNY?" I asked.

"Oh, Thaney," she said, getting up and holding the front of the robe together. "Hi, honey."

Scott's mouth closed, but the grin stayed.

Jessica waded across and touched my collarbone. "We were laughing about when Scott took you down that black diamond in Vermont."

I touched my lip and stared.

"Oh. What happened?" she said.

I dodged her touch and backed away. Scott shrugged and shook his head.

"Ben hooked my lip," I said, growling. "I'm ready to kill him."

Scott laughed again. Short this time, and over the rumbling water he said, "He's a menace. Is that ice? You should ice it."

"Yeah," I said. "That's what this is."

"You want to change for dinner?" Jessica said.

"Unless you want to go in a towel."

"Come on, grumpy," she said, smiling happily, taking

my arm, and leading me out of the room into the breathable air.

I shook free from her grip and headed past the movie theater for the back stairs.

"Where are you going?" she said, following me and still talking in that singsong voice like nothing was wrong.

"You can't go up through the main room like that," I said. "You think this is a fucking spa?"

"Honey, stop it," she said, her voice getting small.

"Stop it," I said, mimicking. "What the fuck? You're in the hot tub with some other guy?"

I stomped up, through the kitchen quick, avoiding the stares of the staff in their whites as they darted around the stainless steel. No one was in the top hall and I took a quick left into the Fishing Room, slamming the door and throwing the old iron bolt behind Jessica. I threw my package of ice down, smashing it on the floor, and turned on her.

"It was Scott," she said. "I wasn't in there with him. I was leaving. He came in. We were talking. You always do this."

"You make me do this," I said.

"You make yourself," she said. "I'm good with people. You know that. I'm friendly."

"Right."

"Come here, you," she said. "Let's forget it. Here."

She tossed her robe on the bed and slipped off the straps of her bathing suit, kissing me and moving my hand to her breast. I couldn't get out of my pants fast enough and she did everything to me that I liked best, and her hair whipped around, stinging my flesh with its wet tips.

It wasn't until I was lying there on my back with my sweat drying and my breathing starting to slow that I even felt that lip again.

"I'm sorry," I said. "I get crazy."

She lay next to me with her arm bent up over her head. I turned and kissed her cheek and traced the smooth arcing scar on the palm of her hand. She flinched and pulled it away.

"Don't," she said, finding her robe and pulling it around her.

"Why? It's smooth. I like it."

"I told you a thousand times. It tickles."

She turned her head away and I propped myself up on one elbow. I took her chin and tilted her face back toward mine. There were tears in her eyes.

"What's the matter?"

She shook her head and lay flat on her back, cinching the tie around her waist.

"Tell me."

She closed her eyes and tears sprung from their dark slits.

"I don't like when you look at me like you did down there."

"I'm sorry," I said. "I told you."

"It wasn't an accident," she said, her face crumpling. "I always said it was, but it wasn't."

"What are you talking about? What happened?"

"This," she said, showing me the scar again.

She took a deep breath and let it out, forcing a smile. "She told me and told me, but I couldn't listen. She had these diamond earrings. Little things."

She laughed, staring up at the ceiling, and shook her head, sniffing.

"And she'd hide them from me so I couldn't wear them. I was six. And part of me thought it was like a game. You know, she'd yell and raise her hand like she was going to hit me, but she'd only spank me and throw me down and hold out her hand and I'd take them off and give them back.

"And then one day I found them in my father's socks and I was out in the yard, playing with some other kids. I was on the swing and they were all looking and pointing because I had diamonds and I was more proud for her than I was for myself, because people where we lived just didn't have diamonds.

"You should have heard her scream. She yanked me off the swing and dragged me into the house. 'Never, never, never,' she said. And she threw the kettle across the kitchen and she just planted my hand on the burner."

Jessica started to sob and I said, no, no, no, and held her tight, and the ache went from my stomach to my heart.

"It's the smell," she said, burying her nose into my ribs, shuddering like a small wet puppy. "I can still smell it. Don't look at me like that anymore."

I held her for a while, looking at the clock, knowing that soon we'd have to go down. Her breathing got slow and regular and I thought she might even be asleep.

I thought back to when we first met. I thought of how she grew up and how that had to be a part of why she was so determined to get to the top. She could have had a lot of guys, someone who could have given her everything, but she chose me.

"I didn't get it," I said, lying back and looking up at the ceiling.

"Get what?" she asked.

"James gave Milo's equity to Scott," I said. "That's why I was crazy downstairs. I'm sorry."

"God damn," she said, spitting her words. "He did it to you again. If he's going to treat you like this, why don't you just give that union the work they want? If James won't give you a piece of the action, I bet they will."

All I could do was laugh.

"Sure, that's funny," she said. "Why couldn't you do something? I'm serious. We got that pool, didn't we?"

"That was different, a small favor. You do business with these people," I said, shaking my head, "and they own you. I bet that's how Milo got *killed.* We're talking the real thing here. He was feeding them information, keeping the project going forward. We snuck in the steel and they blamed him. You make a mistake with that union, you're done."

"And James doesn't own you?" she asked. The corners of her mouth turned down and her eyes wrinkled. She took my wrist and removed my hand from her stomach, looked away, and sighed.

"He said he's got an announcement tonight that we're all going to like," I said in a whisper, twisting my finger up into a lock of her hair. "What if I was the president?"

She turned over, looking into my eyes, still suspicious. "He said that?"

I shrugged. "What else would make me happy after losing Milo's share?"

"If it's true—" she said.

"It's got to be."

"You'd get a huge salary," she said, the pace of her words picking up. "You'd have to be a partner in every project going forward, right? We could still do the house.

We'd have to finance it, but we could do it. You'd run everything, and . . ."

"What?" I asked after a minute.

She gripped my hand, squeezing tight.

"Those goddamn planes," she said. "If you needed one this time, you'd just take it."

"Don't talk about that," I said, touching her face with the backs of my fingers and shaking my head. "Don't ruin it."

13

I DRESSED IN THE CLOTHES Jessica laid out for me. She helped me into a jacket that went over a button-down shirt that was open at the collar. Then she put a Tylenol with codeine into my hand and said I should put down the bag of ice. She wore a conservative pants suit with her hair in a black velvet band that made her look even younger than usual. We walked downstairs, hand in hand. She kissed everyone on the cheek and shook their hands. A pro.

"Don't make a big thing out of your lip," she said in a whisper, brushing some lint off my collar and pushing my finger away from my face. "They'll see it."

Everyone was in the bar, dozens of them, mingling with drinks in their hands. I got into the corner with a double scotch and watched her. People came to her, warming themselves on her smile, the tilt of her head, the sparkle in her eye. Finally, even James found his way. She kissed his cheek and motioned me over with her eyes.

"We're very excited," she was saying when I got there.

James smiled at her and said, "You know. I'm excited

too. Every day I'm excited. I've got the greatest wife in the world and the greatest family."

"And now, on top of it all, this project is going," Jessica said. "It's amazing."

"A lot of hard work," James said, putting his hand on my shoulder. "A lot by this guy here. He and Scott are really the ones that make this company run. He's great, you know that?"

"I think so," she said, touching my other shoulder.

I looked at my shoes.

"Jesus. What did you do to your lip?" James asked.

I said it was no big deal, but I told the story and he had a laugh and told me that would teach me to do anything with Ben that had to do with hunting or fishing. Then he excused himself and went to talk with Jim Morris, our CFO and one of the partners from the early days.

Jessica squeezed my arm and, in a whisper, she said, "You're getting it."

"He said Scott and I made it happen. Scott."

"He gave Scott the money," she said. "He's *got* to give you the title. Scott doesn't need it. You know I'm right about these things."

Bucky cleared his throat. He stood in the doorway looking uncomfortable in a tight blue blazer and told everyone that dinner was being served in the wine cellar.

The walls of the wine cellar were dry-laid stone. Old-world style where the crack between each gray rock was a dark fissure, even in the barrel-vaulted ceilings. They flew five guys over from Italy to make it. The floors were clay, packed solid, and the heavy chain railings that hung suspended along the staircases were completely immovable.

A small fire crackled in a grate set into the wall four

feet above the floor. Sconces glowed yellow from high up on the walls as a complement to the vast iron chandelier hanging over the long table. There were three vaults on opposite sides of the chamber with steps that led to the dusty racks of wine collected from every corner of the world, some of the bottles nearly priceless.

Behind a Flemish tapestry was the elevator where dinner was delivered from the kitchen. On the other side of the rough-hewn table was a sideboard, covered with wine and cheese and fruit. Glasses clinked with ice and the women's laughter was like the tinkling of wind chimes. I circled down the last set of stairs behind Jessica.

She reached back and squeezed my hand and we moved into the room, sitting down at the far end of the table from James, opposite Ben. Jessica gripped my thigh. The wineglasses were already full and I raised mine to Ben. He lifted his glass too, and we drank a silent toast.

The food was served right away, course after course with the chef explaining each dish and the accompanying wine. Duck liver pâté with a Merlot. Endive and walnut salad with a Pinot Noir. Seared lake trout with a semidry Riesling. Crème brûlée with a Finger Lakes Icewine. I didn't taste any of it, and when James began to tap his wineglass with a spoon, I had to swallow hard to keep the food from coming up.

The table went quiet. James cleared his throat and said, "I wanted everyone here because I have an announcement."

James stood up. He was wearing a blue blazer with an open-collared shirt. He put a hand on his wife, Eva's, shoulder and she beamed up at him.

"Everyone in this room has worked together to make something unbelievably special," James said. "King Corp is the largest privately held real estate development company in the world. And, because of the people in this room, we've finally begun construction on the biggest, most profitable mall in the world."

Here James paused for a moment for everyone to clap.

"I won't go into individuals," James said, "because everything we've done, we've done as a team. Our rewards are the fortunes we've created.

"But every team needs a leader."

Jessica was squeezing me so hard I winced. I put my hand over hers and held it tight.

"And for years, I've worked to develop leadership from our younger partners, to pass the torch," James said. "And now we're at a crossroads."

My heart was hammering hard, pushing up into the back of my throat. I was floating, and James's words came from far away.

"We're going in an entirely new direction," James said, grinning at us, his cheeks flushed next to the white flowing hair, his eyes reflecting the points of light in the chandelier. "One I never imagined, but one that makes the most sense.

"We're going public. Over the last six months, I've gotten together a world-class board of directors. Goldman Sachs is ready to underwrite the offering. Part of making it happen was me agreeing to stay on as CEO. Me staying on was critical to the deal, and my commitment to the board is for life."

The fire crackled; otherwise, it was quiet. Going public meant flushing the company with money from stock market investors. It would allow King Corp to grow even bigger, to use those hundreds of millions to buy other companies. But it would also take much of the control away from the family and the partners. A public company had to answer to the shareholders. They would elect the board of directors in the future, who could in turn hire and fire any of us. We would also have to endure the scrutiny of the SEC and their legion of accounting rules and regulations.

"We need officers," James said, "and we've got them. It's time for the next generation. Thane, you'll be the president of the company. Scott, you're the COO. Both of you will report directly to me. Ben, you're the executive vice president of operations. The next generation."

He gave us nothing. No stocks. No options. Nothing but titles for preppies with Ivy League degrees. Shit people bragged about in country club grill rooms. Shit.

I felt Jessica's nails dig into my leg.

Scott jumped up, knocking his chair back to the floor.

"That's bullshit!" he yelled, stabbing a thick finger at his father, poking his chest. "We're not a public company and we're not going to be one. I didn't come back here for this. You're too old to do this. The game passed you by."

"This is *my* company," James said.

"That's bullshit! Who just put together the deal with the bank! Two billion at one hundred over LIBOR!"

"I did! We did!"

"You said they'd never do it! You would have settled for one-fifty and you know it!"

James started around the table. Eva grabbed at his jacket, pulling him back. Jim Morris jumped up and got between them. Ben ran around and grabbed Scott.

"You're not doing this!" Scott yelled, letting Ben pull

him toward the stone stairs. "I didn't work my ass off for this!"

His fiancée, Emily, got up and hurried after Scott. The thunder of his feet going across the catwalk in the upper reaches of the cellar pounded down on us.

I looked at Jessica. She was staring at James. Her mouth was a flat line and her eyes had an empty look, like she was past hating him. Like she knew he was already dead.

14

I PUSHED BACK FROM THE TABLE and followed Jessica out of the wine cellar. I tried to put my hand on her shoulder, but she didn't want me to touch her. On the way out the front door, she grabbed her coat off its hook and pulled it on.

I followed her as she started down the path that walked along the water's edge. She hugged herself against the night chill. Her head was down. Above, the sky was clear.

When the lodge was out of earshot, I said, "You can't just not talk."

She kept going.

Over a narrow part of the lake hung a suspension bridge. Bucky built it by hand. Jessica climbed the stairs and started across. The bridge, a series of wood planks woven together with thick rope, swayed under even her light weight. The sound of her shoes went halfway across and then stopped.

I climbed up and followed, gripping the hairy rope railings and trying my best to place each foot directly in front of the other, fighting the sense that the whole thing was ready to go down. When I got there, she sniffed. Even in the starlight I could see the tears glistening on her face.

I put my hand on hers. It was chilled to the bone, but she didn't pull away.

"I hate him," she said.

"He's given us a lot," I said. "Try to think of that."

"He took more than he can ever give."

"You're so bitter," I said.

"Are you fucking numb?" she said, turning her face toward me before looking back out across the water at the glowing lodge.

"I hurt too," I said.

"It's different for a mother," she said. "I could kill him."

"He didn't cause it," I said.

"He could have saved him," she said. "You know it."

"If he'd known, I'm sure he would have."

Our first baby, Teague, was born about four weeks early. His heart had a bad valve. At first they said he just wasn't going to make it. Jessica went out of her mind. They had to sedate her. I was in a fog, bumping into doorways and stumbling around. Then this young doctor came in and said there was a surgeon in Dallas who'd been doing some groundbreaking things and that we should try to get Teague down there. Right away. Like every minute counted.

They had an air ambulance lined up, but it was the middle of winter and the plane was stuck in Buffalo. Lake-effect storm. Jessica told me to get James's plane and I asked him. But he only had one back then and he was going to South America the next morning. A dove hunt.

He said the air ambulance would make it.

Everything would be fine.

"You think he loses sleep over it?" she asked. "You think he goes through life like a cripple? That's me, Thane. Like I lost my arm. I wish I had. Every day. Every minute, I know my baby is gone. *He* had a hunting trip. My God."

She turned to me and said, "Don't you dare defend him to me."

"You think I don't feel the same way?" I said, raising my voice, shouting across the still water, clutching the railing and rocking the bridge. "You think I don't remember what it was like before? When we'd walk into some party holding hands, people telling me how I had it made?"

"Then I got pregnant," she said. "Is that what you mean?"

"Are you kidding me? That's what you think?" I said. "Who took those classes with you? That breathing stuff and the contractions and all that other Lamaze stuff? Who painted that crib? And his room? Who said we should name him after your Grampa Teague?"

Jessica's father's father was Grampa Teague. A retired air force officer who had a cottage on Canandaigua Lake. He died just before her dad did. She always said if he had been alive, he never would have let her live on that dairy farm. He'd always have candy in his pocket and change he'd give to her, and once every summer she got to stay with him for a week in that lake cottage and when she had to go back home she'd cry herself to sleep for a month.

"You think I didn't want you pregnant?" I said, my voice trailing off in a pitiful whine.

"Sometimes I wonder," she said, and it cut me. She pushed past me and started back toward the lodge.

I followed like a dog.

"A dog?" the shrink says.

"It's a saying."

He nods slowly and says, "Did you feel like a dog? Like her dog?"

I search his dark eyes for an insult, but don't find one. I cock my head and say, "She was probably in control of the situation."

"Like your own mother?"

"There you go," I say, slapping the table. "I knew we'd get to this."

"There were other women involved," he says. "And you seemed to suggest that they were in control too."

"Who? The witches? I said they were reading a script."

"You kind of talked like they had this special power," he says, "to know things."

"Well, shit, man," I say, "they were with the FBI, running around behind the scenes. Tapping people's phones. Following them with infrared cameras. They better know things."

"Can you tell me what they knew?"

"Well, I didn't know then, but I do now."

"Okay," he says. "Tell me."

15

Amanda Lee sat at the far corner of the long boardroom table at the FBI's offices in New York City. She could see the reflection of her fingers on the gleaming walnut surface. Silently she tapped them, wishing that Dorothy Rooks would stop chewing her gum. Agents filled the low-back leather chairs up one side of the room and NYPD detectives filled the other. Their supervisor sat at the head of the table with his sleeves rolled up to his elbows, his tie yanked loose, and his thick glasses sinking toward the end of his nose.

One of the New York detectives got up and pulled the pushpin out of Milo Peterman's photo, taking hold of it only to let it drop into the waste can. The photo of Johnny G stared out at her, pale-eyed, from the middle of the board. The arrogant smile of someone with a secret. A straight nose and the small ears of a boxer. The neck of a bull. Not a bad-looking man, but no doubt there was something missing in those pale eyes. They were the eyes of a man who saw little difference between people and furniture.

"Goddamn backwards," their supervisor said. "Three

years since I've taken over. I've got a meeting in Washington on Friday and that's what I'm saying? We're nowhere?"

Everyone stared at the table.

There was one other woman on the task force besides Amanda and Dorothy and she sat at the supervisor's right hand. An accountant from the IRS with glasses and plain brown hair pulled back tight. She never spoke unless someone asked her a question, but at that moment she had her hand in the air like they were all at school.

"Yes?"

"Dorothy asked me to examine the tax returns of the witness they're working on, Thane Coder, and I found something," she said, looking down at the file in front of her and extracting a page. "He got a priority distribution from a partnership that he claimed as passive income. They tried to say it was for rental income, but that's not really what it was. When a payment from a partnership is—"

"Just cut to it."

"I was."

"How much?"

The accountant looked like she was about to cry. Amanda heard Dorothy grunt.

"Two million dollars."

One of the New York cops let out a low whistle. The supervisor's eyes were on Amanda now.

"And?"

Amanda glanced at Dorothy, who said, "He's got a wife who ain't gonna like that."

"He's extended already," Amanda said.

"What about a wire?" the supervisor said, blinking and pushing his glasses up. "Johnny G's going to want to talk business with someone. If Milo was their man on the inside, then they need another one."

"Maybe," Amanda said.

"Why maybe?" the supervisor asked.

"Coder's been around this stuff a long time," Amanda said. "Beat the union at their own game. He might think he can beat us at ours. When we mentioned a pool he had built as a kickback for another project, he started talking about his lawyer."

"Bull," Dorothy said, snapping her gum. "We'll get him wearing a wire by the weekend."

Amanda closed her eyes.

"Here," Dorothy said, "put him up there."

She took an 8 × 10 glossy photo of Thane Coder out of her briefcase and slid it past Amanda toward the end of the conference table. It was passed along until it reached the detective who had taken down Milo's picture. He got up and used the same pushpin to fix Coder to the board, the connection between the union and King Corp. In the photo, Thane's dark hair was being blown by the wind and the brown eyes in his handsome face had a far-off look. The teeth were slightly crooked. His was a different face than the others. It was the face of someone Amanda wanted to like. It lacked a certain cunning that the others all shared. It lacked that vacant, reptilian stare.

"There," the supervisor said, planting his palm on the walnut surface. "A somewhat positive note. Thank you."

Amanda watched the city cops nudge one another and bite their lips as they cast their eyes at Dorothy on their way out the door. She took the paper from the accountant.

"His 1999 tax return," the accountant said.

"Will he know what we're even talking about?"

Amanda asked. She studied the six-figure numbers on the return and thought of her own two children's college funds and the money her husband had taken out of them in the past six months to begin a direct marketing business selling overseas calling cards.

"He should. He was pushing the envelope. Everyone was back in '99. Remember?"

"He'll know," Dorothy said, snatching the paper. "And so will she. Christ, she had a rock on her hand with its own zip code. She'll understand two million, and I don't think a blaze orange jumpsuit will tickle her fashion sense. This is it. The rest of this bunch may be going backwards, but we just shot to the head of the class."

As they rode down the elevator, Dorothy asked Amanda if she needed to go home for a change of clothes.

"Why?"

"We can't wait until tomorrow. You heard the boss. Friday's the big day."

Amanda looked at her watch. She could hear her husband's nasal whine and the kids' groans. Her stomach dipped.

"We wouldn't get there until like ten o'clock."

The bell dinged and the doors slid open.

"Good," Dorothy said, stepping out into the parking garage with her wiry stride, "we'll get them out of bed."

"Dorothy, we worked through the night last night," Amanda said, catching up.

"And we both went home and slept. Neither snow, nor heat, nor rain, nor gloom of night."

"That's the Post Office."

"We're better than a friggin' mailman, right? You must have missed a few bedtime stories chasing serial killers."

Dorothy slipped into their Crown Vic and Amanda got in the passenger's side.

"And that's a big part of why I'm here."

"'Cause you thought Organized Crime was for housewives?" Dorothy said, snorting before she started the engine.

"Being a partner sometimes means thinking about your partner."

"You mean him, or me?" Dorothy asked, looking behind them as she backed up.

"Both."

"So, you'll go home to your hubby and I'll go up to Syracuse alone. I'll cover for you. How's that?" Dorothy said, screeching the wheels around the tight bend as they shot up the ramp toward the street.

"Fine," Amanda said, crossing her arms. "Swing by my house and I'll get my things."

They drove through the city, Dorothy swerving in and out of traffic and pounding the horn. They were through the tunnel before she spoke again. This time, her voice was even and not as harsh.

"I see the way those NYPD jackasses look at me," she said, nodding her head as if Amanda had asked a question. "You too. Like we're filling a quota. But we can break this thing.

"I know you've got a family and I know I don't. This shit, yeah, it's my life. Fucking pathetic. I talk about my husband and those cats, but they disappear sometimes for a week, him and the cats, and I don't even think about them. This is my life. So, I'm sorry."

"You don't have to be," Amanda said. "I want to bring these people down as badly as you do."

16

AMANDA WENT INSIDE and listened patiently while her husband and kids groaned. She kept her mouth shut and packed a bag, her eyelids at half-mast, not from physical exhaustion, but from the mental grinding. She actually felt relief when the car door slammed shut and they took off down her tree-lined street.

The trip took them less than four hours with Amanda navigating from a road atlas and one quick stop in the dark for coffee and gas. Just before they got to the lane that led to Thane Coder's lake house, the headlights of a car coming from the opposite direction cut in and disappeared past a white farmhouse and some standing corn.

"Bet it's them," Dorothy said, turning. Gravel rattled against the undercarriage.

Down at the end of the lane a set of taillights disappeared around another bend. Dorothy raced. Amanda braced herself against the dash as they shot around the corner. Dead corn stalks stood straight and even in the glow of the headlights. There was a dark opening in a cluster of tall pine trees up ahead and when they drove through it, they came to a set of brick walls illuminated by a pair of post lanterns. The wrought iron gates waited, open for them. Dorothy started through just as the gates began to swing shut. She punched the accelerator and Amanda heard the crunch of metal and plastic as the gates struck the rear end of the car.

"Shit."

Down by the house, Jessica Coder shielded her eyes against their headlights. She looked small in her rumpled suit. Her hair was in a tangle, as if she'd been driving with the window down.

"Can I help you?" she said, glaring at them as they climbed out of the Crown Vic.

"FBI, ma'am," Dorothy said, flipping open her badge.

"We need to talk to you," Amanda said.

"My husband is coming," Jessica said.

"Can we come in?"

"Is it about his accident?" Jessica said.

"We should probably sit down," Amanda said.

Jessica looked toward her house, then studied the two women for a moment before she said, "Sure."

The front door was unlocked and they followed Jessica inside. A young woman appeared and with a Russian accent said she'd put the boy to bed. Jessica took money from her purse and put it into the woman's hand before she slipped out the door with a sideways glance.

Jessica led them into a room that was almost as big as Amanda's entire house. A tall span of windows overlooked the long dark lake. A band of moonlight glowed across its width, and random specks of light winked from homes up and down the thick black hillsides bordering the long stretch of water.

Amanda smelled the musky scent of fresh lilies. There

was a tall vase of them resting in the middle of a coffee table. Amanda and Dorothy sat on the couch, and Jessica sat in a leather chair with her hands gripping the armrests and her feet curled up underneath her. She was a pretty woman, almost girlish except for the small creases at the corners of eyes whose sharpness put Amanda on guard.

"So?" she asked in a voice as small as her figure.

Amanda heard Dorothy snort.

"Mrs. Coder," she said. "Remember Al Capone?"

"I guess."

Amanda rolled her eyes and cleared her throat, but Dorothy wasn't stopping.

"A crime boss. A murdering monster," she said. "You know what he went to jail for? Taxes. That's a big thing in this country. You cheat Uncle Sam, you end up in stripes. Two years in federal prison. That's what you're looking at.

"Both of you."

17

So," the shrink says, leaning back in his chair and folding his hands over his stomach, "what did they want?"

"To screw me over."

"Deep down."

"The one probably wanted to be a man."

"Or?"

"Castrate her father? Isn't that the other Freud thing?"

"What else do men have? In law enforcement that women might not?"

I think about that for a minute in a serious way before I say, "Respect, I guess."

"Hmm."

"Wow. I'm cured."

He almost smiles, but gets it under control right away and in that rumbling voice says, "There are different ways to get respect. Someone does a good job. Maybe they got money or power or fame, but it's all about self-worth. We define who we are in the context of our own reality."

"Deep," I say, wondering what textbook that line came out of.

"Women want respect," he says. "We all do. Your wife

did, right? Isn't material wealth just another way to gain respect? Especially in our world. Conflict, stress, mental disorder come when you do something you don't respect to get respect ... like a snake eating its tail."

"You lost me," I say.

"I don't think I did," he says. "But back to you. The night James told you the company was going public."

"After what she said about me not wanting her to be pregnant, I stopped talking too," I say. "We just went back and started packing our things. I took the bags down the back stairs and loaded up our cars in the dark. When I went to shut the door, Eva King was standing there, apologizing for the ruckus, and telling me we should stay.

"I told her Jessica wasn't feeling well, which was pretty much the truth. Eva told me she knew how hard I worked and that it would all turn out okay.

"She knew James worked me like a dog. There you go, I did it again. Anyway, she knew about what happened—or what didn't happen—to me with football. She knew what I wanted.

"And, she knew the whole president thing was like shooting ducks on their way back to the barn. A setup."

"So you left," he says.

"Yes," I say. "Out of the pan and into the fire, and if I didn't stop to talk to Eva, or if I'd driven a little faster, I might not be sitting here right now."

"How is that?" he asks.

I shrug and say, "We drove separate cars to Cascade, remember? What if I kept up with Jessica on the ride home? If I'd pulled in right behind her, then I'd have been there to greet them and maybe those two witches wouldn't have backed her into a corner. She was smart, but she never had anything like that happen before.

"I'd seen that kind of stuff. We had a partner out in Boston try to lay some fraud crap on James a few years back, got the FBI involved. I guarantee you the minute I heard them talk about jail I would have stopped it and called my lawyer. Then maybe Jessica wouldn't have gotten the whole crazy idea into her head, cutting a deal with the union."

"Didn't you say she mentioned that before?"

"Mentioned," I say, "but this pushed her right over the edge. I think she figured if they were going to treat her like a criminal, she might as well get something out of it."

18

I ALMOST CAUGHT UP TO HER. There was a back way to get home that's a little quicker. The thing about the shortcut though is the twists and turns and the high spots. There's one on Depot Road over by County Line that when you come off it you feel that light-headed rush and the heavy brick that drops in your gut. Right after it there's a hairpin turn and that's where I lost control. I was fine and the car only had a few scratches, but I sat there for a minute, breathing and thinking that it was the second time in two days. I sat too long.

By the time I got there, that dark blue Crown Vic was already sitting there, empty in the driveway right beside the Mercedes with its engine ticking. I bolted inside, thinking maybe they'd waited for me, but Jessica was already sitting there in the living room, swiveling gently back and forth in one of those heavy leather captain's chairs. Her hands were splayed out on those thick leather armrests with the tips of her fingers dug in. Her back was to the fireplace, facing those two FBI witches. They were sitting on the couch with their hands on their knees and their eyebrows knit tight. Jessica was smiling at them, and simpering.

But deep in her eyes was an acid burning I doubt they noticed. My stomach turned, and they all stopped talking and looked at me.

All I could do was stand there with my hands hanging heavy at my sides, knowing that whatever I said, it was already too late. Jessica had some kind of a plan. I'd seen that look.

"We'll do whatever you need," she said, nodding to them and me at the same time.

I sat down on the ottoman next to her chair and held one of her hands. She covered my hand with her other one, patting it gently, soothing me.

"What are we doing?" I asked, looking from her to them.

"Mr. Coder," Dorothy said. "Two years ago, you were paid just over two million dollars by King Corp. You used the money to cover your bets in the stock market. Unfortunately, you never paid taxes on the two million dollars."

"I know that," I said. A seashell sound started humming in my ears. "Those were capital losses in the market. The money was a priority distribution for the leases on the Cumberland Mall. That's rental income. It's passive."

"No," Amanda said, shaking her head slow and almost sad, "it's not, Mr. Coder. We all know it's not."

"My accountant said it was," I said. I was fighting that drifting feeling again.

Jessica squeezed my fingers so hard their bones ached.

"I signed them too," she said.

"A joint return," Dorothy said, a smile sneaking onto her yellow face.

"Tax fraud for something this big, you're looking at two years, Mr. Coder," Amanda said, pinching her lips.

"Remember Al Capone?" Dorothy said. "I told your wife, eleven years in Alcatraz for the same damn thing."

"Look, we can help you," Amanda said. "We just need you to help us too."

Jessica let up and I felt the blood flooding back into my fingers. They tingled.

"We appreciate it," Jessica said, stroking my hand.

I did a double-take, and despite that look in her eye, I stared at her as I spoke and said, "I think we should talk to John."

John Langan was King Corp's lawyer.

"No," Jessica said, her voice was gentle, but she crushed my fingers in the web of her hand, "we shouldn't. They're trying to help us."

She was breathing heavy. Shaking. Willing me to shut up.

I looked at the big window that looked out over the water. Through the ghost of my own reflection I saw the night clouds drifting, their fringes lit by the moon they hid, and the dead black of the earth below. The lake might have been a tar pit, the kind that lured dinosaurs to their death, promising a drink.

"We'll do whatever you need," Jessica said to the agents. "We will."

"All right," I said.

"We'd like you to set up a meeting with Johnny G," Amanda said. Her red hair reflected the yellow light of the room. "To talk about the upcoming contracts for the mall."

"Plumbing, electric, Sheetrock," Dorothy said. "If you give him a whiff, he'll be on it like a crow."

"What about James?" I asked.

"No one else should know," Amanda said, nodding now and smiling, the lines gone from her face. "You won't go through with the deals, just get him into play. If we need James King, we'll talk to him. Meantime, we'll be watching everything. You'll be safe."

"Like Milo?" I said.

"Milo was working for *them*. You'll be working for us."

"The good guys," Dorothy said, flashing a fake smile on and off. "In case you're confused."

Amanda stood up and said they'd be in touch, and that we'd clearly made the right decision. We all walked into the foyer, newfound friends saying goodbye.

When they left, Jessica shut the door and gave me that funny grin she has with one eyebrow lifting just a bit higher than the other.

"That was not you," I said.

"No? What's me?"

"Why wouldn't we call John? That's what you do when things like this happen. You never just . . . just roll over."

"Is that what I did?" she said, laughing and heading for the kitchen.

I followed.

"What are you doing?" I asked, turning toward her.

"Making Tommy's lunch," she said, taking bread, mayo, and a container of boiled chicken out of the refrigerator and setting it on the countertop. "He's been asking for my chicken salad for three days."

I sat down on one of the stools on the opposite side of

the counter, my back to the windows now, and put my elbow on the countertop, resting my head on my hand.

"Cheer up," she said, dumping chunks of chicken onto a wood cutting board and chopping them up with a cleaver. "They just gave us a license to steal."

"Steal what?" I said, my mouth hanging open, my head coming up off my hand.

"The FBI told you to cut a deal with Johnny G, right?" she said, chopping.

"Yeah, so they can arrest him. You know what happens to people who do this kind of stuff? They change their name and move to Utah."

"They must not play the middle then," she said, taking a carrot from the fridge and shaving it onto the board.

"How's that?" I asked.

"The FBI," she said. "They're like lamprey eels. They bore into your flesh and keep you bleeding. You either fill them up and they fall off, or they kill you. So we've got to fill them up."

"Your creepy biology."

"You'll give them meetings with Johnny G," she said, scraping the pulverized chicken and carrots into a bowl and adding a dollop of mayo. "You'll wear their wires until they can't stand it anymore. Hours and hours of talk."

"And when Johnny G finds out? I end up like Milo. Jessica, these people are fucking lunatics."

"Only the talk is worthless. The union, they're businessmen too," she said, her eyes glimmering in the moonlight, her voice lowered as if someone might hear. She stopped stirring and started adding spices, a dash here, a shake there. "That's the middle. We'll cut a deal with Johnny G to push the work to the contractor he wants.

"We'll tell him about the FBI," she said, starting to stir again, her pace quickening with the cadence of her words. "He makes things up, sends the FBI on a wild-goose chase. Then you steer the work to the contractors he cuts deals with *and* we get part of it. Cash on the side. If anything ever goes wrong, we're working for the FBI, right?"

"You're confusing me," I said.

"What we're doing or not doing for the FBI will be so muddled they'll never be able to prove a thing. The bottom line is this, we'll push the work to the people Johnny tells us and he'll pay us to do it. He feeds the FBI fake information when you're wearing your wire. It's perfect."

"I just spent six months getting around this union," I said.

"And getting nothing for it," she said, doling out the chicken salad onto some bread.

"Think about what you're saying."

"Who got you this far?" she said, wrapping the sandwich and sliding it into a brown paper bag. "This is a chance. Sometimes they come around and you have to take them. It's your turn. You can steer that work to the contractors we want, right?"

"If it's not too obvious."

"I'm sure Johnny G can get his contractors to give you bids that are reasonable. Pass me that cookie jar," she said.

"What'd you make?" I asked, taking off the lid and smelling cinnamon.

"Cinnamon oatmeal," she said, stuffing a handful of them into a Ziploc bag. "They do this stuff all the time and things get built down there. Skyscrapers like that Trump thing. King Corp can hire the union-backed contractors and James never even has to know it. We get our cut. The FBI gets a bunch of worthless audiotapes and they can't say we didn't help."

"You heard those agents. They'll be watching. Everything I do. Everything he does."

"I know, honey," she said, adding a bag of chips and putting the finished lunch bag into the fridge before she leaned across the counter to kiss the tip of my nose.

"Time for bed," she said. And then, "That's why the deal has to be done by someone they won't be watching."

She smiled and said, "Me."

19

I look at the shrink, nodding my head.

"What, like a double agent?" he says.

"I told her a guy like Johnny G wasn't going to do business with a woman. You know, all that Italian mobster crap. She looked at me like I was sad.

"She lined it up. Walked right into the union hall. Wouldn't leave until she could see Johnny G. Told him she was just the messenger. He probably bought it. For a little while, anyway. I doubt it took him too long, though, to figure out I had no say."

"Back to your script? No choices."

"That's right," I say.

"Come on. Killing James King, you did that."

"If someone holds a gun to your head and says, 'Shoot the guy that walks through that door or I'll shoot you,' and you do it, is that murder?"

"You got to be accountable."

"Who's accountable for that?"

"Someone had a gun to your head?"

"Goddamn right. They might as well have."

• • •

I took off my suit coat and the shirt underneath and this technical geek stuck the wire to my bare skin. Those two witches stood there watching. I could smell my sweat. I felt a chill, crossed my arms, and put my hands up over my nipples. The redhead's face went pink and she looked down at the floor. The manly one just twisted her mouth up like she'd stepped in something.

It was a hoot, really, walking into this little yellow house right off the interstate that they'd turned into a restaurant and seeing Johnny G sitting there in the back corner booth, his eyes shining like a cat's. He jumped right into it, talking nonsense about a big contractor that he wanted me to steer the work to, a contractor who I knew because they sponsored just about every charity fundraiser you could think of. And the smile that Johnny G wore was laughing as much at us steering the government away from our own corruption as it was at gumming up the works for the honest and legitimate people working for the competition.

I had already convinced James to bid out the entire job to a small list of qualified general contractors, arguing that time was money and with the slow season coming that we could get the benefits of one of the big boys without having to pay the usual premium you had to for one-stop shopping. Johnny G's real connection would be to one of the finalists, and their name would never come up in the conversation that was being taped by the FBI.

I felt like I was watching a movie, sitting there eating caprise salad, fried squid, and manicotti in vodka sauce, grinning at a man I despised. Johnny G didn't make it easy either. He didn't just sit there, smiling like a normal person holding a handful of aces. He had this tick that I'd never noticed before. Every other minute, he'd lick the tip of his finger and touch it to the back of his neck and I found myself wishing like hell that he'd stop. But he never did, so the fun of sticking it to the FBI was watered down by having to conspire with a crooked guy who had a tick.

I walked out of the restaurant feeling small, but things got better back at the cheesy motel where I met those witches and their geeky henchman. They were slapping each other high-fives over their big breakthrough. On top of the world. Better than the rest of us with their shiny badges and their government pensions waiting for them at the end of the game.

"You don't look too happy," Rooks said after they'd calmed down.

"I'm worried about my ass," I said, putting on a scowl and suppressing a silly grin. "You're not the one they'll be looking for when this comes out."

"No one's gunning anyone down," the redhead said, looking at me with those big green eyes and some genuine concern.

"Yeah, tell Milo," I said, wondering what would behoove anyone in their right mind to entrust their life to the FBI.

"We told you," red said, setting her mouth, "that was different."

"Just so you know," I said, "if my wife's signature wasn't on those tax returns, you'd be battling this out with my lawyer."

"It's not too late," Rooks said.

"Dorothy," the redhead said, "please. Can we take it easy?"

When I got home that night we had a little family dinner. Jessica grilled some steaks and cooked up thick fries. Tommy chattered about soccer practice and I tried to keep my eyes focused on him when he was speaking even though my mind wasn't. I didn't feel too bad about it. My old man never even looked my way at the dinner table.

When we finished, Jessica started cleaning up and my son asked if I wanted to watch TV.

"Don't you have homework?" I asked.

"Yeah, want to help me?"

"No one helped me," I said. "That's not how you learn. Go do it."

"Then can I watch wrestling?"

"Sure."

"With you?"

"We'll see."

"Undertaker is fighting Kurt Angle."

"Okay. Do your homework first."

I watched him disappear. Jessica had a bottle of Pinot Noir and two glasses, and she angled her head toward the big leather captain's chairs in the living room.

"He could use a little more from you," she said.

I followed her to the chairs. She poured the wine and handed me a glass.

"And you?" I said. "You give him everything he needs?"

She stared at me for a minute, her eyes filling before she looked away.

"I love him," I said quietly. What I couldn't say was that part of me cringed whenever I saw my son or heard his voice. I hated myself for that, but what I went through with Teague I never wanted to feel again. "Can we not do this?"

"I just think you could be a little easier."

"I know," I said. "I'll try."

She sighed and went quiet, sipping her wine.

"So," I said, swirling the wine around, changing my tone and the subject. "Who's in with Johnny G? Bell Construction? Hogan & Price?"

"How does half point on the gross sound?" she said, arching her brow and raising her glass.

"Jesus," I said. Millions of dollars.

"Cash," she said. "When you take the bids, you'll let them know what everyone else's numbers are. They'll make sure they come in lower. You take their bid and we let them make it up on extras."

It's called low-balling. A contractor gives a low quote to get a job, but once they get into it, they start adding on extras, high-priced addendums they argue weren't part of the original scope of the bid, but things that are essential to complete the project. Like a bait and switch. Risky if you're working for someone who won't budge, a sweet deal if you've got someone like me on the inside who will approve the extras.

"Who?" I asked.

"Con Trac," she said.

I whistled, surprised at a company with that kind of pristine reputation cutting a deal with Johnny G.

"I'll have to get these extras past James," I said.

"But you can," she said. "He's not going to get us this time."

20

I TRIED TO GO ABOUT BUSINESS AS USUAL, but I must have acted a little funny because James called me into his office a few weeks later, after our six-thirty morning meeting, and asked me how I was. I told him fine, just fine, and he looked blankly at me the way he did whenever he was thinking hard about something.

"The bids come in tomorrow," he said.

I didn't say anything. He wasn't asking. On one corner of his walnut desk rested the bust of an African tribal queen, cut from black onyx, a gift that Scott had brought back from one of his safaris. She held her chin high and her eyes were cast upward as if she were silently communicating with the gods.

"I want to take a look at them," he said. "Before we award the work."

"Really? Why?"

The words shot out past my lips before I could shut the gates. The wrinkles in the corners of James's eyes deepened and he smiled at me the way you would a kid who you just fooled with a simple card trick.

"We're going public," he said, like that was something that led to an obvious conclusion.

My gut was in a knot. I looked away from him, away from the African queen, and nodded my head.

"That's fine."

"Tomorrow is opening day of bow season," he said. "I'll be at the lodge. When you get everything together, bring them up. We'll have dinner and go over the numbers."

"It should be pretty cut-and-dry."

"I'm leaning toward OBG Tech," he said.

I swallowed down some bile.

"Whoever's low, right?"

"No," he said, smiling. "This is too important. They'll come in with one of the lower bids and unless it's ridiculous, we'll use them. They're local."

"They've never done anything this big."

"It's about trust," he said, his voice going soft. "You understand that, right?"

"Of course."

"Good. I'll see you tomorrow night."

21

JOHNNY G HAD GIVEN JESSICA a number to call and she did.

"Y-ello?"

"Hi. This is Jessica Coder," she said. "Johnny told me to call if I needed him."

"So what?"

"Well, I need him."

"You're new."

"Can I talk to him?"

"I'll tell him you called when I see him."

"Listen," she said, "I'm sure this is your job, but you get him. I need to speak to him right away. Tell him we're going to lose the Garden State deal. We've got one day to fix it. He's going to want to know. I promise you."

"Yeah. I know."

"You really need to tell him. Tell him I'll be at this number. You got the number?"

"It's on the phone."

"I wouldn't want to be either one of us if this falls through."

"Easy, babe. I'll tell him."

Jessica paced the big room. The picture window looked out over the lake. Early morning. A gray mist hid the far hills. The water was choppy and the color of tarnished silver in the weak light. The cell phone in her hand was slick with sweat, her grip so tight that the tendons in her forearm began to ache. She jumped when the phone rang and snapped it open.

He gave her the name of a lodge in the Poconos, Gander Mountain. She said it would take her about three hours. He told her to come alone.

She was already dressed in baggy olive cargo pants, Timberland boots, and a bulky sweater. Her hair was in a tight ponytail and she wore not an ounce of makeup. It was like the day she met him several weeks ago to offer him the deal. She had walked into the union hall in northern New Jersey wearing baggy jeans and one of Thane's hooded sweatshirts. She didn't want anyone to confuse her with some bimbo in play.

The slick road sang beneath her tires as she listened to a CD by a woman named Carla Werner, over and over, the aching sounds somehow therapeutic. In the mountains of Pennsylvania, the sky began to clear. By the time she got off the highway in New Jersey, the sky was pure blue beyond the canopy of trees leading to the mountain resort. A man with slicked-back hair in a jeans jacket stood at the cobblestone entrance, leaning against a Cadillac, and cleaning his nails with a toothpick. He nodded at her and she followed his car through the trees to a cabin off by itself.

The gravel drive circled a patch of grass grown high from neglect. The fresh smell of rotting wood and leaves all around her. A bee flew past her nose and bumped into the car, drunk in the warm sunlight that fell down through the opening above to warm the grassy circle. In the shadow of the porch, the man in the jeans jacket stopped her and passed a detection wand up and down her body. The jacket hung open as he worked and a black automatic glared up at her from its leather holster beneath his arm.

"For wires," he said, then let the door swing open with a slow squeak.

Johnny G sat at a long table with a checkered cloth, drinking coffee from a thick white mug. A pall of smoke surrounded him. A cloud of pollution that made her cough. He crushed out his cigarette in a brass ashtray and exhaled smoke through his nose.

"You want one?" he asked, raising his cup and motioning with his head to the pot on the stove. "Let me get it. Have a seat."

She sat down and took the coffee in both hands, warming them against the damp chill that had settled on the cabin. Johnny G sat down and looked at her with unblinking eyes. Black holes in their center and black rings around their edges. The filling between was a milky green, the color of a scummy pond that gave no hint as to its depths or the possibility of life beneath the surface. The eyes, or maybe it was the damp, made her shiver.

She told him about the ruination of their plan, and when he asked her what the hell they expected him to do about it, she told him.

"I think you have to get rid of him."

The black holes turned to dots and his heavy cheeks pulled the lips back off his teeth. He licked the tip of his forefinger and swiped it on the back of his neck. She tried not to notice.

"You got some balls, you know that? Look at you. A housewife. You think we're in the fucking movies?"

"Milo wasn't a movie," she said, and she saw the smile freeze right where it was.

Johnny G began to nod his heavy head and it was as if he were listening to the words of someone that she couldn't hear, but she began to nod her head as well. He did the thing with his finger again.

"He's at his lodge," she said. "It's in the middle of nowhere. There's a security system, but Thane can get you in."

"Me?" he said.

"Whoever you send."

"Maybe we just let this thing go," he said, leaning back, his leather coat exposing the thick barrel of his chest.

Jessica said, "This is a two-*billion*-dollar deal. If he's gone, my husband says the two of you will own it."

Johnny G tilted his coffee mug and tapped the bottom edge against the plastic table cloth.

"This coming from you, or him?" he asked.

"What's the difference?"

"Pete," he said, raising his voice, "come here."

The door opened and the slick-haired man in the jeans jacket entered the cabin.

"We got a situation."

While Johnny G explained, Pete licked a small sore on his bottom lip and shot glances at Jessica.

When he was done, Jessica sipped her coffee and said, "I think you should make it look like it was his son."

"How's that?" Johnny said, scrunching up his face and tilting his head, his high forehead shining through the haze from cigarettes.

"They're fighting. Pull-them-off-each-other fighting. The son, Scott, keeps all his hunting things in a locker at the lodge. Thane could get you in. You could use his knife."

"Get a load of her, would you?" Johnny G said, elbowing Pete. Then his smile evaporated and he said, "But do it. I like it. Okay. Tomorrow night?"

"There's a bowling alley on Route 20 just outside of Skaneateles. The Cedar House. Who's coming?"

"Him," Johnny said, nodding at Pete.

"Thane will meet him there at ten o'clock. He'll be driving a black Mercedes convertible. Should he look for that car?" she asked, angling her head toward the front of the cabin.

"No, an Excursion," Johnny G said. "A green one."

Johnny G got up and so did Jessica. He walked her to the door and opened it for her before he clutched her upper arm and yanked her around. She felt his thick lips brush up against her ear and the heat of his breath, smelled the coffee, the cigarettes.

"You walk out of here and it's done. You understand that? You don't go back."

"I understand," she said, and he let her go.

22

So you weren't supposed to do it?"

"I remember reading this thing about time," I say. "It's supposed to be like a river, right? So one little stick can get hung up on a stone and before you know it, there's a mass of shit jamming up the water and the whole fucking river has this new course. Did you ever hear that?"

"Einstein. He said time was like a river."

"Just one little thing. A stick. A parking ticket. It's insane."

"Parking ticket?"

"Johnny G's guy, Pete. He had like twenty parking tickets down in Atlantic City. He pulls off the highway in North Jersey on his way upstate to get a taco or something. A guy jumps out in front of his car in the rain. He jams on his brakes and goes nuts with the horn and starts screaming at this guy. Back and forth they go with their fuck yourselves. A cop comes out of the taco place. He calms them down but runs the plates. There's a warrant out for Pete's arrest. That's it. A parking ticket. A fucking taco."

"And they told your wife that once you were in, you were in."

Now I have to laugh because he still doesn't see.

"Johnny G was ready to walk away," I say. "I didn't know that until later, though."

His eyes blink at me from behind those glasses, the rolls of his brow are furrowed.

I was just plain crazy. Angry. Scared. Hurt. All that crap. A basket case. A lot of women think that when a man cries it shows the sensitive side. Jessica wasn't big on it, though.

She was waiting for me when I got home from work. Wearing my favorite perfume. Aromatics it's called. A smell that reminded me of when we first met in New York City and a red dress she'd wear with nothing underneath. Tommy was at a friend's and up we went, to the bedroom. That was just the beginning, to soften me up. It wasn't always that way. She'd do that sometimes just to do it, but if she wanted something? Well, I guess it helped.

Afterward, I could have slept through dinner and the rest of the night, but she made me put on some sweat pants and a T-shirt and took me outside by the hand.

"They're going to get rid of him," she said, her words striking the silence like a hammer hitting a plow blade.

She sucked in her breath, looked around at the empty land, and said, "We'll build it right here and use those limestone blocks. It'll last ten thousand years. More."

I forgot about the sky and the lake and the world. All I saw was her face, staring hard back at me. Severe and as implacable as those limestone blocks. Her fingers wrapped tight around my wrist now.

"What?"

"James," she said.

"Johnny G is?"

"We get them into Cascade and give them the combination to Scott's locker, for his knife."

"Are you fucking kidding?"

"It's nothing," she said. "You scan your eye, and walk away."

A distressed laugh got halfway out of my mouth before I cut it off.

"Look at this," she said, opening her arms and turning in a circle. "This will be like a castle. How do you think James got what he got? Where he got to? It's the world. You have to fight for it. You have to make deals with people. James did that, maybe not with the union, but crooked politicians and lawyers and businessmen, and look at him. If his son needed an operation, he'd have it."

I was shaking my head, backing away.

"Are you okay?"

"I'm fine," I said, swiping at the corner of my eye.

"Honey," she said, narrowing with resolve as she reached for me. "Don't scare me. We have to do this. We don't have a *choice*. You have to for me. For Tommy. These people. You don't go back. That's what he said."

At that moment, I knew I was the fly. No longer struggling in the web. Spent and resting comfortably when the universe trembles and you see the spider looming, moving toward you. Ponderous at first, then quick and smooth, like a raindrop skittering down the windowpane.

"We're in it," she said.

"I know."

"We have to."

"I know."

She took my hand and led me back to the house. She told me about Pete and how I would meet him tomorrow night in the gravel parking lot outside the Cedar House. I would call James and tell him that one of the bids had been lost by FedEx, that they were looking for it and promised to have it by the next day. That way, he wouldn't be expecting me.

"You'll be fine," she said, and she opened a bottle of Opus, one she'd been saving for a special occasion. The popping cork echoed in the big empty kitchen, and we drank it. Sitting there together on the couch.

I understood where I was in all this. I had a gun to my head. Johnny G. It wouldn't do any good to grouse at her for agreeing, for getting us into this mess. We were in it. Swimming with the sharks. There was only one way out.

So, the next night, while the minute hand on my watch staggered around the face and I strained my eyes through the rain-spattered windshield at every set of headlights that pulled in off the road, I was ready to be a part of it. I knew it had to be done as certain as I knew those were my own pale hands I was looking at in the silent, blue-white flashes of lightning. If James lived, my life would end or be ruined. If he died, I was saved.

When the shape of Jessica's Jeep materialized out of the gloom, the heavy stone in my stomach shifted. I knew before she said it what I was going to have to do. I thought back to the first day we met in Central Park, a warm spring day years ago. I was a young Turk with King Corp and feeling strong. I remembered the American elms, and her textbook. The nematode, fungus, and that beetle, climbing higher into the treetops. Not knowing why.

When my watch read ten and Pete wasn't there, I felt like that beetle. When I saw her car instead, I could imagine that fungus punching through my skin. I was the shell, host to something much more powerful.

I watched her, hunched over in the rain and the wet snow, a dark shadow flitting between our two cars. She slid into the seat next to me and slammed the door. Her mouth was a flat line and the point of her chin jutted out like she was ready for a fight. I knew better.

"He's not coming," I said.

Her eyes widened and her lower lip disappeared beneath the edges of her small sharp teeth.

"We—"

"I'll do it."

She scooped up my hand and squeezed it tight. Cold skin and bird bones. Her other hand found the back of my neck and she pulled me close, kissing me in that wild desperate way that sent a current through my frame.

"He *deserves* it," she said.

I couldn't even answer that.

She whispered, "I should go with you."

"No. You shouldn't."

She sat for a minute, a helpless little girl, looking out through the wet glass as the flakes dropped down, thickening to slush. A big truck sped by, churning up a frigid misty cloud. She nodded and shivered and squeezed my hand again.

"You're right."

23

After a meal of mash and soggy, colorless vegetables, I am escorted across the yard and into the administration building for my next session with the big black shrink.

He is writing, his fat jowls trembling with effort.

When he looks up from his notes, he asks, "How are you feeling?"

"Like I'm ready for a cheeseburger made from beef," I say, sitting.

He nods and slowly stacks the papers before closing the file. He taps its manila cover and says, "You told the doctor before me that at one point you'd convinced yourself that you didn't really kill James King. Now that I know you a little, I wanted to ask you how you meant that."

"For a while, I actually did," I say.

"How?"

"The human mind is a marvelous thing, isn't it?"

"Some more than others."

"I'll tell you."

I took the stairs going down three at a time and almost fell. The image of James struggling and the dark stain of blood on the sheets replayed itself over and over in my mind. I started to slam the door but caught myself and eased it shut. The night air seemed colder. I breathed deep.

The snow was starting to collect on the ground and on the tops of the posts along the driveway. A noiseless blanket. My skin felt tight. A bolt of fear erupted from my core and I started to run. When I reached the woods and its safe smell of rotting leaves, I stopped to look back. I half expected to see someone chasing me or hear some-one yelling for me to stop. A flash of that silent lightning lit up the sky and that instant I could see down along the curving drive. Dark boot prints marked my path in the slush. A tether between me and James's body.

I tilted my head up toward the black sky and blinked. The orange glow from the lodge gave off enough light to see the wet flakes dropping like rain. I turned and kept on running until I got to my car. My lungs felt like bags of acid and my side hurt. Blood pounded through my head.

Out on the main road, a pair of headlights crept toward me. I ducked down behind my car and peered through the spattered windows. The headlights seemed to slow down, then speed back up again once it passed. I stayed in my crouch, watching the red taillights until they disap-peared around the bend, heading north toward the town of Pulaski.

I got in and checked my rearview mirror, clenching the wheel so that my hands cramped, forcing me to flex them. I took it slow, winding my way through the back roads, easing up and over the rise on Depot Road. When I pulled into my own garage, I stood there looking out, fretting over the time it took for the dark tire tracks to fill up with snow. By the time they did, my fingers were numb from cold.

Jessica was in the living room. A fire popped in the grate, the reflection of its orange and yellow light flickering off the shiny surface of the carved mantel. Her feet were curled up underneath her. In her hand was a book. It all looked so normal, and she looked up and smiled at me in a way that made me feel like it had all been a dream.

"Where's Tommy?"

"Asleep."

I nodded and looked down at my hands for the first time, seeing the bloodstains on the soft brown leather. I held them out for her to see.

"You had to," she said.

"Jesus," I said, wincing.

She closed her mouth tight and stood up, taking the gloves off my hands. Without looking at me, she opened the screen and laid them on the fire. When she looked back, she reached up, took my face in her hands, and pulled me close.

"It never happened," she said in a whisper, staring hard into my eyes. "That's what you have to do. In your mind. It never happened. It was Johnny G. His people. They were supposed to do it and as far as we know, they did. You were here. With me."

"Tommy?"

"He's a boy. They can't even talk to him. Don't lose your focus. We had dinner and built a fire. I read my book and you read the paper. Then we made love. It all happened." She paused. "You have to see it."

I felt her hands slipping up under my shirt and her nails dragging along the skin on either side of my spine.

I put my mouth to hers, felt her clenching me. Her fingers undid my clothes.

She took me upstairs and made me forget. She went to the bathroom and came back with a cup of water and something in her hand.

"What is it?" I asked.

"Take it," she said. "It's good for you."

"What?"

I pinched the fat white pill and turned it over in the dim light from the bathroom. Vicodin. From a knee surgery two years ago.

"It'll help," she said. "Trust me."

I started to hand it back but she pushed it toward me.

"Yes," she said.

I took it.

In the morning, I lifted my head up off the bed to look out through the big arching window. The bellies of the clouds were bright pink, their fringes dressed in a lavender mist. They stretched to the end of the lake and on forever after. The thought of James twisting under the pillow dropped like a stone in my gut. My arms and legs went rigid. Jessica woke, touched my face, and looked into my eyes. Her own were puffy and moist.

"No," she said, her tongue slow and heavy. "I told you. It was a dream. You were here."

"Oh God," I said, panic rising. I rolled over and wretched.

"Don't do that," she said, her voice grating my ears. "Don't. You can't."

She hurried me out of bed and into the shower, made me scrambled eggs with crispy bacon, which I picked at.

When Tommy came down, she kissed him on the head and hugged him tight.

"Did you forget to brush your teeth?" she asked.

"Mom," he said.

She just pointed toward the stairs.

When he came back, she said, "Give your father a kiss, he's got to go to work."

Tommy came over, kissed my cheek, and hugged me. I gripped him tight, holding on until he began to squirm. I let him go.

"Time," she said to me. "I've got to get Tommy ready and you've got a lot to do. Go bring home the bacon."

It felt like being pushed out of an airplane, but once I was out, it got better. It never left me, the nausea, the foggy sensation, the image of that death scene flickering up, unwanted on the back screen of my mind, but I was able to somehow go through the motions. I called my secretary and went over the coming week's calendar. I even reorganized a meeting with the leasing group to accommodate an emergency meeting James had called with the Garden State team and the company's new board of directors. Then I started my calls, mostly to contractors eager for a way into the project, talking until I arrived at King Corp.

Ben's office was across an open area filled with file cabinets and secretaries' desks. His door was open and I could see him on the phone with his feet up. We waved to each other and I kept going. My office was just past Scott's. His was all glass and I could see the empty desk.

I said hello to his secretary and asked if she'd seen him.

"He was at the lodge last night," she said, smiling.

"He's got a Jet Management meeting at ten, though, so you might get him on his cell phone on the way in."

I said thanks and went into my own office, quietly closing the door. I had my own private bathroom in the back. I hunched down over the toilet bowl and vomited up my breakfast. I cleaned up, straining to breathe, blinking at the pale green color of my skin in the mirror, then I sat down and turned on my computer.

She was right. I had to push it out of my mind.

My screen was on, thick with unopened e-mails. I just stared. My jaw went slack and my eyes lost their focus.

When Ben burst through my door, I grabbed the edge of my desk and sat blinking at him. When he told me James was dead, I shook my head like I didn't understand.

"Stabbed," Ben said. He had his cell phone in his hand, beating it against his other palm like he was trying to shake some truth out of it. "Scott's knife. That thing from Africa."

He looked at me. His brow was wrinkled. His mouth flat. "And Scott's gone."

I winced and shook my head, glad for an excuse to look as pale as the image I'd just seen in the bathroom mirror.

"Bucky saw him and James talking in the bar last night when he left. They were supposed to hunt this morning. His truck's gone and I guess Emily hasn't heard from him."

"Jesus," I said.

"It can't be what they think," Ben said, shaking his head. "No way. It's got to be something with the union, like Milo."

I just sat there and stared. Through the thick fog, I saw James struggling against the pillow.

"That's what I'm going to tell them," Ben said.

"Who?"

"The police," he said. "They just called. A Detective McCarthy. He wants me to meet him at his office at two."

"Are you getting a lawyer?" I asked.

"Why?"

"I don't know," I said. "That's what people do. I mean, why does he want to talk to *you*?"

"I don't know. He asked for you too."

24

I WENT STRAIGHT HOME.

Jessica was at the kitchen table with the house plans spread out. Through the glass behind her, sunshine played on the lake and the trees up and down the hillsides. She had the architect on speakerphone, and in that metallic voice he was describing a set of marble columns that he'd come across on his last trip to New York City. When she saw me, she looked up with glassy eyes and a lazy smile that made me think about the Vicodin pills. She told the architect that she had to go but would call him right back.

"I'm having the septic field put another hundred yards from the house," she said, running her finger across the plans. "He says we don't need it, but if he smelled as much cow shit as I did he'd want it farther away too."

"The police want to talk to me," I said, sitting down beside her, throwing my face into my hands.

When I realized she wasn't responding, I looked up.

"I didn't want to call you on the phone. This detective called Ben. I asked Ben if he was getting a lawyer. I probably shouldn't have said that, right?"

She reached out and touched my arm.

I stared at her for a moment. Her nod was slow and insistent, and it dawned on me that she was waiting for me to go through the motions of pretending that neither of us knew what had happened, waiting for me to deliver my lines.

Finally, I said, "James."

"What happened?" she asked. Her voice was flat, almost languid.

"They found him," I said, my voice oddly mechanical. "He's dead and Scott's gone."

"What do you mean, gone?"

"It was his knife."

"Oh my God. He killed his father."

I just looked at her, marveling at the strange flatness of her words. Her mouth curled up at its corners.

"I have to go see this cop, right?"

"Of course," she said. "He'll ask you about Scott."

"And the union?"

"Maybe. Does it really matter? You were with me."

She smiled some more, her mind ticking away, enjoying every minute of her game.

I parked next to a rusted blue and gold police cruiser and Ben pulled in next to me in his own car. The New York State Police Department and McCarthy's office were in a one-story brick municipal building just off the town square in Pulaski. The town had once been the site of a major government port project for the Great Lakes. But the port failed, and the highway had been built too far to the east to make up for the loss of commerce. The upper stories of the small brick buildings on the main street either boasted fading curtains or were filled with old plywood. Storefronts were marked by hand-painted signs and the ones still open showed off racks of used clothing, secondhand appliances, or neon beer signs through great sheets of dirty glass. Dust and grit layered crumbling sidewalks, and the broken curb sprouted posts from parking meters long since stolen or destroyed.

Ben and I walked in together with me avoiding eye contact. There were two gray restroom doors right there and I could smell the disinfectant. The woman at the desk took us through a maze of cubicles and sat us down on some scarred wooden chairs outside an office that had McCarthy's plastic nameplate on the door.

Ben hung his head and sighed. The door opened, and there was Bucky with a camouflage hat in his hands. His curly hair was rumpled and his eyes were red and moist, more than normal. Purple crescents hung beneath them. The dark part of his eyes found mine and wouldn't let go. My gut heaved, and I thanked God it was empty. I swallowed and looked down at my shoes, waiting for the shadow of his legs to pass before I raised my head.

McCarthy was fifty. Lean with gold wire glasses. Dark graying hair cut short. An open-collar shirt with a tweed blazer that had a small badge-shaped pin on the lapel. He held the door and asked us to come in. We sat down in the two chairs facing his desk. On top was a stick figure made from golf tees, a dusty phone, and stacks of file folders bursting with papers.

"He's something, huh?" McCarthy said, nodding toward the door.

"Bucky?" Ben asked.

"Yeah," McCarthy said. "Saw some footprints in the snow last night."

"How was that?" I asked.

"Couldn't sleep," McCarthy said, picking up a yellow

pad and a pen off the desk. "Said he saw tracks on the driveway and followed them all the way out to the road. By the time he backtracked, they were filled in. They came from the lodge, went to some tire tracks."

"Scott's?" I asked. I gulped down bile and sat up straight, angling for a better view of his notepad, thinking I saw my name.

"No. One of the maids saw Scott take off around six in the morning."

"Scott would never do this," Ben said. His hands were clasped with their knuckles braced up under his nose, like he was praying and thinking at the same time.

"No? What makes you say that?" McCarthy asked, writing, then glancing up.

"They had a big blowout," I said, looking at McCarthy's phone, my peripheral vision zeroed in on the pad. "James's taking the company public. Scott didn't want him to."

I glanced at Ben, who glared at me and narrowed his lips.

"That true?" McCarthy said.

"That was a couple weeks ago," Ben said, shaking his head. "An argument. You don't stab your father."

"I know," I said and I looked at McCarthy with a frown and a slight shake of my own head. "But Scott was mad. He didn't want this public thing."

"How bad a blowout? Like physical?" McCarthy asked, pointing the pen at us.

"Maybe he grabbed his dad," I said. "No fists or anything."

"We separated them right away," Ben said. "Don't make more of it than it was."

"No, but he's gone, isn't he? Who runs when their

father gets murdered?" McCarthy said, jotting down a note before clearing his throat. "Only the guy who did it. Just so I have it, where were you two last night?"

"Home," Ben said.

"Me too," I said, forcing my eyes away from the pad. "I was actually supposed to go to the lodge to talk with James about the construction on one of our projects, but I didn't get all the bids in, so I called to cancel."

"Who didn't come in?" Ben asked.

"Con Trac," I said. "It came this morning."

"And neither of you heard from Scott?" McCarthy asked, pointing the pen again.

"No."

"Ben said it was his knife," I said.

"Bucky told me anyone could have gotten it," McCarthy said.

"I thought he kept it locked up," I said. I saw the words "THREE FRIENDS" on the pad and scoured for something legible around it.

"Where?" McCarthy asked.

"The whole family, they have these private lockers. Big closets where they keep their own gear. Bucky could show you."

"He didn't mention them," McCarthy said, writing.

There was a knock at the office door. McCarthy got out from behind his desk and opened it.

"The captain wants you," the woman from the front desk said in an urgent whisper.

"I'm interviewing."

"Now," she said. "He said right now. To get you."

McCarthy smiled at us and said, "Excuse me."

"What are you doing?" Ben asked when the door was shut.

"What?"

"What you're doing," he said. "You know Scott would never."

"He was pretty mad," I said. I looked over at him. He crossed his arms so I crossed my own. "Look. I have no idea. I'm just answering the questions. Don't be an asshole."

"You don't."

We sat without talking. It wasn't a minute before the door opened again. This time McCarthy didn't come in.

"Thane," McCarthy said, his face was flushed, "can you come with me?"

"Sure," I said. My heart was thumping and the sound of ocean surf in my ears. I didn't even look at Ben. I just wanted to make it out of the room without tripping.

I followed McCarthy through some desks and down a hallway. McCarthy opened another door. Inside was a long table, two foam cups of coffee, and the women from the FBI.

25

"They said they flew into Syracuse that morning," I say, "to meet with James. Man, that McCarthy's face went red as a beet. You could see the muscles working in his jaw. Looked like he was gonna break his own teeth. They just snatched the whole case right out from under him. You know, the OC task force thing."

"You don't think it was a coincidence that they were there?" he asks.

"I guess. It was weird, though, the way they turned up all the time."

"Witches, huh?"

"Might as well have been."

"What about your friend?"

"Ben? I didn't see him until the next day," I say. "Which was fine with me. Then, when I did see him, I didn't have to worry about the friend thing. That son-of-a-bitch."

I sat down in the wooden chair facing the two witches across the table. Amanda, the redhead, shut the door and sat down next to her partner. They were behind a small table, Amanda in a brown suit, looking the executive.

Dorothy in her windbreaker with that frizzy gray hair busting out in the back of her head. Behind them was a dirty window. No two-way glass or anything fancy, just a view of the barren trees and some train tracks. Like Mc-Carthy, they had notepads, and also a small tape recorder pushed to my side of the table.

"What can you tell us about last night?" Amanda asked.

"Are we talking about James, or Johnny G?"

"Maybe both," Dorothy said, jotting something down.

"Or Scott?" I said.

"Why Scott?" Amanda said, glancing at her notepad, then staring at me.

"Detective McCarthy said he left the lodge in a hurry. James was killed with his knife, right? It doesn't take Perry Mason," I said.

"You're pretty smart, huh?" Dorothy said.

"Smart enough to see the obvious," I said, forcing a smile.

"How obvious is it where you were?" Dorothy said.

"As in, you think I have anything to do with this?" I said, putting my hand on my chest and grinning wide.

"As in, just for the record," Dorothy said, poising her pen.

"With my wife," I said. "In bed. Doesn't get more obvious than that, does it?"

"What can you tell us about Scott?" Amanda said.

I did, trying not to gush.

And it worked. I just kept repeating the story the way Jessica told me, and the more I said it, the more confidence I had in it, the more it seemed like it really happened that way. It was like glue setting, this flimsy liquid that suddenly holds together two big boards. They stared at me and nodded their heads. Every once in a while, they'd look at each other, like they knew something. But it wasn't about me. They kept asking about Scott. They even asked if there was any possible connection between him and the union and Johnny G. I had to say that in this business, anything was possible.

When I left the police office, Ben's car was still there, but I never saw him and I didn't want to. My stomach was still knotted, but the nausea was fading. I knew I did good and I couldn't wait to tell Jessica. I put in the Doors CD and let my hands bang out the rhythm on the steering wheel while I leaned through the curves. When my phone rang, I almost didn't answer, but it was my office and I felt like part of my mind was back to normal. Then the image of James dying hit me so suddenly and so hard, I lost my breath, but still I managed to grab for the phone.

My secretary had this hushed voice and I had to kill the music. With reverence she told me that Mike Allen wanted me to meet with King Corp's board of directors the next day in New York City for an emergency meeting. Mike Allen was the chairman of the board James had put together. He wanted to talk to me about taking over the company before the IPO. My secretary said Mike already had one of the Citation Xs lined up to take me down. Wheels up at ten.

I had to stop the car and get out. I looked up at the sky and clenched my trembling hands. She was so good, Jessica. All I had to do was let her push the buttons and things went right. It was she who coached me into my first partnership. It was she who moved me up the ladder. James King never gave away what he didn't have to, and Jessica had always known that instinctively. Now, I would have it all. With James dead and Scott the main suspect, the board would be desperate for someone to man the helm to get through this IPO. The ether of power would be one more thing to help me blur the thrashing image that didn't want to stop. I got back in the car and stayed heavy on the gas.

26

I COULDN'T SLEEP. The next morning it was cloudy and dark. Jessica got up and went with me, chatting the whole ride to the airport about the architect's columns. Pale green marble, sixteen feet high. When the pilot handed her up the steps into the plane, she looked at me with a smile that sent a hot current through my chest. When the ride got bumpy, Jessica screwed the cap off her water bottle, fished in her purse, and popped something into her mouth before washing it down. When she saw me looking, she said, "Mint." She settled back into her leather seat and closed her eyes, smiling.

I forgot about it with all the "yes sirs" and "no ma'ams" from the pilots. James's pilots. Same thing with the limo driver who was waiting for us with an umbrella to fend off the misty rain. We had a suite at the Palace on Madison Avenue. I dropped off Jessica to meet with her architect, then went downtown to the Goldman Sachs offices.

I was shown to a waiting room with oriental rugs, crystal lamps, and crimson leather furniture. A woman in a tailored suit brought me coffee in a china cup resting on its saucer. After two sips, Mike Allen came in through another door, shook my hand, and sat down next to me. He wore a dark suit with a white shirt and a forest green tie that matched his eyes. His hair was faded blond and combed straight back. His sharp nose and unblinking eyes gave him the air of a predatory bird.

Mike was no silver-spoon baby. He climbed the ranks of the UAW until going out on his own with some Detroit investors to make the drive trains they put in SUVs. He built the company up and sold it for a fortune. Now, he was on the board of a dozen major companies. He was the kind of guy who treated his ex-wife like a friend. He was like that with everyone. From the custodian who swept the floors to the billionaires he hung out with, Mike not only liked, but respected you until you could prove you didn't deserve it.

"We're all sad," he said, lowering his voice and leaning toward me. "But we have an obligation to keep this deal alive. Too many people could get hurt. Goldman has to go through with the IPO. They're committed. We need a leader and I think you're the right person. You know the company, and what it takes."

"I think so," I said, keeping my voice as subdued as his, looking down at my shoes and nodding my head, biting the inside of my lip to keep from heaving.

"You know, he built this company up from a backhoe and two shovels. This project was his magnum opus. So, just go in there and don't let them get you flustered. It's a tough group. Now look, I can't say it's a done deal, but, well, I've got a lot of say in this."

"What about Scott?" I asked.

His pupils dilated and he said, "I don't think he did it, but we can't take a chance with the timing here.

This thing is set in motion. I think you'd be the right guy anyway."

"Thanks, Mike."

"Remember when you returned that blocked punt to beat Navy? You pulled that off and we won. Come on."

Mike put his arm around my shoulder, led me through a short marble hallway, and swept me into a long, tall room dominated by a mahogany table and a massive Tiffany fixture. Around the table sat the board. Eighteen people. Mostly men, older, and wearing their dark suits buttoned up tight.

I smiled at them all and took a deep breath.

I was weary, but strong. Saddened, but full of strength.

In my crazed state, I thought it was my finest moment as a human being.

The elevator collected a few more at each stop on the way down, everyone shifting quietly when a new person stepped inside, looking down. When the doors opened at the lobby, I was the first one out and felt the surge behind me. Someone stepped on my heel and when I turned my head, I ended up walking smack into someone. Hard enough to feel their bones.

Instinctively, I grabbed to keep whoever it was from falling and began a mumbled apology that faded when I saw who it was. Ben's blue eyes got wide and then blinked at me from behind his rectangular glasses. Tiny drops of water clung to his long black raincoat. No umbrellas for him.

"What are you doing?" I asked.

"The board," he said, shrugging. His lips perked up into a little smile.

"They're going ahead with the IPO," I said.

"I know."

"They want me to run King Corp."

"Maybe," he said. He started to edge around me, but I stepped back in front of him.

"There's no maybe," I said. "They're voting now."

"That what they told you?" he said. "We'll see."

I stood straight and looked down at him. He bit the inside of his cheek and brushed past me.

27

I LEFT THE BUILDING and waved off my driver, telling him to meet me back at the Palace. I let some of the cool wet air into my collar and loosened my tie.

After a few blocks, I jammed my hands down into the side pockets of my suit coat. My feet were wet, the Bally wingtips shiny but smattered with crud. A chill shook my bones. Cabs hissed by, screeching to a standstill under red lights blurred by the mist. In the distance a siren wailed and the death scene played in my mind. I took out my cell phone and dialed up the driver, calculating how far he might have gone and how long it would take him to get back. I got voice mail.

There was a subway station up ahead. I jogged down the steps, jostled by a heavy woman wearing sneakers and a plastic shower cap on her head. The rank smell of decay rode the breeze, pumped in and out of the tunnels by the throbbing cars. I studied the wall map. Somehow, I had wandered all the way to the green line. Behind me, I thought I heard someone laugh the way James used to. My stomach soured. I took the six train uptown to Grand

Central and let the mob sweep me up and out onto the wet street and a sky darker than when I'd gone in.

The doorman at the Palace hesitated before opening up, then followed me with his eyes as I dripped my way across the marble lobby. In the elevator, I stared into the mirror at the stringy wet hair and the bulging eyes of the shivering maniac in the soggy dark suit. Me.

The living room of our suite looked down on Park Avenue. On the table in front of the velvet couch rested a silver pail. The neck of a champagne bottle stuck out from the folds of a white linen towel. I blurted out a sound that might have been a laugh and struggled with the gold foil, wanting a drink. The cork ricocheted off the crystal chandelier, leaving a soft tinkling sound in the wake of the pop.

The door burst open. Jessica and Mike Allen. Real laughter peeling back and forth between them that came to a stop when they saw me.

"Thane?" Jessica said, taking one step and then stopping.

There was an awkward moment then and I did my best to smile.

Mike stepped up and said, "Hey, not celebrating without us, are you?"

My mouth went slack. Mike extended his hand.

"Congratulations," he said, grinning. "I knew you'd do it."

"I . . . thank you."

"Thank *you*," Mike said, taking Jessica by the arm. "And I didn't tell you this, but you, both of you, are going to ring the opening bell on Thursday. It'll be on CNN. I tell you, you got the greatest wife."

Jessica splayed her fingers across her chest, bending them back.

"Not me," she said. "I'm not going on TV."

Mike nodded at her, grinning still. He raised two champagne glasses off the tray and held them out to me. I poured.

"How come you're all wet?" he asked, handing a glass to Jessica.

"Just thinking about everything. Took a walk," I said, now filling my own. "Didn't realize it was coming down like that."

"A lot to think about," Mike said, raising his glass. "To King Corp, the man who founded it, and the man who's gonna make it run."

Our glasses clinked and we drank. Jessica shot me a look over the rim of her fluted glass.

"Mike's taking us out," she said. "Why don't you change?"

"Sure," I said, setting down the empty glass. "You two have another. I'll just be a second."

I was stripped down to nothing with the shower leaking steam when she slipped in.

"What happened?"

"I'm washing up," I said.

"Where were you?"

"I saw Ben."

"And?"

"Jessica," I said, reaching for her hands, "I think he knows."

"He knows you're the CEO. That's all he knows," she said, her voice hushed, but urgent. "That's all he could know. It'll be fine."

I shook my head.

"I keep seeing him," I said, "James. Fighting me. The blood. I'm sick."

"Do you think I would have married you if you weren't strong?" she said. "You are."

"I'm sorry."

She put her hand on my cheek and kissed me lightly. "Hurry, okay? Just keep going. Don't think about anything more than getting dressed, dinner. Simple, stupid things.

"Trust me," she said, showing me the smooth scar on her palm. "Horrible things happen. If you just keep going, they fade."

I let the hot water pound the subway stink from my skin and hair and scrubbed up fast. My clothes were all laid out on the bed for me. The olive suit. The rust-colored tie she liked so much. Fresh brown shoes and a matching belt. I forced a smile onto my face and joined them, this time managing to produce a sound close enough to a laugh so that it seemed like I was in on the fun. Jessica had changed into a slim low-cut satin green dress. Her hair was up, exposing her neck and the subtle curves below. The contrast to her normal clothes was stunning.

Mike took us to the Lever House, a long white tunnel with honeycombed walls, deep booths. Elevated at the end of the long room was a trapezoidal hole in the wall and a long table for parties, almost on a stage for everyone to see. Our table. Many of the board members joined us, some bringing spouses. They all seemed to know one another. I kept expecting Ben, and I tossed down champagne like water, but he never showed.

The attention of the entire place was on us. Jessica's eyes sparkled and she kept her arm draped across my shoulders, occasionally toying with my hair or touching her lips to my ear. At some point, the waiter put a grilled piece of tuna in front of me. I swallowed it in chunks, forcing a couple of them down into the disrupted pit of my stomach. I could feel the heat of the wine. A soft buzzing sang out in my ears and I wrapped my fingers around Jessica's leg. She giggled.

We were both drunk.

Halfway across the room, a man getting up out of a booth and moving toward the bathroom caught my eye. He was burly. A white mane of hair. My mouth went dry. I closed my eyes tight and willed the fish to stay down before I opened them again.

"Ow, Thane," Jessica said, knocking my hand off her leg.

"James," I said, the word barely making it past my lips as the man disappeared into the crowd at the bar.

"Dessert," Jessica said in a low voice. "What are you having? Just look at the menu."

Mike tapped my shoulder and leaned toward me from the other side, his cheeks shiny like apples.

"First thing you do after you ring that bell?" he asked. "What are you thinking?"

I looked at him and got my bearings, biting hard on the inside of my mouth to bring me back.

"Fire Ben," I said, then chuckled.

Mike started to laugh. He raised his glass and drank more wine. "Serious."

"I am."

"You can't do *that*."

"CEO can do anything," I said, my heart leaping. "I'm running it, remember?"

I wasn't looking at him or anything. The words sounded surreal in my mind. Jessica was listening, and her face eased around my shoulder, farther into my field of vision.

"He had too much," she said.

She glowed at Mike, and in her big smile I could see the pointed tips of her canines.

28

"Canines?"

"Eyeteeth," I say. "The pointed ones."

I look at him and see the confusion, so I pull up my lip between my finger and thumb and run the end of my tongue around my own pointed tip.

"Like a dog's fangs," I say.

"Are you saying that now?" he asks. "Or was that what you thought back then?"

"No, I thought it then," I say. "I just did. Her eyes would get squinty."

"And that's how she looked when you talked about Ben?"

"I'll tell you when else she looked like that," I say, staring at the bars on the window and a small glinting crack in the glass that I never noticed before. "She had that smile every time we were around Johnny G, and he'd smile like that right back at her."

"And you were jealous?"

"Don't be stupid."

He looks at me without blinking, then looks down at the file. "You never talked about this before, right?"

"Maybe not."

"When were all of you even together?"

"You know how I told her that those union guys wouldn't deal with a woman? And I'm sure they never did. But with her, man, she could cut right through it. She was a beautiful girl. But it was business. That's all."

I am shaking my head. I cross my arms and lean my chair up on its two back legs. The dirty window glows with some watered-down light from the sun, then fades back to pewter.

"Tell me," he says, "about when the three of you were together."

It was the night before we rang the bell on Wall Street.

There was a charity ball at the new Time Warner Center. Everyone who was anyone in the city was there and I guess Johnny G, with all the political connections the union has, was one of them. Two glass towers looking out over Central Park. Fifty-five stories high. *The* new place in New York. Limousines crowding Columbus Circle and white reception tents extending from the front of the building out to the street. Inside, Cirque du Soleil put on a show in the four-story lobby and men in tuxedos carved up animal legs, serving out thin strips of meat onto plates with silver tongs.

We were Mike Allen's guests, and he introduced us to all the big players. Gray-haired men with trophy wives and even a few with their originals. Movers and shakers whose eyes darted at Jessica like gnats. We drank and ate and smiled, making bullshit small talk until we lost Mike in the crowd somewhere near the lamb chop station.

Above us, colored smoke swirled in the spinning

lights. A mime swung from a trapeze and launched into the empty space. He did two flips and came out of it in a swan dive. You could see he wasn't going to make it to the next swing. I felt my heart leap and heard others around me gasp before he caught it by his teeth.

Sporadic applause peppered the hum of a thousand people talking about themselves. Jessica had her head tilted back, exposing her neck and the small swell of her breasts above the line of her Vera Wang gown. Her hair framed her face and a simple tortoiseshell band held it in place.

When she looked at me and raised a glass of champagne, I remembered Mike Allen's words, "a hell of a wife." She was. I was light-headed and only half of it came from the wine. I took her hand, pulled her to me, and kissed her on the lips. When we separated, I saw Johnny G standing there with his teeth showing in that grin. Beside him was a brassy yellow blonde, her brittle hair stacked up high, implants swelling her breasts into globes.

Johnny's face was nearly as red as his crooked silk tie and the ruffled cummerbund. He made a guttural noise and hugged me to him, patting my back and scratching the side of my face with his five o'clock shadow. He introduced his wife, Tina. Jessica shook her hand, but she was looking at Johnny with that smile they shared.

"Life is good, eh?" Johnny said, winking at me, punching my shoulder lightly, spilling some red wine from his glass. "How about all this? Did you get one of those lobster tails?"

He hugged his wife's naked shoulders to him.

"I love a good tail, you know?"

Tina swatted his hand and nuzzled his ear.

"You like lobster?" he asked Jessica.

"Of course," she said, raising her glass before taking a drink. She yawned.

"Then you two have to come with us," he said, wagging his thick head toward the door, licking his finger, and touching his neck.

"We're with some King Corp people and the investment bankers," I said, tearing the meat off a chop. "But thanks."

"So you came with them, you leave with us," he said, shrugging. "I got a place you'll love. Not so noisy as this. Little place on the East Side. Real New York. Lotta TV stars go there. They wrap their tails in capicolla, a little olive oil, and sprinkle it with Grappa."

Johnny kissed his fingertips.

"Come on," he said. "You'll be my guests. Anthony Congemi's gonna be there."

"Who?" I said.

"*The Young and the Restless*," Jessica said.

"Yeah," Johnny said. "That guy."

"We're with people," I said, tossing the bone onto the plate and taking another glass of champagne from a passing tray. I winked at him. "But thanks."

Johnny's face grew dark. He looked around. "Yeah? They're not gonna miss you, right? Come on."

He took his eyes off my face and turned away with an arm around his wife's shoulders, staggering toward the entrance.

Jessica smiled like a little girl, raised her eyebrows, and squeezed my hand. "Oh, come on. Real New York. A million billion miles away from the cow shit."

I shook my head, but when she tugged on my arm, I followed.

Johnny had a limo outside, a stretch Mercedes with two men in the front who were each the size of a small building. We sat on the seat across from the bar. Johnny spread out in the back with his legs splayed out, his feet pointing in opposite directions, and a glimpse of his hairy legs above the sock. His wife pulled a red fox shawl tight around her neck and snuggled up to Johnny.

"Have a drink," Johnny said, motioning his hand to the bar.

"What do you drink in one of these things?" Jessica asked.

"Grey Goose," he said. "There's chilled glasses in that fridge. I'll have one with you."

Tina poked out her lower lip and looked at Jessica with drooping eyelids as the two of them made a silent toast.

The drive was quick. It was a small glass-fronted place on Third Street and late enough in the evening so that the traffic was thin and the limo could pull right up to the curb. Before we could get out, two more behemoths in tuxedos skittered out of the restaurant and opened the door for Johnny to step out.

It was a long narrow place and crowded. Smoke curled up to the ceiling, adding to the thick fog. Cigar embers glowed, illuminating heavy jowls, gold cuff links, diamond watches and rings. The laughter was guttural, like the greetings the men gave to Johnny as they rose from their tables, kissed his cheek, and hugged him tight.

"They sound like they're on the friggin' toilet," I said into her ear.

Jessica wrinkled her nose.

"Are youz with Johnny?" an older woman with high curly hair and thick glasses asked. We nodded yes and she reached for our coats with a birdlike arm, gathering them to her like firewood.

"This way here," she said.

There was a big round table in the back with a "Reserved" card in the middle of its white cloth. She picked it up, gathered Johnny's wool coat, his wife's dead fox, and disappeared through a small door in the back. We ordered drinks from a young waiter fingering the middle button on his shirt. Three people waited behind the bar to make them up and send him right back.

Those who hadn't gotten a hug on Johnny's way in proceeded to queue up in the main aisle to have a moment with him at our table. He introduced them all. A judge who wasn't a judge. An accountant under federal indictment. The actor named Congemi, who everyone but me recognized and who kissed Jessica's hand. A fund-raiser for the governor's upcoming campaign, and a lot of younger men with slicked-back hair, Rolex watches, thick New York accents, and four-hundred-dollar Hermès ties.

I was drunk and so was Jessica and it all felt ragged and surreal.

We never ordered, but the food started to arrive. Platters of squid, deep-fried zucchini blossoms, stuffed mushrooms, roasted peppers, squab, chicken livers, cold shrimp, mozzarella and tomatoes were set down, picked over, then taken away to make room for more. Each dish was better than the next. I unbuttoned the top of my pants and kept eating. Bottles of wine were opened and decanted over candle flames, heavy and rich with the scent of spices, wood, and fruit.

Then the lobsters came. Four burning plates held high with two tails on each, mummified in capicolla and prosciutto. The waiters huffed out the blue flames and faded away. I put my hand on my stomach, took a deep breath, and exhaled. Tina had abandoned her fork for a cigarette long ago, a little one about the size of a toothpick, but Jessica and Johnny showed off their teeth to each other and started to work.

I picked up my own fork, sawed off a hunk, dipped it into the small glass dish of drawn butter and put it into my mouth. I was hungry for the first time in days and it was too good to stop. I finished one whole tail and most of the other. Jessica ate only two bites, but she chewed slowly and seemed to enjoy the conversation Johnny and I were having about the Yankees bullpen.

There was a panacotta and some fruit and coffee, and we dug in with spoons. Cigars came in wooden boxes, Cubans, and port, very old. Jessica took a cigar and let Johnny light it from across the table. I raised an eyebrow at her and shook my head. More smiles. The smoke and the din of laughter, clinking china, and groaning men started to swirl in my head. If I was drunk I knew Jessica had to be too.

I leaned her way, put my lips to her ear, and said, "Time."

"For what?" she said, leaning away from me, grinning, and sticking the cigar in her mouth.

"To go," I said, in a low tone.

"He's tired," she said loudly to Johnny, exhaling a blue cloud.

Tina cackled. Johnny slapped me on the back. Tina kept cackling and then she farted. Johnny laughed so hard his face turned bright red.

"Come on, kid. There's a club in SoHo the girls will love. You need a boost?" He reached into his coat pocket and put a little gold box on the table in front of me. Clipped to its cover was a small spoon.

"I'm done," I said, waving my hand. I sat up straight. "Gotta ring the bell tomorrow. Open Wall Street."

Johnny blew out a little spray of port and started laughing and choking all at once, pounding on the table with the flat of his hand.

"I'm sorry," he said, wiping his eye with the corner of his linen napkin and leaning into his wife. "I loved the way you said that. Like you're playing in the Super Bowl or something. I love it."

Jessica was grinning too, covering her mouth with her own napkin, her eyes wrinkled and twinkling. I laughed along with them and shook my head.

"I know," I said. "I'm drunk. What the hell, right?"

I got up, took a step, and grabbed the back of Jessica's chair to stay upright. From the corner of my eye I saw Jessica take the gold box from Johnny. She palmed it and tucked it behind her back. I was hazy. All of it was.

"I gotta go."

"Okay," Johnny said, sucking on his cigar, then blowing a big blue plume my way. He squinted. "We'll take care of the missus."

Jessica looked up at me, grinning, and said, "Oh, come on. It'll be fun."

"We're going."

"Ta ta," she said, sticking the cigar in her mouth and flickering her fingers goodbye.

I grabbed her wrist without even thinking, and yanked her out of her chair. I wrapped my other arm around her waist, dragging her toward the door. Her cigar bounced on the floor, scattering orange sparks. I heard Johnny bellow. We were halfway down the bar when the actor stepped in my way. A big hand clamped down on the back of my neck, two more grabbed my arm. I dropped Jessica and spun, swinging.

I hit a nose and heard a pop. Warm wet on my knuckles. My feet went out from under me and the floor came up fast, striking the back of my head. A woman screamed, and there was a gun in my face.

29

He doesn't say anything, but he takes a breath and lets it out slowly through his nose, nodding his head like it all makes sense now.

"My dad used to take care of the sludge pits at Allied Chemical," I say. "I was like every kid, you know, bragging about what my dad did, how important he was. My claim to fame was that my dad had to wear one of those space suits with a breathing mask and a hood and rubber boots. I used to beg him to go to work and wear one of those masks.

"So one Saturday, after my mom finally stepped in and gave him the order, he took me out there, got me a suit that he rolled up and tucked into some boots, and we walked around those milky green pits, and I'll tell you I was scared to death but flying high as a kite. It was a blue sky day. You could see the little white puffs of cloud reflecting off the surface of the sludge. So we walk around for a while, breathing through these masks with him poking at the retainer walls with this long metal pole, and I finally calm down enough to notice this old braided rope hung around his shoulder and tied to his waist.

"Just a crappy old thing like the ones you'd climb in gym class that smelled like horsehair, greasy and bristly and worn at the same time, and I asked him what it was for.

"'You fall in that pit,' he said, 'you don't come out if you ain't got a rope.'

"I asked him why someone couldn't just throw one in, and he said, 'Once you're in the sludge, it's too late. The sludge gets on everything. You can't hang on to anything and you couldn't tie off a rope if someone threw it to you. You gotta have your rope going in.'

"So I said, 'Well, I don't have a rope.' And I looked at that cloudy pit, swirling, crawling slow like a snake's skin when it's getting ready to move, and I took a few steps back.

"'No, you don't,' he said, like it was the first time he'd thought of it, and he turned and climbed over the wall and I practically knocked him over getting out of there."

The shrink tilts his head and wrinkles his brow.

"You ever have someone put a gun in your face?" I ask.

He shakes his head and says something quiet.

"Huh?" I say.

"Not in my face."

"I was in the sludge," I say. "Get it? Deep. No rope. No help. All I could do was try to keep my head up."

I felt my face burning at the sound of them all laughing, like it was no big deal to put a gun in someone's face. It sobered up Jessica too. We went back to the hotel and rang the bell on Wall Street in the morning, neither of us feeling very good.

Mike Allen took us in his own limousine to Teterboro, where the Citation X was waiting for us. Jessica gave him a kiss on the cheek and disappeared into the plane. I grabbed the railing and stepped up.

"Can I talk to you for a minute?" Mike said.

I shielded the sun from my eyes to read his face and stepped back onto the tarmac.

"What's up?"

"You're kinda quiet," he said.

"Rough night."

"Look," he said, putting a hand on my shoulder. "I know how hard this all is. I know how much he meant to you and I know this all probably seems a little coldhearted."

I smashed my lips together, shrugging.

"Great leaders, they overcome. You're like my Hannibal, riding an elephant through the Alps. The funeral's tomorrow."

"I know."

"You've got to get this project built," he said. "We've got shareholders. The Street doesn't care about funerals. Are you in the black or in the red? Did you make your earnings? That's it."

I looked him in the eye and shook his hand.

Then I got on the plane and listened to Jessica talk the whole way home about the plans for the house and where the new columns would go. She had some meetings with the carpet people in town so she dropped me at the office and said she'd pick me up in a few hours.

Before I got out of the car, she said, "I want to make a party, okay?"

"For what?"

"You," she said. "Us. At Cascade. Mike thought it was a good idea. All the partners. The contractors. The bankers too. Something upbeat in all the gloom."

I put my hands in my lap and stared out the window

at the traffic going by. Some people were already done for the day.

"The funeral is tomorrow," I said, my eyes losing their focus.

"It won't be for a couple weeks," she said. "It's for you, you know. To bring everyone together. That leadership thing Mike Allen keeps talking about."

"Can we really just keep doing this?" I asked, searching her face.

Her lips turned down at the corners. "Listen to me. Scars fade away."

She held up her palm.

"Just keep going," I said, looking back out the window, nodding my head.

"You'll be okay."

"And Ben?"

"Ben too," she said. "She ran off with that professor with the kids *and* his bank account. Did he do anything about that? He put his head in the sand like an ostrich."

"What if he wants to talk about it?"

"You tell him you can't talk about it. You need some time. That happens with things like this."

"He knows," I said, the words slipping past my teeth.

"Come on, Thane," she said. "You've got work to do. I'll pick you up at seven."

I told her okay and went inside and called our general counsel into my office. Together, we called the president of Con Trac to tell him that we were awarding them the Garden State job and that we wanted them to start immediately. He was pleased, but did a poor job of feigning surprise. We agreed that the lawyers would paper the deal by the end of the week.

I had more e-mails than I could get through and several letters that needed dictating and it *was* healing, to just keep going, grinding through the paperwork like a termite. Somewhere in the middle of it, I realized that I couldn't see. The lights were off and it was dusk outside the windows. I turned the lights on and kept going. It was sometime after that when my office door flew open.

"I'm sorry," Ben said, throwing himself down in the leather wingback chair facing my desk. "It's all crazy."

I looked at him for a moment, my hands clutching the arms of my chair. The air vent on the ceiling hummed quietly and traffic swished by outside.

"You don't have to be sorry," I said. "Remember how we used to race every day, all summer long on that two-mile run?"

He shook his head and said, "I know. It's not about them choosing you over me. It's just, I can't believe all this."

"Mike Allen told me that James would have wanted us to finish the job. That Garden State was like his magnum opus. I know what you're saying, but let's just get it built."

Ben was looking at me, puzzled.

"I just don't think Scott . . ."

"Ben," I said, looking down at the papers in front of me, picking through the pile, "I can't do this. We have to work through the scars. They fade. I want you to go down on-site. Con Trac starts digging on Monday."

"Con Trac?"

"They were low," I said.

"I thought OBG because of the local thing?"

"Con Trac was low," I said, sifting through the papers in front of me with my fingers. "I just got off the phone with Lance Parsons. It's done."

I found a copy of the Con Trac deal with James's notes in the margins and looked up. Ben was staring past me, out the window. I waited.

He nodded his head and got up.

"Hey," he said. "Remember when they caught us burning down the coach's tower?"

"Yeah," I said, shifting in my seat.

"And they brought us in and I told them I did it and I didn't know the other guy, just some drunken frat brother I met on Marshal Street?"

"Because it was your idea. That's what you said, and I bought the pizza and beer for the rest of the year."

"It *was* my idea, yeah," he said. "But that's not the only reason I did it. I did it because you were my friend, and it was the right thing to do."

I looked up at him, squeezing out a smile, knowing the expression I wore had to be stupid.

"Scott's my friend too," he said.

"Yeah, I know."

30

"My mom always used to say that it was a good thing to have it rain at a funeral," I say.

"We always had music," he says. "To lift the spirits."

"I guess that after someone's in the ground, the next time it rains it makes you sad all over again."

"You think that's true?"

"I don't know," I say. "But I think every time I ever had to bury someone, it rained."

I felt mist from the rain on my face. It was a soft rain, and the sky was fairly bright. Most of the leaves had turned and fallen though, so the hiss of water sounded worse than it really was. My arm was around Jessica, my other hand gripped a wide umbrella, balancing it overhead. Each step brought a little flood out from under the edge of my shoes into the grass. They'd need a shine.

The casket gleamed beneath a blanket of pink roses, and the priest swung an incense lantern back and forth, chanting in Latin. Across the grave was the family. James's wife, Eva, standing with the other kids. All grown. All living out their lives in different corners of the country, places like Dallas, Palm Beach, San Diego. There was an empty, gaping space on Eva's right. Where Scott would have been.

Bucky stood just behind the family. His face gray and his mouth a straight line, like it was drawn onto his face with a charcoal pencil. The bags under his red-rimmed eyes hung low, but those dark irises stayed pointed at me the whole time. Finally I looked right at him and nodded. His face stayed set in stone.

When the priest was finished, the family began tossing little scoops of dirt from a silver pail onto the casket. My knees were locked up, but Jessica tugged at me until I was turned around and walking away from the grave, dodging headstones and the deeper puddles in the grass.

On the hilltop overlooking where we'd parked was a stone crypt that read "Barrows." As we rounded the corner, we could see a dark blue Crown Vic. A thin ribbon of smoke curled up from the exhaust pipe. Paper cups of coffee sat on the dash, steaming up the windshield. Through the rain-speckled window, I saw the gray-haired witch pop something into her mouth and start licking her fingers. The redhead took a sip from her coffee cup.

Jessica grabbed my arm and pulled me up the steps and behind one of the Grecian columns supporting the pediment of the crypt. She took the umbrella from me and retracted it, then clung tight and pushed me up against the column.

"What the hell?" I said, under my breath.

"Shh," she told me.

After a minute, Ben came out from under a cluster of pine trees standing over some old graves. His blond hair was dark and matted from the rain and his head darted around before he jogged the last ten steps to the witches' car and slipped into the back. The taillights glowed for a moment and then the car crawled off down the gravel drive.

"Shit," I said.

"Uh-huh," Jessica said, nodding her head as if this was exactly what she suspected. "A sneak."

I just looked at her.

She looked at me, frowning, and said, "I never told you what he did after his wife left."

"What are you talking about?" I said, my chest feeling suddenly tight.

"He's not such a friend," she said. "I tried to forget it. I knew he was depressed about her leaving, and the kids."

"What's that got to do with you?"

"Come on," she said, opening the umbrella and starting off down the steps.

"What?" I asked, catching up, taking the umbrella from her, but keeping it over her head as we walked.

"You were in New York," she said, her hands deep in her coat pockets, shoulders hunched. "He showed up at the house and said he needed to talk. He was crying. I felt bad for him and he asked me to have a drink at the Sherwood. On the way, he pulled down into Sandy Beach and turned the car off."

"You didn't tell me?" I said, the pressure now pushing up through my throat and out my ears.

"He tried to touch me," she said, stopping and looking up at me. "He said he used to think about me. I got out to walk home and he grabbed me and put his hand . . . up under my dress."

"Where the hell was I?"

"You had a dinner with Latham & Watkins. Scott

Gordon. I knew you were working on the Toronto deal and I didn't want to upset you."

"I'll fucking kill him," I said.

"See? That's why I didn't tell you," she said, hugging me to her, resting her head against my chest.

"Fuck him," I said, squeezing her and thrusting my nose into the soft bed of her hair. "He tried to rape you?"

"This is worse," she said. "This is all of us he's doing it to."

"James's little puppet," I said. "I could do the same goddamn thing to the puppet. You know that?"

"I know," she said, rubbing her forehead against my tie. "And you might have to. But if we do, I'll tell you when. We have to do it right."

31

That's when I knew she really meant it," I say.

"You didn't realize before?"

"Look, we were like brothers going through school," I say. "Yeah, we drifted a little. Our wives never got along. You get busy with kids and things."

"But he was a threat," the shrink says.

I shrug and say, "You don't go after a guy's wife. But as much as anything I think that after you do something like what I did to James, you realize you don't really have anything to lose. What's it matter, right? If you get one life sentence or a thousand?"

"Every time you committed a crime you were taking another chance," he says, "making it more likely you'd be caught. You had to know that."

"Did I?"

"Didn't you?"

"It was like that night we just left that fund-raiser with Johnny G, like we could do whatever we wanted, and if you didn't do what you wanted, then why be there? That's what Jessica said and I thought she was right. You gotta live.

"We had those planes," I say, looking out the window, my mind lifting off into the gray sky, snatching at that feeling of freedom. "Even in the middle of it all, we'd just go wherever we wanted, do whatever we wanted. It was like, I don't know, like we were gods. Mount Olympus. Over the clouds. We did it because we could."

I look at his shabby yellow sweater, the shirt collar with frayed edges, the pounded-down ten-karat gold on his ring, and say, "That's how people live, you know. Movie stars and billionaires. Like everyone else is down on earth in the stink, groveling and fighting for the crumbs."

As a kid, I would always draw the water with a bright blue crayon, a color I never saw until Bermuda. The rocks too, huge volcanic slabs like a children's drawing. Jet black. The weather forecast in Syracuse was for a week of clouds and cold and rain and Jessica said, "Let's get out of here." She got Amy to watch Tommy for three days so he didn't miss school, and booked a suite at the Coral Beach Club. We flew in there, just the two of us, like we were going across town for a cup of coffee. She said we both needed to get away and she was right.

When you land on an island in a big private jet, people move quickly for you. They hold doors open and wave you on. There is a hurried air about things, people's hands keep working, even while they're stealing glances at you and your beautiful wife.

A limousine took us to the club. We stopped on the terrace for a minute to inhale the smell of living plants and the salt air shouldering its way ashore. The pink beach glistened under the bright sun and birds chattered in the trees above. Out over the water a white raptor with a tail streaming behind it like a kite dove a hundred feet with a splash.

By the time we got to our room, the bags were there, open and waiting. A breeze wafted the translucent white curtains, tickling the edge of the king bed, which I thought we should use right away. But Jessica wanted to get into the sun and she pushed me away with promises of something special that night.

I never got to find out what it was, but all that afternoon, out there on the beach, I stared at her in that white bikini just as hard as the pair of teenage kids who walked up and down the beach nonstop.

"This is my second most favorite place," she said, her words sleepy.

"What's your first?"

"You know I love Como. I want to live there some day. The Italians know how to live. The food. The wine. God I love it there."

"When the project's done, we'll go," I said.

"Good."

She fell asleep smiling.

I soaked up the sun, watching her until I saw the manager coming across the beach in his blue double-breasted suit, kicking up tufts of sand with his black Gucci shoes. When I realized he was heading for us, I sat up in the lounge chair and took off my sunglasses.

"Mr. Coder?" he said, his British accent subdued. "I'm quite sorry to disturb you, sir, but it seems there is an emergency at home."

I stood up with my heart pounding and my stomach all balled up, thinking that it had happened to us again.

Jessica woke up. She sat up and looked at me over the top of her sunglasses. Her back was rigid.

I pulled on a shirt, buttoning as I jogged alongside the manager across the beach, past the pool, and inside the glass doors. Halfway across the marble lobby next to a tall white pillar was a bamboo phone stand.

There was an ice machine whirring in the corner and a parrot chuckling as it stepped headfirst down the side of its brass cage by the window. I put one finger in my ear and said hello.

"You better get your fucking pal under control and I mean now!"

It was Johnny G. For an instant, I was relieved and I signaled to Jessica as she came breathless into the lobby that everything was okay.

"Jesus, Johnny. What are you talking about?"

"This fuck partner of yours. He threw Con Trac off the job. Shut down the whole fucking project! If we didn't have all this fed heat from Milo I'd— And you're on a goddamn beach?"

"Look," I said in a hushed tone, wondering how he'd found me but knowing I didn't want to ask, "there's nothing I can do from here. I'll be back in two days."

"No, you don't seem to get how this works," Johnny said. "You're working for me now. You don't drop out on some sunshine vacation in the middle of this. You get your ass back here now, and I mean now."

"You mean now?" I said, raising my voice, puffing up my chest and looking into Jessica's eyes. "You think that works with me?"

There was silence on the other end. I heard him breathing, a nasal, sleepy wheezing.

"I got a little tape recording," he finally said. "That tricky little slit of yours, talking about don't worry, my *husband* will take care of James King."

More breathing. Jessica, the potted palm trees, and the wicker furniture had all gone out of focus for me. The parrot's laughter came from far away.

"I'll come as soon as I can," I said.

"Hey," he said, "how'd you get down there?"

"We've got a corporate jet."

"Yeah," he said, "that's what I heard. You get your ass on it. I'll be picking you up from Teterboro myself.

"Tonight."

32

W E'RE FINE," Jessica said.

I ranted at her on the way back to our room, but it was like I wasn't talking. She was all business, nodding her head and getting our things together, telling me to call the pilots, check out, and get us a driver. When we pulled up next to the hangar in Teterboro, Johnny G was standing there with his hands jammed into the pockets of his brown leather jacket. Beside him in a windbreaker was a baggy-eyed man with slicked-back hair.

"That's Pete," Jessica said, peering over my shoulder and out the small airplane window.

"Now he shows up," I said. "He didn't need a taco tonight. Look at that guy. Jesus."

Pete fingered a bright red sore on his bottom lip. Johnny had his head tilted back so that I could see the dark caves of his nostrils. I had no idea how they got themselves out onto the tarmac, but when we descended the steps of the plane, Johnny embraced me and patted my back as if we were brothers reuniting for a family funeral. Pete stood back and played with his wound. Neither of them even looked at Jessica.

"Look, I can handle this," I said. "It's not going to help things with you guys around. I know him. It'll be a lot better if he doesn't see you."

"He knows us," Johnny said, shrugging. "We'll just give you a lift to the site."

"I've got a car."

"Just a lift," Johnny said, turning toward the terminal. "Moral support."

I told the pilots to wait and we followed Johnny. He and Pete had pulled up their green Excursion into the covered drive just outside the terminal's lobby. I thought about telling Jessica to stay, but kept my mouth shut. She and I got in the back of Johnny's truck. By the time we got out to the site, the sun was down, the sky's glow fading.

The skeleton of the mall stretched nearly a quarter mile end to end. It rose up three stories and in the center there was a seven-story tower. Clusters of bright lights on posts illuminated different areas where dozers and cement mixers churned up the dust. A slew of rumbling portable generators drowned out the crickets and poisoned the air with the stink of diesel.

"I thought it stopped," I said.

Johnny turned around in his seat and said, "For our guy it did. You see any Con Trac steel?"

By steel, he meant equipment, dozers, Caterpillars, and mixers. Pete pulled up to the gates and a uniformed Pinkerton in a hard hat came out of a small shack with a clipboard and a radio.

"I got Thane Coder from King Corp," Pete said, angling his head.

The guard peered past him. I moved my face into the light and waved.

"You got ID?"

I handed up my license. The Pinkerton examined it, then called into his radio before opening the gates. We pulled right up to the tower area where the work was in full swing. Beams swung from cranes out of the dying light and into the halogen glare. Mixers pumped concrete into the foundation. Most of the equipment had green and white OBG emblems. My blood boiled.

I jumped out and grabbed a foreman.

"Where's Ben Evans?" I asked.

The man pointed up, the top of the tower. There was a platform there among the girders and I could make out three men poring over a makeshift table. There was a simple cage elevator with big red and green operation buttons. I got in, pushed the green, and lurched upward. The Excursion got smaller and smaller. Everyone stayed inside, but I thought I could make out Johnny G's face looking up through the windshield.

When the lift clanged to a stop, I unlatched the cage and stepped out into the night air. From there I could see the string of lights on the George Washington Bridge and, beyond that, the glow of New York City. Ben and two men in OBG hard hats were looking at plans, occasionally leaning over the platform's railing to point at some detail of the work. I walked up to the table and stood there, waiting for them to notice me.

The two OBG guys stopped first and looked back and forth between me and Ben until he realized something had changed and he looked up from his plans.

"Thane."

"What's this?"

"What?"

I snatched the helmet off the head of the man closest to me and jabbed my finger at the OBG emblem.

"This!" I shouted.

He looked at the OBG guys and asked them to leave us alone for a minute. They scrambled into the cage and hummed out of sight.

Ben took a deep breath and said, "They were stealing."

"Who? What?"

"Con Trac had the union in here. There were two trucks full of fiber optic cable and now there's just one. They cut the lock on the fence."

"It could have been anyone," I said. "You can't just throw a company like Con Trac off a job like this."

"I did," he said. "That was just one thing. These guys were showing up and sitting around playing cards. It's bullshit, Thane. You told me to get it built. Here I am."

"We've got a deal with Con Trac," I said. "You bring them back."

Ben looked at me for a while, then he looked off toward the bridge. The elevator returned, clanging into place. Ben's chest rose and fell, quickening. Finally, he looked at me.

"I see," he said, stepping toward the cage.

I stepped in front of him, looking down a couple inches through the rectangular glasses into his burning blue eyes. I had this image of me shoving him right over that two-by-four railing, ending it all right there. An accident. He slipped.

"You see what?" I said, through my teeth.

"Everything," he said.

33

I breathe deep and exhale through my nose, then say, "The Apaches used to say that you measure the strength of a man by his enemies."

"You think Ben was your enemy?" he asks.

"Johnny G was my enemy. I switched sides, is that what you want me to say? I'm saying it. My enemies were my friends."

"The most dangerous kind," he says.

"Dangerous? Dangerous was Bucky," I say.

"The hunting guide guy?" he asks.

I nod and say, "Even James knew there was something about him. Relentless. One time we were on this hunt in the mountains in New Mexico and this big storm whipped up out of nowhere. It was getting dark and the guides were calling everyone into camp.

"The wind came screaming through the chinks in the lodge, not a big lodge like Cascade, just a log cabin, and when the last group came in, three inches of snow blew in through the door before we could get it shut. That's when we realized these two cops from Boston were missing. They stayed to quarter out an elk while their guide doubled back on the trail of a wounded bull with the man who'd wounded it.

"James asked the New Mexico guides who was going out for them, and their eyes got big and they told him it was eight miles up and down two passes to where they were, impossible in a storm like that to make it to them, let alone come back. Bucky didn't even say anything. There were some arguments and some pretty bad feelings and no one noticed what he was doing until he shouldered his pack and disappeared out the door. Ten minutes later, it was dark as tar and the guides started in on some vodka, and using the word 'suicide' like he'd already hung himself from the rafters."

He looks at me and waits.

"No one knows how he did it," I say, drumming my fingertips on the tabletop. "The cops weren't even conscious. It was five a.m. when he came through the door with one of them over each shoulder.

"I'm not stupid," I say. "I wasn't trying to get caught."

"No one said that."

"This guy was unbelievable," I say. "And once he was on me, I guess I didn't stand a chance."

"How did he get on you?" the shrink asks.

"I'm pretty sure I know."

34

IT WAS TWO-THIRTY IN THE MORNING when Bucky woke up. Still in the pit of the night, but time for him to be on the move. Judy, his wife, lay on her back with a flared-out paperback still in her hand. Her reading glasses had somehow made it to the nightstand. Bucky liked the outdoor air and he slept with the windows open unless it dropped into negative numbers. The nighttime high thirties of October were actually what he preferred, but it didn't keep him from hurrying across the wooden part of the floor to the warm slate surrounding the stove.

After stoking the fire, he washed up quick, slipped into his camo, and started breaking eggs into a pan. He made them scrambled and cooked six sausage links until they were good and brown. There was a cup of oatmeal to be stirred and toast to be buttered while everything cooked and the coffee brewed. It was enough to overcome the pine scent that permeated their home.

Out on the road, he straddled the dividing line, confident that no one else was about. He was heading north, to the big lake. It had taken him several days to puzzle it out. No one had heard from Scott. His truck had disappeared, but he never carried cash and, according to one of the deputies Bucky knew in McCarthy's office, none of Scott's credit cards had shown any activity.

Bucky knew all of Scott's friends and he was certain from the tone of their voice that none of them had seen him. Then the answer hit him, and he was as certain of where Scott had gone as if he was a wounded animal. Bucky didn't always have to see the tracks. He could look at the lay of the land, a watercourse, a ravine, the rise of a hill, or a patch of brambles and just know.

The beam of his headlights cut through the harbor fog, sweeping across an army of white hulls wearing blue plastic covers that reminded him of shower caps. Most of the boats rested on their trailers, but some were simply propped up on blocks. Pleasure craft, owned by lawyers and doctors and architects from town. But not all the boat slips along the dock were empty. There were a handful, like Bucky, who ran their boats late into the fall to take advantage of the steelhead runs. It was cold, tiresome work. Not the stuff for greenhorns.

Bucky eased past the corrugated steel building and shone his headlights through the fog and down on the docks. His thirty-two-foot cruiser, *Reel to Reel*, was missing. The faded blue ropes hung limp from their posts. It didn't make him smile, but his eyes narrowed a bit and he stroked the long edges of his mustache, deciding whose boat he would take and deciding on Frankie Denoto's. He knew Frankie left the keys wedged down between the cushion on the captain's seat and he was the kind of man who always had two full tanks of gas.

Bucky called and left a message on Frankie's answering machine, then unmoored the fishing boat and hopped onboard. The chugging engine filled the damp morning air with petroleum. The fog was thick enough so that his fumes stayed with him until he got out into the fat part of the harbor. He could feel the space on either side of him and make out the upcoming harbor lights, colorful pinpoints in the mist. He started to outrun his own fumes and drank in the smell of fish and water, slowing to ease his way through the break walls, keeping well between the green and red light towers.

There was some chop outside the harbor. He trimmed his motors as best he could, but there was no escaping a rough ride to Canada. Halfway over, the sun poked its orange rim over the starboard horizon. The fog began to melt and soon there was nothing in sight but water and sky and the weakened sun glaring down at the fishing boat through a high haze.

His face and hands were numb by the time he saw the island, and the thin curving line of smoke confirmed his suspicion. On the north side of the island there was a small inlet with a channel deep enough to get through if your motors were trimmed all the way up. Bucky saw his own boat and eased up next to it on the other side of the single dock. On a rise in the lee of some towering blue spruce was a snug cabin that was the source of the smoke.

Bucky climbed the winding trail of pine needles. In the glare of one of the small square windows, he saw the flicker of a face and the black barrel of a gun. When he got there, he stood for a minute on the porch, listening, then let himself in. Scott looked up from a bowl of cold cereal and a mug of coffee. The black-barreled twelve gauge rested up against the sink.

"Christ, I couldn't believe it, Bucky," Scott said. "I

close my eyes and there he is, lying there in all that blood."

Bucky went to the stove, took a chipped mug off its hook, poured himself a cup, and sat down.

"You didn't do that, did you?" he said. He'd told himself he wouldn't ask, but found that he couldn't help it. The question just came out.

Looking hard into Scott's eyes he could see the answer, horror at the thought of harming his own father.

"How many times did I tell him we needed more security?" Scott said, slamming his palm on the table. "Carl at the office, that's it, which is great unless Carl is fixing the boiler and some nutcase walks in through the front doors with an Uzi.

"Huh," Scott said, huffing out something like a laugh. "The lodge? Who didn't have an eye scan done? There had to be a hundred people who could have popped that lock and walked away. If it was even locked. He wouldn't listen, Buck, and they got him. Of course they got him. It's a miracle they didn't get him before."

"They think it was you," Bucky said.

"Because I took off?" Scott said, casting a wild look Bucky's way. "That's stupid."

"And your knife."

"Stupid," Scott said, shaking his head.

Bucky nodded.

"They got Milo and they got him," Scott said. "I figured I was next. So I got out of there. I didn't even tell Emily. They'll leave her alone if she doesn't know anything.

"Christ, it took long enough for you to find me. You getting old?"

Half a grin broke out on Scott's face and Bucky smiled back.

"I don't know if it *was* the union," Bucky said, his face drooping again.

"Bucky, you know it wasn't me."

"I know that."

Bucky looked down at his coffee and took a swig. In the bottom, the grinds swirled like black smoke before settling back down. He looked up and spoke in a quiet, even tone.

"I saw man tracks that night," he said. "In the snow. About a size thirteen. First thing I thought of was Thane. He was supposed to meet your dad and I figured they finished late and he took a walk. When I saw what happened, I knew whoever killed your dad made those tracks. The snow covered them by then and the goddamn police have their heads up their asses."

"Thane?" Scott said.

Bucky looked at him.

"He's like a brother," Scott said.

"Crazier things happen," Bucky said.

"Did you tell the police?"

"Sure," he said. "But they think I'm trying to protect you."

Scott sat for a while, staring at the floor before he said, "What do we do, Buck?"

"I'll be honest," he said. "I've been thinking about it and if he did do it—"

"Maybe he didn't, right? I can't believe it. Size thirteen could have been anyone."

"Maybe," Bucky said. "But if he did, or if he's somehow hooked up with the union, he'll make a mistake."

"I can't just keep sitting here," Scott said, bursting from his seat and pacing the floor.

"When you're on to a big whitetail," Bucky said, following Scott with his eyes, "the closer you get, the more wary he gets. When you get in range—you know this—you just stop. You don't move a muscle. Then, just when you think he might have given you the slip, he'll twitch an ear, or flick his tail. Then you got him."

Bucky looked out of the small square window. The sky was full gray now, the clouds churning their way to New England.

"No," Bucky said, finishing his coffee, "we stay still, and we watch.

"He'll slip."

35

For KING CORP, opening day of deer season had always been a holiday. The night before, there was a big dinner for the partners and the most important clients. Wives were invited and welcome to hunt. Between the lodge and several renovated outlying farmhouses, there was room for almost a hundred. The dinner would be held in the massive hall that opened out onto the water, its three-story beams stretched to the distant roof like one of the great European cathedrals.

Jessica was using the annual event for a coronation, that party she had talked about having.

Invitations went out to all the most important bankers and CEOs of the major retailers and construction companies across the country. The fleet of four Citation Xs was scheduled to bring the VIPs in and out. James's old friends, the ones from his earlier days as a sewage line contractor, were dropped from the list, and only the most important people inside the company were invited.

"You didn't invite Vitor?" I said, looking over the list at the breakfast table. "He makes the white lasagna."

"I thought lamb chops," Jessica said, laying fried eggs

onto two plates and carrying them across the kitchen to Tommy and me. "Roses for the centerpieces."

"Can I go?" Tommy asked.

"Drink your orange juice, pal. It's a thing for work, but in a couple of years, you're gonna be old enough to hunt and you'll be right there with me," I said, reaching over and mussing his hair. I looked over the top of the list at Jessica. "How could you not invite Vitor?"

"People don't eat pasta that late anymore," she said, setting the plate down. "This is about you, us, our friends. James's gone."

I scowled at her, glancing at Tommy.

"What?" she said. "Tommy and I talked about it. It's like the *Lion King*, the circle of life. Everything that lives, also has to die."

I winced and shook my head.

"You take care of the hunting," she said, patting my back. "I'll handle the food and the guest list. It's too late now anyway."

She pinched the list and tugged it out of my hand. I picked up my fork. She sat down at the computer she kept on a desk in the corner of the kitchen to check her e-mails. Jessica didn't eat breakfast.

"I could call him," I said, wiping up the last of the yolk with a piece of toast. "I like Vitor."

Jessica kept on typing, scanning the screen.

"Get your book bag, Tommy," she said.

I sighed, got up, and put my dishes in the sink. Our bags were packed and waiting at the front door. I loaded up the H2 that Jessica bought to replace my Escalade. When I told her we were ready, she came out with her hands jammed into a brown shearling coat and whistling,

Tommy in tow to be dropped at school. Going up the driveway, I let him sit on my lap and steer the Hummer.

It was a busy day at the lodge. There were nonstop questions for both Jessica and me, and we set up our base of operations in the conference room of the main entrance of the lodge with the staff coming and going like bees.

There was also Garden State business to attend to. A day couldn't go by without some kind of equipment or material mysteriously disappearing. A half million dollars' worth of copper piping, metal scrap as good as cash. Two dump trucks. A dozen generators. One day we even lost ten Porta Pottis. Jessica assured me that we were getting our cut from any leakage, and I assured my employees that it was just part of doing business downstate.

It was sometime after lunch that I realized a lot of the unanswered questions about the opening day hunt could only be answered by Bucky. Which hunters were riding in which trucks? What time did the first drive begin? Were we serving coffee in the European tower-blinds?

"Have you seen him?" I asked Marty, the lodge manager whom James had lured away from the Ritz-Carlton in Naples, Florida.

Marty shrugged and said he hadn't. Not all day.

"Have someone find him," I said. "We need some answers on this stuff. And Marty, make sure there's a dozen yellow roses in the master bedroom."

"Not red?"

"You ever smell a red rose? They stink. Do yellow."

I didn't see Marty again until four o'clock. I was downstairs in the larger group conference room with Dave Wickersham, one of the architects who had helped design the lodge. Dave had his notepad out and a schematic of the room on the table. I pointed to the area where I wanted the treadmills and the plasma screens. Since I was running the company and Cascade was company property, I could do as I pleased, and I intended to make the place my own.

"I always wondered why James never did this," Dave said, marking it down.

"Why walk on a treadmill when you can walk outdoors?" I said. "Remember?"

"God, those damn hikes," Dave said, shaking his head. "Up and down and through that goddamn swamp over by the Hughes place.

"But," he said, after looking off into space for a moment, "I guess you got to see things."

"You can burn more calories on a treadmill," I said, "and you can see the TV."

Dave looked at me over the tops of his glasses for a second, then said, "That's right."

Marty came down the stairs and I asked Dave if we were all set. We were. He left and I turned to Marty. His eyes darted here and there.

"He's not here," Marty said.

"Who? Bucky? What do you mean, not here?"

Marty shook his head and said, "I looked all over the place, the fish shack, the duck barn, all over. No one's seen him and then I went to his house. His Suburban wasn't there, but I asked Judy and she said he's down in Endicott on a hunt."

"What hunt?"

"Some old friends. Harold Sincibaugh's crew."

I choked down a laugh. "It's opening day tomorrow."

"I guess he wasn't thinking," Marty said, wringing his hands.

"Get his ass on the phone," I said, raising my voice.

"They don't have one," Marty said. "I asked."

"Where's Russel? Luke?"

"With him."

"Fuck. Who *is* here, Marty? This is your fucking staff too. Isn't it?"

"James never let me get involved with Bucky's guides."

"And did James have to spoon-feed Bucky on every fucking detail? It's opening fucking day! We've got the dinner tonight."

"I don't know," Marty said, taking a step back. "Maybe he didn't think he was supposed to come."

"Marty," I said, closing the gap between us and gripping his shoulder, "you get someone down there and get his ass back here tonight. I mean *tonight.*"

"You want me to go?"

"You can't go, we've got the dinner. Get someone. Who's left? Who in this place isn't related to Bucky?"

"Adam could go."

"Good, whoever," I said, letting him go with a little shove. "Just get him back here."

Marty hurried off. I went upstairs into the great hall where the dinner would be and told Jessica about Bucky.

"I think white, don't you?" she asked, holding a red and a white napkin up in the light.

"He puts everyone in their stands," I said. "He keeps everyone together when they move through the woods or the whole thing gets gummed up."

"Honey," she said, standing up and stroking my cheek with the back of her fingers. "No one cares. They can sleep in."

"Guys are going to want to hunt."

"Who? Chris Tognola from Deutsche Bank? Howard Reese? Tim Kingston? Please."

"Jim Higgins will."

"The Bass Pro Shop guy," she said, clucking her tongue. "People come here to see the lodge."

She put the napkins down and glanced around, making sure we were alone. Her eyes narrowed. She lowered her voice and said, "If you're worried about what people think, maybe you should get rid of people who don't do their jobs. And, if they're living on company property, maybe they shouldn't be."

"Bucky?"

"*Anyone* who tries to make you look bad. Anyone who thinks you're not running this place," she said, moving a wineglass to the other side of the plate. "You let people snub you and this won't last long. Kick him out."

"His house?"

She gave me a grim smile with those teeth, put her finger in my chest, and said, "The house belongs to the company. You run the company. What did James used to say? Eat or be eaten, right? You're at the top of the food chain now."

"Judy's there," I said.

"I got thrown out of my house," she said with a shrug, huffing on a spoon and wiping it on her sleeve. "I survived."

She put the spoon down, looked at me, and asked, "What did you do when you played football and somebody took a cheap shot at you? Forget about it until they did it again?"

She turned and walked away in the direction of the kitchen. I watched her disappear, my face hot and pressure building in my brain. I jogged downstairs to the parking garage where I found Adam wearing his Carhartt jacket, jeans, and big rubber boots climbing into his pickup truck. I got in on the other side.

"You going with me?" he asked. His round cheeks, which were always bright pink, turned red, and his eyes widened behind their wire-framed glasses.

"We're not going to Endicott," I said. "Take me to Bucky's."

"His house?" Adam said, and he started the engine.

36

Bucky's wife, Judy, was in the trophy room, reading a book by the fire. Bucky's mounts stared down with their dead glass eyes. A stone sheep. A monster Cape buffalo. Two big turkeys in flight. There were dozens of animals from six of the seven continents.

"Judy," I said, "I'm sorry, but you have to leave."

"What do you mean?" she said. She was a quiet woman with frizzy brown hair and glasses. The kind you would expect behind the desk of a public library.

"You have to leave," I said. "Adam will help you pack some things. I only have ten minutes, so you'll have to hurry."

"What? What happened?"

"Bucky's fired," I said. "This is a company house. I can't allow ineptitude any more than James did. If Bucky did this to James on opening day, James would have done the same thing."

I spoke quietly, but with force. When I saw her hesitation, I raised my voice. "I mean now!"

She looked at Adam, whose cheeks were now shiny and purple. Adam clasped his hands together and stared hard at the mud on his big rubber boots. She got the idea and twelve minutes later she and Adam were loading several bulging suitcases into Judy's truck while I talked on my cell phone and pretended not to watch.

Adam and I watched her truck wind down the drive and disappear out onto Swamp Road. My heart was pumping fast and hard. I could see Jessica's smile in my mind's eye, the one she shared with Johnny G.

"We still got that big backhoe out in back of the duck barn?" I asked Adam.

"Yeah," he said.

"You know how to run that thing, right?"

I knew he did. I'd seen him and Bucky tearing down various barns and old farmhouses over the years as James consumed his neighbors, slowly expanding the preserve.

He nodded.

"Get in," I said. "I'll drive."

I took him over to the barn and out in back where the machine rested in the tall brown grass.

"Take it over to Bucky's," I said.

"Well, what for?"

"You're going to knock it down."

"Bucky's house? I can't do that," he said, his mouth hanging open, his eyes wincing.

"Then you're fired," I said. "You can get out too."

Adam had an old farmhouse on the property, where he lived with his young wife. She had diabetes. A drain on the company's health insurance.

"Or else you can knock it down and take his job."

"Me?"

"Am I not speaking English?" I asked.

"But it's his house."

"It's the company's house," I said, my voice rising. "I run

the company. Either you tear it down by midnight or your place will be next. How's that? Are you getting me now?"

Adam backed away from me toward the machine. He climbed up into the seat, keeping his eyes on me. I got into his pickup and followed him as the machine bounced along the shoulder of Swamp Road, back down toward Bucky's. He sat on the machine outside Bucky's house for a while with the old rusty exhaust pipe pumping crud into the air.

Finally, I looked at my watch and hopped down out of the truck. I shooed him down off the machine, raised the front scoop, and drove it straight into the corner of the house. I backed up and did it again, three times, until the roof sagged to the ground.

I got down and, raising my voice above the chugging motor, said, "You got that now? You fucking get it?"

Adam licked his lips and nodded. He waited until I was well away before he climbed up, then he rotated the machine around and began pounding down the roof with the bucket. Once he got going, he worked with the skill of a mason, touching just the right spots to bring everything crashing down.

Glass shattered. Wood splintered. Concrete popped and grated. The day was fading, but as I pulled away in his truck I could see his red face glistening in the rearview mirror like a beacon.

The guests were starting to arrive and drinks were being served at the long mahogany bar outside the massive great hall where banquets were held. People stood clustered together or sat in the furniture groupings of mission oak and dark leather. There was a festive buzz in the air and as Jessica and I walked arm in arm into the comfortably enormous space, people came to us to smile and shake hands and offer their congratulations.

I took a glass of champagne off one of the girls' trays and drained it in time to take a second after Jessica took hers. Every time I turned, one of those girls was going by with a tray and not many of them got past without taking an empty glass away and leaving me with a full one. I felt the bubbles lifting my spirits and it seemed to me that that party was the first gathering since James's death that wasn't tainted with mourning.

The room was crowded and noisy and in my ears it began to sound like ocean surf. My teeth lost all feeling, and in a discussion with Howard Reese about the World Bank, I became remotely aware that my words weren't coming out quite right. I got quiet after that and noticed that Marty was up on a chair pinging a water glass with a spoon. It took about five minutes before it was quiet enough for him to announce that dinner was served and would everyone please go to the front table to find their place cards.

I started toward the dining area, saw Jessica, and gripped her hand in mine.

The big oval table in the middle of everything was where James always sat with Eva, Scott, and Emily, and the most important guests from outside the company. Out past the mullioned windows stretched a spacious deck, then the black water and the peninsula beyond. Jessica and I took our places, James's and Eva's seats, in the middle of everyone with our backs to the windows.

I sat down on my hands and pressed my lips tight. The room leaned one way, just a bit, then the other. I lowered my eyelids halfway until Jessica nudged my ribs with her elbow. Everyone was looking. It was time for a toast.

"I thought you said traditions didn't matter," I said, leaning toward her. "Now it matters all of a sudden? Shit."

She forced a smile at me, her eyes darting around the table. I stood up, bracing my hand against the table. A hundred faces scattered among a sea of round tables, each offering up a trio of candles surrounding a bloom of yellow roses. I raised my glass and felt them lean toward me. I opened my mouth to speak, then stopped and narrowed my eyes.

Beyond the glimmering candlelight, in the open area of the bar where the stairways led up to the bedrooms, the lights had been dimmed. But my eye caught the movement of someone coming down the stairway, descending almost mechanically with his hand on the cast-iron railing.

When he reached the bottom landing, I felt a tight ball in my gut. I couldn't make out the features of his face, but could see from its pale glow that it was regal and topped with a flow of white hair.

I felt Jessica's fingertips on my arm.

I saw the nose. The high cheeks and the strong jowls. The eyes glaring, snowy eyebrows pitched toward the floor. I looked at Jessica and flicked my eyes toward his shape until she looked too. The glass slipped from my hand and smashed somewhere in the distance.

I stepped away from the table and fell back over my chair. I heard small screams and a wave of murmuring.

Jessica stood over me with a pale face, tugging on my arm, helping me to my feet.

"We're fine," she said, raising her hand to the crowd

and sweeping a strand of hair behind her ear. "Please, everyone eat."

She braced my arm over her shoulder, straining under my weight. My feet fumbled underneath me and my eyes lost their focus as she led me away.

37

Do you still see him?" he asks.

"That's what those pills they gave me are for," I say, "right?"

"They're more for depression, I'd say. Were there others you haven't told anyone about? You said you see your wife. In your cell."

"When I close my eyes I do," I say, closing them for a moment to show him. "But you mean like James, right? Like ghosts?"

"Is that what you think he was?"

"I guess that's what made me crazy, huh?" I say.

"Were you?" he asks.

My lip curls up at this. "You people say I am. What's a label, though? Fiction. With money you can create any fiction you like. 'My wife designed the wing on the museum.' 'I'm a hell of a polo player.' 'She's a brilliant art collector.' Crap like that. Everyone swallows it."

"Did you have a fiction?" he asks.

I lace my fingers together behind my neck and lean back. "The happy couple. Horatio Alger. In control . . ."

I let the chair fall forward with a crash and I lean across

the table. "I was seeing dead men, for Christ's sake. Johnny G was in my shorts. The FBI had Bucky on a leash, tracking me down like a bloodhound."

"Interesting choice of words."

"What is?" I ask, sitting back.

"Bloodhound."

"Why? Blood on my hands?" I asked.

"Was he really with the FBI?"

"They were all working together against me," I said. "That's why Ben had to go."

He riffles through his papers, studying them with a frown, then looks up and says, "Together? All of them? This is something new."

"Not to me."

38

BEN PULLED UP THE DRIVE, rounded the bend, and saw Bucky's blue Suburban resting in front of rubble. The log house looked like a squashed matchstick sculpture. Jagged ends of wood sprouted from the twisted mass of piping, wires, and sheet metal.

A head popped up from the middle of the mess. Two dark eyes and a thick, drooping mustache beneath the rim of a camouflage cap. Ben cut his headlights and got out.

"Bucky," he shouted.

Bucky disappeared for a moment, then came from around the side of the mess with a shotgun in one hand and a gazelle mount in the other. He held the stuffed head by the good horn. The other was broken, but Bucky still opened the rear window of his Suburban and laid it in.

"You want me out?" Bucky said, staring baldly. The shotgun in his hand wasn't aimed at Ben, but it was pointing in his general direction. "A lot of this stuff is mine."

Ben shook his head. "You don't understand. Adam told me what happened. He had no right."

"James's gone, though, right? Now it's just you and him running things."

"Buck," Ben said, shaking his head, looking hard into his churning eyes, "I am not a part of this. I tried to get the board to put me in charge. Jesus, he put the union on the job at Garden State. We fought them for fifteen years and now they're down there running a poker game in the job trailer."

"I guess we all got our problems," Bucky said, motioning his head toward the broken heap.

"We're on the same side here, Bucky," Ben said.

"Who's side is that?" Bucky said, lowering the gun and walking toward the pile.

"You don't believe me, do you?" said Ben, following.

"They treated you both like family," Bucky said, pushing a beam up out of the way and stepping in to retrieve a clock radio with one hand and a reading lamp with the other.

"Look at this," Ben said, taking a business card from his pocket and handing it to Bucky.

Bucky set the clock down on the ground and took the card, holding it at arm's length to read it.

"Yeah, so? I talked to them already. They think it was Scott. Is that what you think?" he said.

"I've been talking to them," Ben said. "Trying to convince them what's really going on here."

"Which is?"

"The union, I think," Ben said. "Thane helping them, maybe."

"Who else could have got in?" Bucky said, picking up the clock and taking it and the lamp to the back of his truck. "I saw man tracks. Thane's size. They came from the lower entrance by the gun room. There's a scanner there to let you in."

"I can't see Thane," Ben said, still trailing him. "Letting one of them in, but not doing it."

"There was just one track," Bucky said, standing still in the fading light.

"Maybe he let them in another door."

"Maybe a skunk don't spray."

"Can we prove he went in?" Ben asked. "Does the scanner record the activity anywhere? The time and who used it?"

"I think it's just like a lock and your eye is the key, but I don't know," Bucky said. "I couldn't find out. It's that Eye Pass company. They wouldn't tell me anything, one way or the other."

"You're not an officer of the company."

"Yeah, so?"

"So, I am," Ben said. "I don't know if it's there, but if it is, I'll find it."

He held out his hand, and Bucky took it.

39

Amanda dashed into the room, tugging a wrinkle out of her blouse. Everyone else was already seated at the conference table. She sat down next to Dorothy and ignored the stares, fixing her eyes on the supervisor's shiny bald head. Even he was looking at her in an off-center way.

She looked at her shoulder and saw the Pop-Tart crumbs. She brushed them off and looked up at her supervisor's eyes magnified by the thick lenses. He cleared his throat and began to speak. Amanda had a hard time paying attention to the laundry list of uneventful details. An argument between a hit man and his cousin. A forged check by the wife of a street thug. A wiretap that shed light on nothing more than a teenage romance and a preferred brand of condoms.

Finally, they came to her. Amanda looked at Dorothy, saw the flat line of her mouth, and stood up.

"Well, the plot thickens," Amanda said. All eyes were on her. "One of our sources is claiming another source is the one responsible for James King's murder."

"What source?" the supervisor asked, his mouth agog.

"Ben Evans—his picture isn't up there—thinks Thane Coder either killed James King, or helped someone from Johnny G's organization do it. But Evans himself could be involved. We need more resources. To watch them all."

"Was Johnny G or Peter Romano anywhere close to this lodge?"

"Johnny was at a political fund-raiser," she said. "Pete was in a holding tank in Morristown, New Jersey, for some unpaid parking tickets."

"Shit."

"Evans is the other friend?" one of the NYPD cops asked.

"Of James King's son," Amanda said.

"Who we *thought* was the killer," said another.

"And no one can find," the supervisor said.

"Someone's working with the union," Amanda said, nodding toward Johnny G's glossy photo in the middle of the board. "I don't know who. The son. This, Ben Evans. The union is all over that project."

"Probably our former football star," Dorothy said, leaning back in her chair with her hands laced behind her head. "Coder's dirty. Taxes are just the start. So is the wife. Comes off like a Girl Scout, but she's a snake. Cold-blooded."

Amanda shot her partner an annoyed look, even though her interruption was no surprise. Dorothy had voiced her opinion on the drive home last night.

"Based on?" the supervisor said, his magnified eyes unblinking.

"Had a little dinner with Johnny G he didn't tell us

about," Dorothy said, popping her fingers into the air, as she counted off the reasons. "Only alibi for that night is the wife. And, the caretaker says there was a boot print in the snow outside the lodge the night of the murder, Coder's size."

"The lodge has a retina scan security system," Amanda said. "We've asked for a warrant to see if there's any record of who accessed the system and when."

"Monte?" the supervisor said, looking at the agent the team relied on for any information technology.

Monte shrugged and said, "Depends on the level of the system. Some have it, some don't."

"Why didn't we check this from the start?" the supervisor asked.

"We had the son's bloody knife and him on the run," Dorothy said. "No one thought about someone sneaking in. The son was in there already."

"We missed it," Amanda said.

"*We* didn't," Dorothy said.

"You two got a problem?" the supervisor said, eyes darting between them for clues.

"Bucky Lanehart, he's a hunting guide at the lodge," Amanda said. "I'm betting he'd say anything if it helped Scott King. No one else saw those prints. They conveniently melted."

"Size thirteen," Dorothy said. "Coder's size."

"He says."

"Footprints are a hunting guide's specialty, wouldn't you say?"

Amanda saw the grins around the table. They were obviously happy it was her instead of them who had to listen to Dorothy's junk.

"We've put time into Coder already," Amanda said.

"My gut tells me he's all right. I don't know. If Coder were discredited in any way, Ben Evans would end up running the company. If Evans is the dirty one here, I'm sure the union would prefer to have him running the company instead of Coder."

That set off a round of murmurs, everyone speculating, until Dorothy said, "Your gut sucks."

The room went quiet.

Their supervisor cleared his throat and said, "Get the warrant. See what the scanner says and we won't have to worry about anyone's gut. If it was Coder there that night, then he's lying."

40

AT FIRST I THOUGHT the house might be burning. The sky over the trees was thick with dark smoke aglow in the setting sun. When I drove through the gates, I saw the house standing tall and clean. It was the lot next door where the smoke came from and it wasn't a fire. Five big excavators belched black diesel exhaust into the air. The earth was torn open. Dirt piled high. A steady stream of dump trucks filled their beds and rumbled off up the dirt lane to the main road, grinding their gears and disappearing into the dusk.

I pulled into the garage and walked around the outside of the house. A section of fence had been removed, and there was a path beaten in the grass between the lower level of the house and the work site. Through the sliding glass doors I saw a table set up on sawhorses that was covered with plans. Around the table, wearing orange hard hats, stood Jessica and two construction men in muddy boots.

I looked over at the work. The thundering machines shook the air and the fresh scent of raw earth mingled with the exhaust. I realized now that the red steel bore the Con Trac emblem. I took two steps toward the site, drawn by its enormity, then retreated back toward the house, where the plans were being laid.

"What the hell?" I said, before they could turn their heads.

"Thane," Jessica said, easing my way and planting a kiss on my cheek. She had on work boots too and a fleece-lined jeans jacket. "We got started."

"The house?" I said, eyeing the crusty men in their Carhartt overalls.

"Johnny said they had a couple machines that could dig the foundation in two days," she said. "It's not costing us a dime."

"Oh, it's free, right?" I said, raising my voice.

She checked me with her scowl. I motioned my head and we went upstairs. Jessica closed the door quietly and turned to me, frowning.

"I thought you'd be happy."

"To see a hole in the property?" I said.

"I'm saving us almost a hundred thousand. Johnny said they could just come up and dig it quick while they were between things on the project. I don't know why you're doing this."

"Johnny?" I said, shaking my head, searching her face. "When the hell did you talk to him?"

"On the phone," she said. Her jaw was set, warning me.

"You don't just dig a foundation like this on an off moment," I said. "It costs thirty thousand just to move those machines up here. You've got ten million dollars' worth of equipment out there. Nothing's free."

"Well, technically," she said, "they're not here."

I threw my hands up and spun toward the big picture

window, catching a glimpse of the red monsters tearing into the ground with their steel-toothed buckets.

"Great. That's great," I said, wheeling back to her. "I'm two weeks behind schedule already and we've got ten million dollars' worth of equipment in the backyard. You have no idea what you're doing."

"Let me get you a drink," she said.

"I don't want a drink. I want you to stop pushing."

"Pushing got us here," she said, taking down a bottle of wine, driving the screw into the cork and yanking it out. "Think about if you'd pushed the night our baby died."

I stared at her, noticing the red rims of her eyes, the bitter sharpness of their focus.

"You gonna do that?" I said, my voice cracking.

"Want to play Xbox?"

We both turned. Tommy had come downstairs wearing a backwards orange Syracuse hat.

"How about when we get home?" I said. "We're going to go out for dinner. Get changed, okay, pal? Lose the hat."

He shrugged and went back upstairs. We stared at each other.

"Are you taking those Vicodins?" I asked her, lowering my voice.

"Because I'm saying what we both already know?" she asked.

"Because you're acting out of control," I said.

Her face contorted, then relaxed. She smiled.

"It'll be fine, okay?" she said. "They're here already. They'll get it dug and then get back to the project. I'll go tell them to hurry. Why don't you get out of that suit and we'll go to dinner. Tommy's hungry."

I shook my head and sighed and went upstairs to change into jeans. In the bathroom, I went to look in the mirror. It was gone. Bare wall, torn through to the gypsum in the places where the glue was. There was a mirror on the back of the door, inside her closet. I went there. Gone. I went into the guest bedroom and the bathroom there. Gone.

"Tommy," I said, and my son popped his head out of his room, smiling.

"Is there a mirror in your bathroom?"

His face fell and he shrugged. I went in, past the big TV and its tangle of wires and control sets and into the bathroom. No mirror. Downstairs, the decorative mirror in the entryway had been replaced by a painting.

I went into my library. From there, through two windows, I could see down into the main room on the ground floor. There she was, down there with those men, planning her dig. Her face was bright with her dark hair tucked back behind her ears as she pointed from the plans to the machines, and they all shared a laugh.

I sat down at my desk and turned my attention to the jewels of light on the far shore as they went out one at a time. The lake got dark and the machines shut down, one by one, until the silence pressed in on me. I heard her saying goodbye, then her footsteps on the stairs. She was behind me.

"Ready to go?" she asked, still upbeat.

"Is Rosalie's okay?" I said, getting up.

"Sure. I'll get Tommy."

We shared a silent dinner, radicchio salad, pasta, and lamb chops, that went down in lumps. It wasn't until somewhere in the middle of my third bottle of wine that I felt like I'd made a big deal out of nothing. I noticed

Tommy, batting a square of ice back and forth on the table with his fork and knife as it melted.

I made a goal for him by touching my thumbs together and putting my fingers at a right angle to them.

"Shoot," I said.

He did and made it. The ice shot up over my hands and hit my face and we all laughed.

"Honey," Jessica said. "We're in a restaurant."

"Okay," I said. "Only two more."

Tommy fired ice at me and we had some more laughs before I told him game over and he better go wash the red sauce off his face. We watched him skip off.

"I'm sorry about getting on you," I said after a minute, taking her hand.

She kind of smiled and I noticed her makeup for the first time. It was off just a bit. The lipstick bleeding past the edges of her lips. Black eyeliner thicker on one side. Rouge not quite blended in.

"Hey, what happened to the mirrors?" I asked.

She stiffened, looked away, and said, "Just a decorating thing. I read about it. Some Bauhaus thing Julia Roberts did."

"I thought that was everything inside out, Bauhaus," I said. "Pipes outside the walls and stuff."

"It's just something," she said, tucking the hair behind her ears.

"Do you want to talk about it?" I asked.

"Let's not ruin a nice dinner."

"I don't mean with me," I said.

"A shrink?" she asked, puckering her face.

"We've both got, like our fingers in a dike," I said, "holding it back."

She looked at me and motioned her eyes toward

Tommy, who was back from the bathroom. She shook her head and emphatically mouthed the word no.

I paid the bill and we drove home listening to Radio Disney. I played *Ghost Recon* on the Xbox with Tommy, then let Jessica read to him. I waited, lying on our bed in my boxers. After a while, I heard her in the bathroom, the rattle of a pill bottle, then moving around in her closet, before the lights went out. There was a slice of moon outside the window, so when she stood beside the bed I could see the silk teddy, shimmering white and cut high on her hips.

"Being on top is hard," she said. "People try to knock you down, try to take it away. You have to fight. We have to take care of ourselves, of each other."

She put her mouth to mine and kissed me deep. In the middle of it all, she let out a groan, digging her nails into my back and breaking the skin. I didn't even care. When we broke apart, I lay panting until I fell asleep. I don't know if it was two minutes or twenty, but sometime soon she shook me awake. The room glowed in the pale white light from the moon. The twisted sheets and the pillows, damp with sweat, had been pushed to the edges of the mattress. Her head was tucked under my arm with the tip of her nose touching the edge of my chest.

"I was thinking," she said in a voice I had to strain to hear, "about what I said. About taking care. We should put some money aside. Just in case."

"Okay," I said, groggy. "Sure"

"The money is gushing out on that project," she said. "The banks have no idea where it goes. We could set up a company offshore."

"Offshore?" I asked, rolling up on one elbow. Wide awake.

"I mean, what if we had a hundred million dollars in an account?" she said. "We'd never have to worry."

"That's the truth," I said, chuckling and shaking my head.

"It wouldn't be that hard," she said, raising up on one elbow, her eyes wide.

"No," I said. "You just take it."

"Exactly," she said, gripping my arm.

"Come on."

"People do it *all* the time," she said, whispering, urgent.

"And go to jail."

"I think you just have to hide it, like in a Swiss bank. You could get it, but you could even put it back if you had to.

"I'm going to find out."

I shut my eyes and lay back on the bed, breathing through my nose. The marks on my back were beginning to sting.

41

"How's your son?" Johnny G asked. He had a small brown bag of pistachios in his hand. He was popping the nuts into his mouth one at a time, tossing them a foot from his face, extracting the meat, and spitting out the shell.

They were on an empty road in the swamp behind the Meadowlands and they walked in the great expanse between streetlights. The NYPD cop had his hands jammed deep into the pockets of his leather coat.

"Good," the cop said after a silent moment. "Thank you."

"Amazing, ain't it?" Johnny G said. "From all the way up here to all the way down there in the Sunshine State, me keeping him safe."

Johnny spit out a husk and shook his head, taking a deep draft of the smelly air.

"He'll be out in April," the cop said quietly.

"And then what will I do?" Johnny said with a laugh, mussing up the cop's salt-and-pepper mane. "Who's gonna keep me two steps ahead?"

The cop's frozen face kept its focus on the distant city lights.

"Not you, huh?" Johnny said. "Well, you did good while it lasted. Who knows? Maybe he'll break his probation?"

Johnny slapped the cop's back. The sneer he saw made him chuckle. "Yeah, my uncle always used to say to me, he'd say, 'Johnny, you can bone a guy's wife, but don't ever mess with his kids.' That's what he said and I knew he was right, but I always thought he meant kids like when they're riding tricycles and shit, not out having gunfights with crackheads. But I guess it goes for kids no matter how old. A man loves his kids, right? Do anything."

The cop said nothing. He just kept walking with his hands jammed down deep and his cold frown.

"I don't want any more killing," the cop said, angling his eyes at a 767 roaring up out of Newark, drowning out the whisper of the cattails.

"Funny, though, isn't it?" Johnny said. "Cop like you with a bad guy for a kid, all those big bucks down south there wanting him for their bitch. You know where my son is? Dentist out in Sacramento. How about that? Met a girl from there at school. Fixing people's teeth while yours was selling crack to kids. Life's funny.

"So, when you say that, about no more killing," Johnny said, spitting so hard he lost the meat too, "I know you got some good shit for me, and I got a poker game waiting so let's have it."

"They know about Thane Coder," the cop said, looking at him.

"You told me Coder was working for you," Johnny said, grinning. "A big witness, you called him."

The cop sighed and said, "I'm just telling you what I hear."

"Go ahead."

"The guy, Ben Evans?" the cop said. "There might be some database to prove Coder got either himself or someone into the lodge the night James King was killed. There's a retina scanner to let you in."

"Nice friend, huh?" Johnny said, popping in another nut.

"Which one?"

"You're right," Johnny said, shucking with his teeth, spitting, and chewing slowly. "Kind of deserve each other, don't they? Like you and your boy."

"You gonna do that?" the cop said with a sigh. "Why?"

Johnny narrowed one eye at the cop. "You don't like it? Go get your scumbag kid some protection somewhere else. You're lucky I'm not making your wife service the crew at the job site."

The cop's hand whipped out of his pocket, slipped inside the coat and came out with a .357 that he pointed in Johnny's face. A big jet screamed overhead and the gun trembled.

Johnny smiled and when the roar of the plane finally faded, he said, "There's two types of cops that pull guns. The ones who shoot and the ones who never will.

"You missed your chance a long time ago."

Johnny's smile never faded as he pushed past the cop and strolled back to his waiting car with one thing on his mind. Ben Evans.

42

"Jessica was right," I say. "When you're on top, everybody's gunning for you. It's kill or be killed. It just is."

The shrink just looks at me and blinks a couple of times behind his heavy face.

"How was he going to kill you?" he asks.

"They have the death penalty in this state," I say. "You know I had to do what I did with James, so I was exposed. You don't have to stab someone or pull the trigger to kill him, but it's all the same, and Ben was trying to kill me."

I knew it wasn't good that Mike Allen wanted to see me in New York. That's what I was thinking when we walked through the small terminal at Teterboro and I saw two limousines waiting outside the plane instead of one. Jessica got Amy to watch our son so she could go with me and she made for the limo in the rear.

"You're not coming?" I asked.

"You've got business," she said. "You don't mind if I get some things, right?"

"What things?" I asked, tilting my head, trying to figure if she had a little more rouge on than normal.

"Who knows?" she said. "Shoes. A dress maybe. Some Victoria's Secret."

I smiled at that and gave her a kiss, and waved as she pulled away. But when our two cars reached the Jersey Turnpike, hers went north while my driver went south. I immediately dialed her cell phone and asked what she was doing, that I thought she was going to Manhattan.

"We're taking the GW," she said. "My driver thinks it's faster than the tunnel."

The project was north too. So was Johnny G.

"Oh," I said. "Okay. See you at dinner. Eight, right?"

"You'll be fine."

When we came out through the Lincoln Tunnel, my driver headed south. Mike Allen had the penthouse of a building next to Battery Park and overlooking New York Harbor. The elevator was paneled in pink granite and chrome and when I got off, the doorway to Mike Allen's place stared at me like the vault to a bank. Two great doors. Polished metal. And, instead of a doorknob, a chrome wheel with five thick spokes.

I rang and a tall sharp-faced butler answered the door and led me in. The spaces were vast and white, rooms punctuated by the minimal amount of odd-shaped leather chairs or, in one case, a single amorphous orange statue. Windows rose from the floor to the height of the ceiling. Mike Allen appeared from the kitchen wearing a yellow golf sweater and spiked shoes that clicked loudly against the marble floor.

"Thane?" he said. "Drink?"

He rattled a gin and tonic at me, the lime swirling in the ice. Over his other shoulder was a wooden golf club.

"Sure."

He winked at the butler and motioned me toward another elevator.

"Watch. It'll be there before we are," he said, the doors rolling shut.

When the elevator doors opened, I had the strangest feeling of having shifted into another place and time, just like a dream, but I was awake. Green trees, some twelve feet high, and shrubs framed our view of the perfect blue sky resting peacefully over a brilliant green golf tee. I could smell the grass, and as we walked up the mound, complete with a bench and a ball washer, I could smell the dirt as Mike's shoes tore into the turf.

"A little spot I like," Mike said, smiling and obviously pleased by the look of wonder on my face.

A woman dressed in a yellow maid's uniform appeared from around the trees and handed me my drink before disappearing without a word. As we reached the top of the tee, the New York harbor opened before us. The Goethals Bridge spanning Staten Island and New Jersey. Ellis Island. The moldy green Statue of Liberty. There was a bucket of balls beside the bench. Mike teed one up and whacked it into space.

"So, we got problems," Mike said as he teed up his next shot.

"It's a different world down here," I said.

Mike looked up from his ball and smiled at me, showing all his teeth.

"You know why this isn't a phone call, right?" he asked. "You know how I feel about you, but we've got real problems. Ben—"

"Jesus, him again," I said, throwing up my eyes and my hands at the same time, spilling part of my drink.

"He's got a following," Mike said, his smile losing

steam. "He's respected in the industry, and this is a public company. A week after the IPO, the stock hit twenty. Yesterday we dropped below eight. It makes us look real bad. People are talking about the project. The union."

"You can't get things built down here without them," I said. "People know that."

"I know, but they don't move the opening date out twelve months," Mike asked, smacking another ball before looking for the answer. "The banks get nervous."

"We moved the opening in Boston," I said, fighting to keep my voice from slipping into a whine.

"The drinking. There were a lot of people at that dinner when you passed out," Mike said. He spoke softly, letting me know that he was my friend. "Stuff like that makes it hard."

"Mike, I got drunk with some friends."

"You think they were all your friends?" he said. "Look, this thing isn't over yet. That's why I wanted to see you, but you've got to do something. Talk to Ben. Work something out. If you two can join forces, you can work through this."

"And if we don't?" I asked, even though I already knew the answer.

Mike smiled and said, "Aw, come on. It's like politics. You make alliances. You guys go way back. You'll be fine."

He took aim at his perfectly dimpled white ball and smashed it. I watched as long as I could, until it was the smallest fleck of a shadow, and then swallowed up by the enormous space.

43

I SAT AT THE BAR OF DANIEL drinking vodka tonics until my teeth were numb. The waiters all wore the same dark suits and the same pink ties with thin orange stripes, but the leather bar stool was padded and comfortable enough for me not to want to move. When I saw the bartender's eyes jump, I turned around to catch Jessica slipping out of a mink coat at the maître d' stand.

Her hair was as rich and dark as the coat and held back with a thin diamond band. She wore a low-cut pearl-colored dress and thin heels. The uneven makeup, though, left her looking like a call girl. I stood and greeted her from across the room. She came at me with open arms, kissing me on the mouth.

The maître d' asked us if we'd like to sit down and we followed him into the dining room, where tall columns and long thick drapes made the ceiling seem miles away. The middle of the room was sunken marble. He led us along the gallery to a table nestled into the corner looking out over the rest of the room. I started to sit, but Jessica was frozen, her head looking away and down.

"Could we please sit somewhere else?" she said, still looking away.

"This is our best table," the maître d' said with a light chuckle. "Especially for Mr. Coder."

I looked from Jessica to the maître d' to the ornate gold-framed mirror.

"How about there?" she said, pointing in the opposite corner, a table surrounded almost entirely by the walls of a full-size Turkish tent.

"That's for parties," the maître d' said. When he saw the hundred-dollar bill I was holding out for him he hesitated. "I have one due at nine-thirty."

I peeled off nine more bills.

"This way, please," he said with a bow.

We entered the crimson tent with its gold vertical stripes and pointed top. Three waiters were hurriedly removing all the service but the two on the end where we sat.

"Romantic," Jessica said. "Thank you."

We ordered a bottle of Dom and I told them to bring me a fresh vodka tonic in the meantime. Then we were alone.

"What's wrong?" I asked, finishing my drink.

"It didn't go well with Mike Allen?" she asked.

"It's fine," I said. "Politics. They want me to play nice with Ben."

Jessica's eyes narrowed and she stared down at the table. A waiter brought me a fresh drink.

"Ben," she said when he was gone, gritting her little teeth.

"Just business."

"Was it business what he tried to do to me?" she asked, her eyes blazing.

"He's not my friend."

"No, he's not," she said, shaking her head. "He's worse than anything you ever thought. Worse than what he did to me."

I reached over and put my hand on her wrist.

"I saw Johnny."

"The GW Bridge," I said, shaking my head. "Why didn't you just tell me."

"I'm trying to help us," she said, raising her voice, tugging free.

"The guy is a mobster."

"The guy is our partner," she said, glaring. "It's business."

I snatched up my drink and swallowed it whole, slamming the glass down and glaring right back at her.

"That's right," she said. "Medicate yourself. Just slip into oblivion."

"You're the one who can't even look at yourself. Take another pill."

"Ben Evans is going to try to get the records of the retina scanner for the *F-B-I*," she said, leaning forward, seething.

"You're the one who told me to do it, scan my eye and walk away."

"It would've been nice if you told me there might be a record," she said.

"You're the one pulling the levers," I said. "You pull the wrong one and you want to blame me."

"Not so loud," she said, hissing as she looked around and leaned my way. "All you do is gripe, and I'm working to keep this all together. To keep us together."

"Us?" I said.

The waiter arrived with a silver bucket and began fussing with the champagne. I told him to give me the bottle and leave the glasses. He frowned, but took one look at my face and did it. I popped the cork, firing it into the side of the tent, and poured from the smoky neck.

"To us," I said, twisting my mouth and raising my glass.

"You've got to get rid of him," she said.

"Sure I do," I said. "That's easy, right?"

I leaned over the table and grabbed hold of her forearm, hissing my words. "I'm not killing anyone."

"I'm not killing anyone," she said, mocking me with her whine.

I tossed down the champagne.

"Have *another* drink," she said.

"Thanks, I will," I said, refilling my glass. "I'll work something out. Split things with him or something. Get him on our side."

"Split things with him," she said, curling her upper lip and jerking her head side to side, like a puppet, as she spoke. "Best buddies.

"Oh, God, you fool," she said.

My fist hit the table and everything jumped. People down on the floor craned their necks, looking in through the big opening. A waiter peeked around the corner, then disappeared.

I stood up and so did she. We both walked toward the door, swatting and nudging each other with elbows as we went, moving fast. She stopped for her coat. I swept past her and burst outside, into the night.

44

"I remember being on vacation one time in Barbados," I say. "I was on the terrace in the morning, looking out at the ocean. Having coffee.

"This little green lizard scoots along the rail, comes up to a bug and snaps it up. It had these huge eyes and they just stared out empty while it chewed. So, then it starts down the wall and a bird swoops down from a palm tree. Gulp. No more lizard."

I sit staring at him for a moment before he clears his throat and says, "And?"

"It's just nature. Big things eat little things. Bigger things eat the big things, it just keeps going."

"But we're not animals," he says.

"But that's where we come from, right?" I say. "That's our nature. Our heritage. Slugs in the slime."

"What happened that night?"

I shrug and say, "We went back to the hotel and made up. She had it all figured out. There are a thousand ways it could have happened different, but Ben was like a June bug in a campfire, buzzing into those flames no matter what."

I shake my head and stare at the tabletop between

us. It's milky blue, and the fluorescent lights above have marked it with their glow.

"I never told anyone what happened," I say.

"I know," he says quietly. "I think you should."

I called the Eye Pass offices in the morning. I went to the top, but the CEO was on vacation. His assistant gave me the name and number of someone she thought could help. It was a tangle of secretaries and assistant managers. I tried to stay calm, but by the time we got to the plane at Teterboro, I felt like I was back at the beginning.

By the time we landed, I was making some headway. The person I wanted was the director of technology. She was in a meeting, and her secretary promised to have her call the minute she got out. I had a dozen Japanese bankers waiting for me at Cascade. Tommy was already in school so Jessica rode up there with me. We were crossing the bridge where you can see the lodge across the water when the Eye Pass woman called me back.

I told her what I wanted. She told me they did have a record of the system functions from Cascade. It was the private property of King Corp, and my chief operating officer had just left with the memory stick containing all of it. Ben Evans. It was the only one they had. I snapped the phone shut and told Jessica we were too late. The Eye Pass offices were in Rochester, Ben could be at the FBI offices in less than two hours.

"We should turn around," I said, stopping in the middle of the drive.

"And do what?" she asked. She was staring straight ahead, calculating.

"Go get him," I said. "We've got to."

She just sat, her face unmoving except for her eyes. They flickered back and forth.

"You go to your meeting," she said.

"And just let him go to the FBI?"

"We have to bring him to us," she said. "If we try to get him, he'll run. If we can bring him here . . . that's what we have to do."

"But—"

She held up her hand. "Go to your meeting. Come on. You're late. Trust me."

I pulled up to the main doors of the lodge and we went inside. She told me not to worry and peeled off, closing the door of the library behind her.

The Japanese tossed around nine-figure numbers like they were no big deal. In my mind, they really weren't. None of the numbers would matter if we didn't stop Ben.

I was looking at the top bank guy, my eyes only half focused, when the door to the conference room cracked open. I saw Jessica's eyes. She poked her finger through and motioned to me.

I excused myself, bowing and apologizing profusely, slipped out, and followed Jessica into the library. Her eyes were shining.

"He's coming," she said.

"Here?"

"To the West Lodge."

The West Lodge was the original cabin built by James when he first bought the surrounding property. It was in the middle of the woods nearly a half mile from the main lodge.

"How did you get him?"

She put her hand on my arm. "I just did."

"What's he think? He's sleeping with you?"

"That I'm in trouble. He was on the Thruway. He's coming now."

"Let me end this," I said, nodding toward the meeting.

"Take your time," she said. "He just left Rochester. We've got a couple hours. Don't do anything weird. Wrap it up around four and let them all know you're going out hunting."

The Japanese were okay with ending things at four, they were jet-lagged anyway and wanted to have a drink in the hot tub before dinner. I made a big show of telling them that I was going out into the woods to deer-hunt. I threw on some camouflage, grabbed a radio, and my twelve gauge Benelli from the hunting locker that used to be James's. I was breathing hard and shallow, feeling like I needed to think, even though Jessica was doing the thinking for us both.

She was waiting for me in the H2, hunched down in the backseat so no one would see her leaving with me.

The preserve is a large rectangle made up of woods and water running between rumpled drumlins that stretch north and south. In the southwest quarter, on top of one of those long, fingerlike hills, was the West Lodge. At the bottom of the western side and southern tip of the drumlin was a thick deep swamp. Along the rim of the swamp was a muddy deer trail.

When we pulled up to the lodge, Jessica pointed into the woods and said, "Wait up there. After he goes inside, you come down and wait on the side."

It was James's personal tree stand, built halfway up an ancient birch adjacent to the old lodge. A three-by-four-foot wooden box, painted in camouflage and built fourteen feet up, tight to the tree. From the road, you couldn't really see up into it, but in the stand I would have a perfect view of the driveway in front of the lodge.

We went inside, and Jessica had me start a fire.

"Like I've been here, waiting," she said.

The intimacy of it burned me and I wondered if she did that on purpose.

I knew she did when she said, "Forget about what he tried to do to me at Sandy Beach. This is about us. Our family. If you don't do it, we're dead.

"We're worse than dead," she added.

I nodded, trying to swallow the dry lump in my throat. We argued over whether or not I could shoot him up close, finally she gave in and realized it would be better for me to shoot him from a distance. I didn't want to see his face. I couldn't.

"Then just stay in the stand, God damn it, but don't miss. Go," she said, kissing me deeply before she pushed me out the door. "Stay down."

The tree stand wasn't thirty yards from the driveway, an easy shot for anyone. I was supposed to wait until he came out. She was going to talk with him, and make sure that he had the memory stick with him. If he did, she would turn the porch light on as he left.

Then I'd do it.

The sun was already melting from orange to red as it disappeared into the inky web of trees lining the next ridge over. As I walked down the trail, the woods were quiet except for the soft crush of my steps.

I climbed the ladder and eased into the cushioned seat, breathing heavy, but quiet. I sat back to wait, knowing that it would be twenty minutes before the woods came back to life with the sound of nuthatches and squirrels foraging. The distant splash of the first doe stepping from her secret hummock into the swamp.

I began to unwind what was happening the way you might untangle a snagged fishing line, picking at one little knot only to find that it was the smaller part of a much bigger problem. There was none of the usual tranquillity for me that came from sitting quiet in the woods. No connection with the natural world. I was floating in it, but part of something twisted and dark.

When I heard the sound of a car crunching up the gravel drive, my heart seemed to expand in my chest, spurting adrenaline like a leaky radiator. My breath was staggered and the muscles behind my ears trembled. I ducked down and froze, working hard to muffle my tattered breathing.

When I saw the white Lexus through a seam in the side of the stand, my stomach ached. Ben got out with his hands jammed into the pockets of an L.L. Bean corduroy coat and disappeared inside the small lodge. His jaw was set and from under that thatch of dirty blond hair was an angry scowl. I got back up on the seat and rested the barrel of my gun on the stand's railing, finding the red laser dot of my sight and fixing it on the front door.

I never let my eye leave that sight and I spent the year it seemed like he was in there wishing that somehow that porch light would stay off when he left. But when the door did creak open, the light went on right away.

I followed him with the red dot, square in the center of his body. He was halfway to the car when Jessica burst out onto the porch and screamed at me to do it, God damn it. Now.

I closed my eyes and pulled the trigger.

45

My chest was tight and the air was suddenly too thin. I opened my eyes quick enough to see the pale shape of Ben's face flicker back at me before he darted off the driveway and down a winding path.

"Get him!" Jessica screamed.

I nearly fell out of the stand and somehow lost track of the time it took me to get down that ladder. I ran upslope, to the spot on the driveway where Ben had disappeared. Down the hill on the opposite side of the stand, I could still hear Ben crashing through the sticks and leaves. Maybe I'd hit him. Maybe not. Branches snapped. I saw movement and ran down the path, the gun pressed to my shoulder, frantic for a clear shot.

His shape blurred into a small space unblocked by trees a hundred yards away. I fired again. The explosion of the shell was immediately followed by the thick slapping sound of a shotgun slug. Ben tumbled, but then he was up and running again. I fired wildly at him, running. He angled downhill, dove to the ground, and plunged into a thick stand of brambles and scrub brush. There were deer trails through that stuff, muddy lanes that you couldn't much more than crawl through.

I got to the place I thought he'd gone in and stopped. I put my hands on my knees and tried to slow my breathing so I could hear. By the time my own huffing subsided, there was nothing. No crickets. No frogs. The small things were either hiding from the coming winter, or dead. Twenty feet away, the trees and scrub were melting into the gloom. It was nearly dark.

I looked up to the driveway and saw Jessica's silhouette peering down at me. I stalked around the edge of the brambles, first down toward the swamp, down the trail along the water, then all the way up the other side to the ridge where I could see the black shape of the lodge down the driveway, my vehicle, and Ben's Lexus coupé right behind it. Jessica spotted me and jogged my way, clutching her arms to her chest to keep away the evening air. I crunched down the edge of the driveway toward her, stopping every few feet to listen down into the brush. Nothing.

"Where is he?" Jessica asked, breathless. "Goddamn it, what were you waiting for?"

"I don't know," I said in a whisper. "Come on. I'm pretty sure he's hit."

In the pockets of my coat were some camo gloves. I put them on and opened the door to Ben's car. The lights went on and a small bell rang until I pulled the keys. I shut the door and looked around. Down on the other side of the drumlin, through the thick tops of the trees, I could see headlights coming down Swamp Road. I could hear its engine rumbling. I choked back my panic and stood frozen, holding my breath, listening as it approached the driveway below, staring wide-eyed at Jessica's pained expression.

It went on past.

"You've got to find him," Jessica said.

"I need a light."

"Do you know how to do this?" she asked.

"Just follow the blood."

She shadowed me back to the lodge. I went in and found a long metal flashlight, Jessica got one too, then returned to the trail, staying on it halfway down the hillside. I was confused as to exactly where Ben had gone into the scrub, but certain that it was the right patch. It ran from the edge of the driveway down almost to the swamp and was nearly two hundred feet thick.

A voice made me jump and spin, scaring a small yelp out of Jessica.

"Thane, this is Marty. Thane?"

I had forgotten I even had the radio in my pocket. I took it out, trembling and held it to my face.

"Go ahead, Marty," I said, swallowing bile.

"Are you on your way in? I think these guys are ready to eat."

"Let them start if they are," I said. "I hit a big buck and I'm tracking him."

"You want me to send Adam?"

"No," I said, staring at Jessica. "Don't send him. I've got it. I want to do it myself. Don't send anyone. Just start dinner and tell them I'll be there."

"Adam could—"

"Marty! I'm fine!"

There was silence for half a minute, then static before Marty's voice came on again.

"Okay. Sorry."

I looked at my watch. It was nearly six-thirty. Dark now, except for the beam of our lights and the thin glow from a crescent moon that had suddenly appeared halfway up the eastern sky. From the path, I swept the light through the woods in the direction of the scrub. There were several small, cavelike openings where crisscrossing muddy trails went in. I started with the closest and looked hard at the mud. In the light's beam, I examined the pattern of pointed tracks made by deer hooves.

I wasn't the tracker Bucky was, or even Adam, but I knew enough to know that wherever Ben went in, with mud this thick, there would have to be some sign. A disturbance of the pointed pattern of deer hooves. I walked downhill to the next trail and saw it right away. A shoe print. I got down on my hands and knees with the light and could see the smooth smear marks of where he'd slipped in on his knees. I found a partial print from his hand. Then I saw something that made my heart skip a beat. Like strawberry reduction splashed on top of chocolate frosting, the rich spatter of red blood made a cherry pool on the dark mud.

"Look," I said, glancing back up at Jessica and jabbing the light at the ground.

He was hit.

46

THE BLOOD WAS A STRONG, dark red. A chest wound. I stabbed the light's beam into the tangle of scrub. Thin shadows wavered, shrank, grew, then melted into the night. Nothing.

"Stay here," I said in a whisper to her.

I anticipated some kind of protest, but she just closed her mouth tight and nodded.

With the shotgun in my right hand and the light in my left, I slowly crept into the web of thorns and branches. I found another spatter of blood, then another. The beam from Jessica's light passed over and around me as she searched from the edge of the brush. My heart pounded and the air came out of me in a ragged stutter. I stopped at every pool to search ahead with the light, dissecting the darkness, searching for the crouched shape of a man lying in wait or maybe even crumpled in a dead heap.

I was in the very middle of the scrub under the small canopy of a strangled apple tree when I saw something that made me hyperventilate. A man-sized, egg-shape depression molded into the mud. Blood everywhere. A shiny crimson pool in the bottom deep enough for me to dip my fingers into. I felt its warmth. I whipped the light around me in every direction, spinning on my bottom, kicking at the vines and brambles clinging to my legs.

My breath floated up in smoky white puffs. My mouth was cotton-dry. He was here. Somewhere. Maybe only ten feet from me in the darkness. I shivered and circled my light again, this time stopping on the twisted horizontal shadow of an old rotten log. A ribbon of a creek ran beneath it and I heard its faint gurgle. I raised the gun, bracing my back against the trunk of the apple tree and meticulously ran the light over every inch, expecting Ben to explode from the shadows like a quail.

After five full minutes, I got on my knees again and moved toward the rotted log. Just as I touched its soft moist side with my knuckles, the scrub behind me exploded with a thrashing. I whipped around again and saw his shape, flailing. He was up on his feet and working downhill. He had doubled back on his own trail and waited for me to go by. It was a good time for him to make his break. I was imprisoned in the thick overgrowth with no chance at getting off a shot.

I stayed low and crabbed back the way I came. There was no mistaking where Ben was, the sound of his struggle with the brush filled the night and he began to roar and howl like a madman. He was getting close to the swamp and I had to do something. I pushed upright into the tangle and fought downhill.

Briars slashed my face and hands and somewhere along the way I dropped the light. I redoubled my grip on the gun and pushed on. If he beat me to the trail along the swamp, he might make it to the road. I remembered the car that had just gone by.

But even with his head start, Ben, with all that bleeding,

couldn't match my strength. I lowered my head and bulled through the tangle. I heard Ben break through.

I was too far away. I'd never catch him.

That's when I heard a crack like a baseball bat, and his scream. Jessica shrieked too. I heard someone tumbling and splashing into the swamp, and I thrashed even harder.

Five seconds later I broke through. Jessica was there on her knees in the mud, gripping her flashlight, aiming it down the trail at Ben's stumbling shape. I raised the shotgun, breathed in, let the tiny red dot find the middle of his form, and fired. He dropped, but started to rise before he flopped off the edge of the path and back into the swamp. I ran.

By the time I reached him, his limbs were still. Only his chest pumped up and down. His hair, like his clothes, was a snarl of dirt and blood. His eyes were white and they stared wide at me, full of horror. They began to glisten in the moonlight. Tears.

"I got him," Jessica said, breathing hard from behind me. In the beam of my flashlight, she showed me hers. Its rim was bloody and mashed with red meat and dirty blond hairs.

I moved closer. Ben's head was split from the flashlight and blood ran down his face. His hands clutched the right side of his lower ribs. The seams between his fingers leaked dark gushers of blood that ran and swirled into the swamp water.

"Jesus Christ," he said, his gurgling voice pitched to hysteria.

A sob escaped him. The sucking sound of snot and air.

"You're my friend," he said, the words barely understandable.

I stood no more than six feet from him now, the thick shotgun barrel aimed at the center of his chest. The gun began to tremble and then shake. My sight grew foggy and I shuddered, sobbing right along with him.

I don't know how long I stood there before I realized she was there too, beside me. Her hand gripping my arm.

"Do it," she said, squeezing her fingers to the bone.

I shook my head no and swore to Jesus.

And pulled the trigger.

47

I blow the air out of my lungs.

He looks at me. His fingertips have strayed to his beard. He strokes it.

"What?" I say.

He shakes his head, like he's breaking free from a bad dream. "Did you do it? Pull the trigger. Or did she?"

"Does it matter?" I ask.

"No," he says, "I guess it doesn't."

"Let me ask you, does a friend try to pick up your wife? Does he dig up shit for the cops?"

"I'm not the judge, man."

"No?" I say. "I see your look."

"Keep going," he says. "It's good to get it out."

I sigh and say, "Whatever. Was it her, me? Both of us? All I know is, she had a plan. I followed her that far and I guess that wasn't the time to stop."

"Killing your best friend?"

"It was easier than James."

"How easy?" he asks.

"Easier to do. Easier to think clearly. Assimilation. It's like that experiment. They put glasses on these people. The glasses turned everything upside-down. In about three weeks, they woke up and saw things right-side-up again. The brain adjusts."

He looks at me like he's expecting a punch line.

"A learning curve," I say. "It's like a secret place in the woods. Once you find it, you know just how to get there the next time. We knew exactly what we had to do."

I touched my ears, which were ringing from the shot.

"We've got to get rid of him," she said, reaching into his pocket and extracting the silver memory stick, about the size of a lighter.

I watched her throw it overhand out into the black water where it disappeared with a small splash.

"I know how," I said. "I know."

My hands shook and the smell of rotting leaves and thick mud pressed in on me. I rested the shotgun against a tree, lifted Ben by the ankles the way you'd lift a wheelbarrow, and set off backwards.

"Where are you going?" she asked.

"Quicksand," I said.

"I'll help."

She picked up his arms and we carried him through the swamp. My own camouflage boots were rubber and came almost to my knees, they were practically made for dragging a body through the wet dead grass. With Jessica's help, it wasn't hard to take him away from the road, deeper in. There would be no blood trail in the shallow water.

It was nearly a quarter of a mile, the place I knew we had to go. When Jessica tripped and dropped him and he got caught up in some thorns, I dug in with my heels, and pulled him free. She got a grip again and deeper we went.

Two winters ago, I had been part of a deer drive in this section of woods and swamp. When the drive was over, somehow Russel and Scott ended up on the other side of the main artery of water that ran through the swamp. There was no wind, and there was a spot in the water where we could see to the bottom. It looked about three feet deep. The leaves and sticks were dusted with mud. Both Scott and Russel were already wet to the waist from slogging through the swamp, so it was no big deal for them to hold their shotguns up over their heads and wade in.

But when Russel got three quarters of the way across, he simply disappeared. There was a great cloud in the water and bubbles of methane broke on the surface. Scott hadn't been far behind Russel, and with his feet still on the solid creek bed, he reached forward, grabbed the shotgun Russel still clung to with both hands, and with a herculean wrench, dragged him up out of the muck.

Russel looked like he'd been dipped in chocolate, and Scott and I had a good laugh at him when he finally stopped choking. The two of them walked the long way back around after that and Bucky told us later that the swamp was full of soft spots like that, where the muck was sometimes ten or fifteen feet deep. He said if Scott hadn't grabbed him right away, a crane couldn't have pulled Russel out of that muck.

"You get four feet into that stuff and it sucks you under like a vacuum cleaner," he said. "The more you fight, the harder it sucks you."

There was a twisted birch tree right by the lip of the creek at that spot and even in the wan light it was easy for me to find. We carried him down along the shallow edge of the creek and stopped when I got to where I knew the soft spot was. There were some stones the size of bread loaves in the side of the bank and I was able to pry five of them loose.

"For his pockets," I said to her.

We stuffed the stones into Ben's coat, under his arms. My fingers were numb from the cold, but I managed to button up his coat tight to his neck. In the large pocket on the side of my pants I had a length of clothesline for dragging dead deer out of the woods. I took it out and wrapped it around the waist of Ben's coat, tying it tight so the stones couldn't slip out.

"What do I do?" she asked.

"I got it."

I sat down at the edge of the water, soaking my bottom. From there, I could shove Ben's body toward the soft spot with my feet, while keeping myself on the relatively solid part of the creek bed.

"Put your hands on my shoulders," I told her. "I'm going to push against you."

I felt her grip me to the bone and stiffen her arms. I braced myself and pushed with my feet. Ben rolled over into the deeper water and bubbled under. We kept doing this, moving farther into the creek until I was sitting in water up to my chest and he was beneath the water's surface. My eye started to twitch.

"What are you doing?" she asked.

Maybe the hole had somehow filled in.

But on the next shove, I felt Ben's body slip quickly away from my feet as if something had snatched him. She helped pull me out and we scrambled back and stood at the water's edge. A small troop of bubbles rose to the surface and popped in the moonlight. The stink of methane filled the air, then floated away.

Everything went still.

Deep inside me, an exhaustion waited to pull me down into my own kind of grave, but I knew we had more to do. We trudged back along the swamp through the moonlight, our muddy hands locked together. We found the spot where my gun and Jessica's flashlight were. I scooped up the spent shell. My flashlight was easy to find, shining there in the brush, and I used it to find the other shell casings from the shots I'd fired on the path. With them in hand, we marched back up the hill to the H2.

"What about his car?" I said.

"Don't touch it," she said. "What's the difference where they find it, as long as they don't find him."

"They won't," I said. "You drop me, then you can take this home."

"Won't someone wonder where it went?" she asked.

"They won't even know," I said. "It's dark. I'll take one of the Cascade Suburbans tomorrow."

As the massive building came into view, I slowed to a stop on the bridge. I put the window down and tossed the spent shotgun shells along with Ben's keys into the lodge pond with a kerplunk.

When we got to the lodge, I pulled down into the lower entrance and got out. We said goodbye and then I went into the lodge through the same doors I'd gone through the night I killed James. I stripped down in the mudroom, leaving my boots and taking my outerwear directly to the washroom to throw them into one of the machines with a cupful of soap. Naked except for my boxers, I went into the hot tub room—which was now empty of the bankers—and used the shower.

When I wiped the steam from the mirror, I saw that my face looked like it had been on the wrong end of a wet cat. Long red scratches and welts crisscrossed my cheeks, and even after five full minutes of scrubbing with a washcloth, my fingers still bore the faint shadow of mud underneath the nails.

I went to the locker and pulled on a pair of corduroys and a flannel shirt, then slipped into some Timberland shoes before going upstairs. I was just in time for dessert with the bankers.

Marty came into the dining room from the kitchen, wiping his hands on a towel.

"Jesus," he said, wincing at my face. "You get him? Adam heard the shots."

I shook my head with a laugh, raised a glass of red wine to the Japanese bankers, who laughed along with me.

"No," I said, winking at Marty. "All that and the damn thing got away."

"It was two days before they found his car," I say, "and they didn't really know how long it'd been there."

"But they figured it out."

"Bucky did," I say. "Eventually."

"How did you feel?" he asks. "Waiting for them to find it?"

"Part of me felt good to have him out of the way," I say.

"You weren't worried?"

"I didn't think I was going to get caught."

"Really?"

"Or if I did, at least not until we had a way out."

"You were working on that?"

"She was."

48

Fᴀᴛ ꜰʟᴀᴋᴇꜱ ᴏꜰ ꜱɴᴏᴡ ꜰᴇʟʟ from the dark sky spattering the windshield. Jessica had seen Halloween nights when it was seventy degrees. This one was cold. Tommy sat in the back of her Jeep wedged between Darth Vader and Spiderman. She took a right on Genesee Street and braked for a ghost, a ladybug, and the father carrying a flashlight.

"Can't you just drop us, Mom?" Tommy said from the backseat.

"So you can spray people with shaving cream?" she said, shooting him a glance over her shoulder.

Tommy shrugged.

"You don't have to get candy," she said. "You can watch your movie and go to bed. I'll make hot cider."

"Mom."

She took a left on a street of houses and pulled over at the curb. They got out and Jessica told her son to put on his coat.

"Zombies don't wear coats, Mom," he said. "They're dead."

"Well, this zombie has a mother who doesn't want him

to catch pneumonia," she said, reaching into the truck and tossing him his coat. "On."

"Andy doesn't have a coat."

"Andy has long underwear, don't you Andy?"

"It's like a long-sleeve T-shirt."

"See?" she said. "Long sleeves. On."

They headed up the street, Jessica in Timberland boots, jeans, and a parka lighting their way over front lawns with her own flashlight. They took a right on the next street and started up the hill. Jessica shivered and took a black knit cap out of her jacket pocket, pulling it down over the tops of her ears.

She waved to the other mothers, calling out hi, and at one corner stopped to talk with Neil, the father of a boy on Tommy's basketball team. A big man with awkward feet and hands jammed deep into his yellow North Face pockets. Part of her thought it was sweet, a dad shadowing the kids on Halloween. Thane was at the lodge, partly because of some more bankers, but also because it gave him an excuse to be out there in the woods, brooding.

Her cell phone rang. She looked at the number, expecting Thane, but seeing a New York City area code. She excused herself and waved the boys on with her light, calling for them to go ahead as she snapped open the phone.

"You wanna see Johnny?" asked the gravelly Bronx accent on the other end.

Her skin crawled. She hesitated, then said yes.

"Okay," the voice said. "He'll be at Mickey Mantle's on Fifty-ninth Street. He'll meet you at the Essex House next door at ten, ten-thirtyish. Get a room and he'll find you."

Her throat was tight.

"I'm," she said, wanting to explain how far away she was, when the phone went dead. "Shit."

"Sorry?" Neil said. He had bumbled up alongside her, training his flashlight on his two kids as they dashed from one porch to the next.

"Oh, I got cut off. Sorry."

"That's all right. They said 'shit' in *Spy Kids*. We usually don't take the kids to PG movies, but we thought, you know, they hear it on the bus."

"Neil," she said, "have you got room in your car?"

"A little."

She told him it was a kind of emergency, no one dying, but something she had to do right away. Neil said he could take the boys home when they were done. Jessica told Tommy, who shrugged and asked if they could double back to the big white house because they were giving out full-size boxes of Milk Duds.

Jessica walked double time back to her Jeep, dialing King Corp's chief pilot on the way. She didn't want it to be this way, having to drop everything. She had a child, but they didn't care about that. Still, the fact that she could just order up a private jet and be down in New York within two hours gave her a lift. She went home quick, called her sitter, and threw some things into a bag. She held up three outfits before deciding on a black tapered pants suit with a gray silk blouse. Sexy, but serious.

Thane's old leather shaving kit was under the sink. The dust had been knocked off it during the past two weeks. After his knee surgery, his doctor friend had given him four refills of Vicodin, in case. Two weeks ago there were three. Now the second was getting low, but Jessica needed to get through this. Then she'd stop. She took one, put three more in her pocket, and headed out.

The plane was waiting in the hangar. Frank, the pilot, asked if Thane was coming.

"He drove down to the Garden State site earlier," she said. "He was already in Binghamton looking at some equipment."

"Drove?"

"He was halfway already, I guess," she said, shrugging.

They taxied out into the snow, the wind already buffeting the plane. They lifted off and headed straight up. The plane bucked and shuddered, twisting in the gusts. The strobe of the wing lights illuminated the flailing snow outside the windows. She dug into her bag and took another pill. The tension melted away. Floating.

They landed a half hour later. On her way through the terminal, she stopped in the ladies' room. Shielding her eyes with her hand from the mirror, she slipped into a stall. When she came out, she washed her hands, keeping her eyes focused on the sink. It was her eyes she couldn't stand to see. Those black rings that no amount of makeup could hide. The crevices at the corners. Age, and something more.

From the back of her limo she watched the skyscrapers of Manhattan before spiraling down into the tunnel. People owned those buildings. People with money. The kind of money she was going to have.

The Essex House had a suite looking out over Central Park. Fifteen hundred dollars, but she put it on the corporate card and left a message at the desk for John Garret. The furniture was upholstered in emerald green velvet with ornate arms and legs that were painted gold. She tapped her foot while the bellman placed her bag on the stand in the bedroom. When he left, she tore the sheets off the bed and covered the mirrors.

She was breathing hard by the time she opened a bottle of Pinot Grigio from the bar and poured herself some. On top of the pills, it acted fast. Standing by the curtains with her forehead against the cool glass, she was halfway through the wine when she heard a soft rapping at the door.

She straightened her back, tucked her blouse down into her pants, and absently brushed her slacks. She cracked the door just a bit, then swung it open. He pushed inside, bringing an overpowering smell of Grey Flannel. His hair was slicked back and the milky green eyes glowed at her like opals. The tan suit and white shirt did what they could to disguise his bulk but nothing could hide a neck that thick.

Even with heels, her eyes were only level with his chin. She returned his minute smile with one of her own.

He tossed a black duffel bag down on the floor.

"Five hundred thousand," he said. "Don't be calling me for it next time. I'll call you. A deal's a deal with me."

"I wanted to talk to you," she said.

He looked at his watch and said, "You got five minutes. I'm late for a card game."

"Would you like a drink?" she asked. She turned and walked back into the room. She refilled her own glass and poured one for him.

"No," he said, when she offered it. He looked at his watch again. "You got four."

"You know I had to fly down here from Syracuse?"

"So?"

Her heart pattered.

"We've got a deal we want to know if you're interested in."

"What deal?" he said. His hands hung at his sides, fingers curled up like an ape's.

"We want to move some money."

Johnny snorted. "You and every politician in the city. We said cash from the start. There's your cash."

"Not that," she said, angling her head toward the duffel bag. "A hundred million."

He turned his head as if to get his left eye closer to her. The wineglass jiggled and she brought it to her lips.

"Con Trac bills us a hundred million in extras. We pay it," she said, taking a swallow. "Then, Con Trac gets a consultant bill from a Swiss company for ninety million that they pay."

"You mean eighty."

"Oh," she says, looking at her watch. "I guess my time ran out."

"What are you? Sarah Bernhardt? The fucking feds are up my ass," he said, scowling.

"It's ten million," she said. "Found money. Thane wanted to run it through the project down in Miami Beach. They'll do it for ten and be happy. I just thought."

Johnny's face softened. He grinned and stepped closer. Softly, he said, "You got anything else? To sweeten the deal a little?"

He reached out and touched her shoulder.

49

We sit in silence for a moment before he asks if I can talk about what I think happened.

"Nothing. That's just what kind of an asshole he was," I say, shaking my head. "I was pissed at her. Just going down there like that. I actually came home that night, to surprise her. Tommy was sitting there with his buddies watching *Texas Chainsaw Massacre* or something and Amy's on the phone talking to her boyfriend. I asked him where his mom was and he gave me this empty stare. But then you have to admire her nerve too."

"She didn't come home?" the shrink asks.

"I was the one who told her the easiest way to pull it off was through Con Trac."

"She did come home?" he says.

"Of course."

"When?"

"Let's just say she didn't spend the night," I say. "I told you she was bad, but not that. Not what you think."

"What do I think?" he asks.

"I see your look."

"Is it possible you're projecting?"

"She told me what he said about sweetening the deal," I say. "Why would she tell me that if she did anything? That wouldn't make sense. What are you looking like that for?"

"What do you mean?"

"Like a dead fish or something."

"What do you think is really going on here?"

"Why don't you just save us all a little time and let me in on it?" I say, leaning forward. "Or don't you really have a clue?"

He purses his thick lips, nods, and says, "How do you feel about being alone?"

"Fine."

"I thought you missed her?"

"Her. Her. Her. You think I'm weeping for lost love or some crap?"

"There's no shame in admitting the fear of being alone," he says. "Most of us are."

"I am perfectly fine."

"Okay," he says, puffing out his fat cheeks and letting out the air. "Let's shift gears."

"Oh, no. Please let me talk about how much I miss her," I say, clasping my hands together. "It's cleansing."

He tilts his head down and looks through the tops of his glasses, waiting for me to stop before he says, "You said it was two days before Bucky found Ben's car. Did you do something to lead him to it?"

"Me?"

"It's pretty heavy," he says, "doing that to your friend."

"Like I wanted to get caught?" I say, my mouth open at the ridiculousness of the suggestion.

"Is it possible?"

"Trust me. It had nothing to do with me."

• • •

I always thought of the boardroom in a big company as a place for flanking maneuvers, charges, betrayals, and retreats. High ground is essential. So are allies. The boardroom at the King Corp offices was on the third floor, a long dark wood table surrounded by windows and a cluster of easels with artwork depicting the various projects from around the country. A mall. An office building. A hotel. All pen and ink with rich green trees and perfect people in the foreground, usually pointing toward the impressive creation.

Mike Allen came to see me, which in itself is never good news. The chairman doesn't come to see the CEO any more than the principal sits in on a teacher's classroom. We met in the boardroom. When I offered him coffee, he held up a paper cup with a plastic lid and shook his head.

"Sit."

I made a point of pouring myself a cup from the sideboard before I did. Then I took a sip and leaned back in my chair, smiling at him.

"You know why I'm here," he said.

"New York isn't an easy place to do business," I said. "Did you know we had the chance to build the South Street Seaport? You know James, though. He'd never play ball with those guys."

"And you are?"

I put my coffee down and leaned forward. "Mike, it's part of the cost of doing business. Everyone down there knows that. When you don't . . . what do you think happened to James? Milo?"

"Have they made threats?"

"I thought you didn't want to know about all this," I said. "Just get the project done. That's what you said."

"I heard two engineers had their trucks stolen from the site last week," he said. "We're twenty-four days behind. I got told yesterday that if it keeps going, this thing could run two years over. I don't have to tell you the interest costs on two billion dollars over two years."

"Who told you two years?" I asked, making a face and shaking my head. "Some engineer? A banker?"

"Someone who knows."

"You can say Ben."

"I don't play games like that," he said, gripping his coffee and flicking off the top with his thumb. "We've got a leakage rate of over twenty percent."

"Morris," I said. King Corp's CFO.

"I asked him, Thane. He didn't volunteer."

"You think you would have gotten those numbers if it was James instead of me?" I asked. "How the hell am I supposed to run this thing when I can't trust the people I need?"

"That's not really the issue, is it?" Mike said. He sipped his coffee and set it down carefully. "I look worse in this than anyone. Trust me. Remember those dinners we'd have after the SU games? The party we had at Grimaldi's after the Nebraska game? I've always been there, your biggest supporter. But this is business."

"What's that mean?"

"We've got to get it right. This can't keep going on."

"As in, what?"

"There are people on the board pushing for a change," Mike said. "Time is running out."

"Let them," I said, standing up. "Go ahead. Let any one of those stuffed turkeys run this job. Let Ben."

"Why do you say Ben?" he asked, tilting his head.

I felt a current in my stomach, like he knew.

"He's the fucking problem here. What's he done to help? He's the one supposed to be down there, not running around up here. I said fire him. You said no. Now I'm fucked."

"Easy," he said, holding out his hands, palms down like he was going to levitate the table. Then he turned them over. "We gotta do better. That's all. It's like a coach. What did you do when they yelled at you? Quit?"

"I'm not quitting, Mike," I said. "I just want them to know. Take it if they want. See what they get."

Mike rested his hands on the table and looked at his cup.

"Thane," he said. "You don't have anything going on, right? I mean, I've seen it happen. But, it's something we'd have to fix right away. It's something I'd want to fix."

I stared at him until he looked up with those pale green eyes. He was a good man.

"No, Mike."

That made him happy. He clapped me on the back and we traded well-known inspirational quotes from Vince Lombardi and then he left and flew back off to New York. My office was between the boardroom and Morris's. On my way past, I noticed my secretary's empty desk. I stopped and looked inside. Darlene was at my computer.

"What are you doing?"

She jumped and put her hand on her chest.

"We've been having problems syncing the schedule on your BlackBerry with the computer. You scared me."

I crossed the room and yanked the plug out of the wall. The computer snapped off. Darlene frowned and stepped back.

"I don't want anyone on my computer," I said, glaring

at her until her eyes filled with tears and she rushed out of the room.

I slammed my office door shut behind me and made a beeline for Morris's office. He had a paneled alcove with a high ceiling just down the hall from where James had been. My eyes caught that dark end of the hallway. An oriental rug rolled up and sagging against a desk. Picture frames leaning on a lamp. An unplugged coffeemaker.

A shadow flickered.

I swallowed and looked away, asking Jim's secretary where he was. She said he had someone in there. I knocked once and walked in. One of the young leasing agents jumped to his feet and I held the door for him. Jim Morris blinked up at me.

I stared.

"What did you want me to say?" he finally said, blinking again.

"What did James always say?" I said. "Chain of command."

"He said he was trying to help."

"You think that helped?" I said, raising my voice.

He looked down and shook his head.

I exhaled through my nose and said, "Did you get the overages from Con Trac?"

"I was going to talk to you about that. It's—"

"Pay it."

Jim twitched his nose, moving his glasses up higher on the bridge. He took the bill from a stack of papers on the edge of his desk and held it out to me, blinking.

"I know what it is," I said. "This is a two-billion-dollar project. We're in with Con Trac, which, by the way, was the company James told me personally he decided to use.

Now I'm stuck with making it happen. I trust his judgment, Jim, and I'm sure you do too."

"Three months from now, we have to give the bank an accounting. You know that," he said. His eyebrows were doing a jitterbug above the rims of his glasses.

"You think I spend all my time out there in a tree stand?" I said. "The Japanese are ready to step in as soon as anyone blinks."

"Well," Jim said, raising his eyebrows up high, "I'm glad you're thinking about it."

"So, pay it," I said.

I walked out, thinking about that money, which led me to thinking about Johnny G, so I wasn't really paying attention when I got in my Hummer to head to the lodge. I didn't notice the FBI car until they pulled out around me and swerved right in front.

They wanted to talk about Ben.

50

Bucky woke up and heard cars instead of birds. His face tightened, then his stomach. He rolled his eyes toward Judy. Her back was to him and he eased out of the sagging bed, avoiding the corner of the old striped mattress where the sheets had pulled free during the night. The floorboards of the small rented room creaked, and with the bottoms of his feet he could feel the gaps in the rough-cut wood. Framed by the dusty yellow curtains and split diagonally by the long crack in the window was Main Street.

Bucky washed up in the tiny sink, then squeezed through the back staircase out of the crumbling brick building. He puffed into his hands, crossed the gravel lot, and climbed into his blue Suburban. He picked up his cell phone, dialed Ben, and got voice mail again.

"Ben," he said, after the tone, "it's Buck. I have no idea what happened to you, but call me."

Bucky hung up and called into the King Corp offices, asking for Ben there and getting more voice mail. He spent the rest of his drive figuring and by the time he reached the lodge, the adrenaline was running hot. He punched the code into the access gate for deliveries. It didn't work.

He banged his fist against the metal box and headed back down Swamp Road, past the ruin of his house, then onto the long winding road that the greenhorns had to use to get to the lodge. After crossing the bridge, he turned down the service entrance and went in through the kitchen. Robin, the pastry chef, lost the color in her face when she saw him.

"Bucky?" she said.

"Where's Adam?"

Robin hesitated, looking from one of Bucky's hands to the other. "I think in the wine cellar."

"Thane?" Bucky asked.

"I don't know," she said. "I know he has something here tonight. Some politicians. You— It's good to see you, Bucky."

"You too," Bucky said, and rounded the bend, heading down the stone steps into the cool dry cellar.

Adam was bent over a shelf of wine casks trying to plug a leaky spout. The red wine spewed out, dousing him and staining his clothes. Bucky grabbed a cork off a higher shelf and snatched a wooden mallet out of Adam's hand. He struck the spout, blasting it free, replaced it with the cork, and with one resounding stroke plugged the hole. Adam looked up at him with an open mouth, eyes big through the round glasses. His face went from pink to red, outshining the stains on the white apron he wore over his flannel shirt and jeans.

"I'm lookin' for Ben," Bucky said.

"Thane didn't see you," Adam said quickly, wiping his pudgy hands on the apron covering his big belly, "did he?"

"Where's Ben?" Bucky said.

Adam's mouth was moving now, jiggling the rolls of his neck. But his only sound was a constricted gurgle.

"You shoulda turned that backhoe on *him*," Bucky said, pointing his finger at Adam.

"He was gonna wreck my house too," Adam said, choking. "I had to, Buck. He was gonna do it anyway."

"You think I woulda done that to you?" Bucky said, his forehead knotting.

Adam cast his eyes at the floor.

"Ben," Bucky said.

"Not for three days, Buck," Adam said, untying the apron, and using it to mop up the mess.

"What about Thane?"

"I don't know when he'll be here," Adam said, talking fast, wiping the cask. "He just comes and goes. He's running everything, Buck. My wife's back in school. Tuition's six thousand dollars. It's not the same without you, though. The hunting's not too good. Thane wanted a fresh roast for the governor's people. I even took a flashlight out with my Winchester, but I had to go to the freezer. Thane, he wounded a big buck down by the West Lodge the other night. Didn't get him. We could've used that. He was a mess."

Adam went on mopping the wine. Bucky just looked at him until he stopped.

"James's gone," Bucky said. "Then Scott. Now Ben."

"Ben?" Adam said, looking at his wine-soaked apron.

Bucky just looked. Adam kept his eyes down and shifted his feet, making little slapping sounds in the puddle of wine.

"You call my cell phone if you hear from him," Bucky said. "Anyone out hunting this morning?"

"Not till this afternoon," Adam said. "Some of the politicians."

"Okay," Bucky said, staring at him, "listen, I'm going to take a drive around. If Thane shows up, you call me on my cell phone. I don't want any trouble."

"Buck," Adam said, gripping the apron and twisting it, "if he finds out."

"So you better call me," Bucky said.

Adam swallowed, then glanced up and back to the floor.

Bucky took the stairs two at a time and left a trail of dust with his Suburban. There was a lot of ground to cover if Thane was going to be heading for a tree stand sometime in the afternoon. He came out off the driveway on Scope Road, drove through the woods, and into an area they called the Upland Fields, bouncing along the dirt tracks, his chest restrained by the seat belt. He kept his eyes moving, the way he would if he was looking for game, his eyes roving for signs.

He came out of the high grass and rumbled past the pheasant barn. He had planned on going right on Swamp Road and scouring the gravel road around the goose pond, but when the Suburban hit pavement, he turned left, not knowing why, and raced up the gravelly spine of the drumlin toward the West Lodge.

Ben's car was waiting for him.

51

I WATCHED THE REDHEAD, Agent Lee, get out and walk up to my window. A van pulled up behind their car and honked. Agent Lee flashed her badge and motioned for the car to go around.

I rolled down the window and said, "Are you crazy?"

She told me they wanted to talk. I told her to go ahead.

"Your friend is missing," she said.

"Ben?" I said, raising my eyebrows and letting my mouth fall open.

"Can we sit down somewhere?" she said. "We've got an office in the Federal Building"

I told her mine was around the corner. She said that would be fine and they followed me back to the circle in the front of the building. I showed them into my office and offered them chairs around the small conference table opposite my desk. Agent Lee looked up at the shelf behind the desk. Old trophies and framed photos of me, Jessica, and Tommy skiing, scuba diving, on a boat, at a football stadium.

I asked if they wanted a drink. They said no, but I

asked Darlene to bring me a coffee before sitting down at the table.

"We heard about your little dinner with Johnny G," Agent Rooks said.

"Right," I said, staring at the red light on the recorder that she had set on the table without asking. "You said interact with him. We saw him at the Time Warner Center. A charity thing and he asked us to dinner. What you wanted me to do, right?"

"Only you forgot tell us," she said, forcing a grin.

"I'm supposed to track you down?" I said, looking at the redhead. "No offense, but I'm trying to run a company."

"You're a family man," Agent Lee said, nodding toward the pictures on the shelf.

"Of course."

"Sometimes people forget," she said. "Work and everything."

"There's a balance," I said, gazing up at the pictures. "That sailfish was number three in the world. Working hard lets you do stuff like that."

"Hard days and long nights," Agent Rooks said. "That's what my dad said. I think I saw him at my graduation. I'm pretty sure it was him."

I looked at her for a moment.

"So," I said. "Ben."

"We had a meeting," Agent Lee said. "He stiffed us. No calls, and no one's seen him."

I shrugged and said, "He's supposed to be down at the Garden State project. I haven't been able to get him either, but it's been nuts down there."

"We've got people down there," Amanda said. "They haven't seen him."

"On the site you have people?" I asked, raising my brow.

"How close was Ben to Scott?" Rooks asked.

I sucked in my lips and my eyes shifted from one of them to the other.

"Like brothers," I said. "All of us. Since back in school."

"What about the union?" Amanda asked.

"Well, stuff has been disappearing down there on the site like it's a free-for-all. I never even thought of Ben. I mean, he's in charge down there, but . . ."

"You said you've been trying to get him," Rooks said. "He works for you, right?"

"Things are crazy right now," I said. "It's like the Cumberland project we did in Albany. Everyone just scrambling. You have to let people do their jobs."

"To trust them," Agent Lee said.

"Hopefully you can," I said. "Is there something you know that I don't?"

Rooks's dark eyes bore into mine. I knew she knew. I knew she wanted to say it. I swallowed and stared right back.

"There's a connection between the union and King Corp and James's murder," Agent Lee said, drawing my attention away from her partner's glare. "That we know. It could be Ben. It could be Scott."

We were all quiet for a minute. Darlene brought my coffee in and set it down in front of me. We all stared at it.

"Or me?" I said quietly. "That's not what you think?"

Agent Lee looked me in the eye. And bit back a nervous smile.

"That would be pretty ballsy," Rooks said. "A cooperating witness on the take."

Agent Lee cleared her throat and said, "We've seen the fallout in these things before. One guy, we found his head in a Dumpster with three bullets in it. Sometimes it's hard to say no."

"You think that's what happened to Ben?" I asked.

Rooks shrugged and said, "It's like squeezing a ball of dough. Shit starts squirting out between your fingers all over the place. It's a mess."

"The thing is," Agent Lee said, "we know it's coming apart. It's heating up. The bodies. The stealing. That's just the thunder.

"So, if you see Ben and he's got something he can tell us, you could do him a favor. At this point, no one's going to get out of this without getting burned. But when the whistle blows, and if he's on the right side, well, we could help him, still."

"But that whistle's gonna blow any day," Rooks said. She looked over at her partner and added, "Wouldn't you say?"

"I would."

I looked at her, put my arms on the table and leaned toward her, my face softening. I actually thought about it. Coming clean.

She waited.

I opened my mouth to speak, then realized just how stupid that would be. I closed my mouth, sat back, and said, "If I see him, I'll let him know."

52

Bucky turned off the engine and got out. He worked his boots into the gravel and stood for a minute, letting the quiet settle in on him. He inhaled the woods through his nose and let it out slow. A red squirrel chattered and somewhere down in the thorns a deer crashed through the brush. Three geese flew overhead, late for breakfast, silent except for the sound of their wings in the air. Dead leaves whispered, then went quiet.

Bucky circled Ben's car and swiped his finger on the windshield. The sun still glowed white through the clouds and made a dull glare that showed the small smudge. A light film of dust from dry dead leaves had settled on the car.

There'd been no rain. That meant it was two days' worth of dust. The car had been there since the last time Bucky had spoken with Ben. Bucky took a faded blue bandanna from his pocket and used it to open the Lexus's door. No keys. No blood. Only the smell of leather. He closed the door and stepped into the middle of the driveway, where he knelt to read the tracks.

Too many scuff marks and too dry to make any sense.

He stood and walked back down the driveway until he came to a low soft spot, still brown with autumn mud. That he could read. His own tracks were freshest with hard crisp edges on the tread marks. There were Ben's tracks, or portions of them, the car's tread narrower than a truck's. Someone else had been there at the same time. The dried dirt of this other track was made about the same time as Ben's. Bucky would have a hard time telling someone exactly how he knew, but he knew it wasn't magic. To him it was as obvious as an overbaked loaf of bread to a baker or a good wind to a sailor.

He touched it to make sure. Truck tracks. Wide. Maybe an H2.

Maybe Thane.

Bucky went to his truck and returned with a digital camera, snapping three shots of the tire tracks from different angles. He didn't know if he could convince anyone else to be as certain as he was about the time of the tracks, but the picture would let him try. The first thing to do was search the lodge and Bucky did that. There was no sign that anything bad had happened.

He walked back to the Lexus and began to survey the ground in widening circles outside the car, searching the dusty grit. Halfway to the cabin he found it. A dug-up spot in the gravel. Someone jumping into action, moving toward the swamp. Running from something. Bucky looked for a sign of what. His eyes crossed the driveway and continued on through the woods until they came to rest on the tree stand.

He went through the woods to the base of the stand. In the mud, size thirteen boot prints. Resting on a bed of brown leaves ten feet away was a single spent shotgun shell. Bucky picked it up with a stick and examined it before putting it down. It was fresh, fired from a twelve gauge. Probably two days ago.

The picture started to come together. He went back to the disturbance in the grit and searched the bank on the swamp side of the driveway.

Five feet away, he spotted a patch of leaves that might have been scuffed up. He moved toward it, then knelt and looked along that same direction down the bank, shading his eyes even though the light from the pewter sky was dull. Five feet farther there was another scuff mark. He sifted through the leaves, moving them one at a time until he exposed a small corner of a dead leaf that had been pressed into the dirt by a flat curving object. The heel of a shoe. Ben's shoe.

Twenty feet on, his heart jumped into his throat. A round spot, the size of a nickel, spotted a dead maple leaf. He scooped it up and held the leaf close. He knew before he tasted it, but wanted to be sure so he scraped a bit off the brown button of dark matter with his pinkie nail and put it to his tongue. He felt his saliva glands kick in and his stomach turned.

Blood.

The path, now that he knew it was a path made by a man, became easier to follow. The disturbed spots in the leaves stayed five feet apart. A running man. A place where he'd fallen. More blood spots.

Bucky stopped, blinked, and looked up at the sky. The tiny wet flecks it spat were a reminder that his time to read the woods would be short. He was more than halfway to the swamp when he saw a big scuff mark. Leaves and dirt dug up in two divots so great even a greenhorn could spot them. Another sudden change in direction. Bucky scanned the woods in the direction opposite where the dirt had been sprayed. He staggered forward, fearing that the sudden change in direction was the result of a direct hit.

The dark brown spots became splotches, confirming the new wound. Bloodstains jumped out at him now from the forest floor, getting bigger as he went. Bucky saw the brambles and the triangular opening where the game trail went in. He jogged toward it, knowing the way he knew with animals that wounded things ran downhill, taking the path of least resistance. He didn't have to examine Thane's boot prints or the hand marks in the mud where they both had begun to crawl. The rain was coming down in full drops now and the wind began to lift the leaves from their resting places and carry them tumbling away through the trees like mad little demons.

Every so often, Bucky would check the mud for the man tracks, but for the most part, he kept his eyes on the thick tangle of branches around him. He was looking for the frayed ends of broken twigs, the spot where one or another of these two men made their mad break to get free from the tangled undergrowth. When he saw the first pale filaments, he pushed through the brush and looked down at the mud below. Ben's shoe prints, clear enough for a child to track. Snapped twigs and sticks and broken vines.

Bucky stopped and made a careful examination of the mud. There were no boot prints, only Ben's shoes. Bucky stood up to look around and his spirits rose with him. Ben might have escaped. Bucky thought of all the possibilities. There was a lot of blood, but the wounds could have been muscle. If it were fresh, Bucky could have told exactly what part of the body it was from by looking at it. But dried as it was, he could only guess and he preferred to hope.

He followed the new trail through the brush to the path along the swamp, then followed Ben's shoe prints toward the road. Another good sign. Ben had known where to go for help. They stopped at the water's edge.

Bucky saw the broken grass and the confusion of hand and boot tracks in the mud. His stomach turned, knowing what it meant. Part of him wanted to stop reading the signs. Rain pattered against the black surface of the water. Bucky got down on his hands and knees again, willing a sign that continued along up the trail. There was nothing. He stood up and paced the shoreline, thinking.

He imagined a final struggle, Ben lying dead, and Thane trying to figure out what to do with the body. There was a small flat-bottomed boat up by the road bridge. Bucky jogged to it and saw right away that it hadn't been moved. He hustled back to where he'd found the last shoe prints, blinking up at the rain. His heart and lungs burned.

If he was going to find anything, it had to be now. He paced back and forth at the spot he knew Ben had been murdered, peering into the woods and swamp, frantic. He found Thane's boot tracks and some smaller prints, a woman's, read them, and reread them to no avail. Then he splashed back and forth in the teeming rain until there was nothing but his own muddy ruts on the trail and even they began to fill with milky brown pools.

He sat down in the mud and stared out at the rain-blasted surface of the swamp water until the drops began to drip from his mustache and he wiped his mouth on the back of his soaking sleeve. And it was then, when he'd given up hope, that he saw it.

His son Russel, coated in mud from head to toe. A soft spot in the creek bed. Scott and Thane laughing about it, until he told them about the deadly suction.

Bubbles in the swamp.

53

I CANCELED MY DINNER with the politicians and I was almost home. Wind pushed at the H2 as I drove along the rise above Sandy Beach. I looked down the dirt road bisecting the farm fields. A road like the one in Van Gogh's last painting of the field where he killed himself. The road to nowhere. The road Ben tried to take Jessica down. To talk about his wife running off.

According to Ben's story.

The construction site next to our house was an open wound. Two enormous mounds of dirt rose toward the sky. The trucks and excavators were long gone. Even the deep teeth marks of their tracks had begun to erode. A single trailer rested on cinder blocks. A beat-up bulldozer and a white pickup truck slept beside it in the red glow of dusk. I lost sight of both as I pulled down into the circle drive.

Inside, I called Jessica's name. In the entryway, I glanced at the mirror that wasn't there. Its replacement was a woven Navaho rug. Bright red and orange. Colors that didn't match the space. I ran upstairs, then down. Tommy was holed up in the game room with a friend, playing Xbox. He jumped up and hugged me, then got back to the game.

In the walk-out great room beneath the main floor, a dozen renderings of the new house, the castle, rested on easels. A mini-boardroom. In the center of the floor was a drafting table, riddled with plans. A card table beside it bore the replica of the new house and the old, a scale model that cost ten thousand dollars.

A muddy track came in from the sliding doors that looked out on the lake. The track circled the tables. I shook my head and stopped in front of a watercolor rendering of the new house, the way it would look from the water. Three stories of flat-cut fieldstone. A round turret in the center. Tall broad windows. Dormers. Parapets. Sweeping slate roofs. A stone terrace with a formal pool and geometrical shrubs. Affluence. Power. Perfect order.

The scent of raw earth snuck in through the crack in the sliders. I went to close them and saw Jessica in a hard hat on the foundation with a man in a rusty Carhartt jacket. His arms flying through the air. Her hands were planted on her hips. The sun's last rays gave the scene a rose-colored hue.

They didn't notice me until I was moving toward them with my arms extended for balance, careful not to fall into the basement hole or the deep trench on the outside. A ponytail poked out from her hat and she wore jeans, a sweatshirt, and muddy work boots. The man with his back to me was Dino, the GC for her project.

He turned when he saw me and threw his arms in the air.

"Thane, you tell her," he said.

"Tell her what?"

"See this line?" he said, squatting down and squinting

along the line of his extending arm and all five fingers. "She wants it framed, but I can't. Not straight. We've got to dig it out and pour this thing over."

"The Con Trac guy said you could fir it or something," Jessica said. Her eyes were moist and pink-rimmed.

Dino set his mouth and shook his head. "It's too far off. You build on this and you're going to have a crooked house. I'm not doing it. You're mad now, but you'd hate me worse if I did it.

"Look," Dino said, skipping across one of the planks that bridged the concrete wall to the outside ground.

He raised a massive board and fed it across the trench on the outside of the foundation to me. I held it and he marched back across the plank holding the other end.

"When are you gonna fill that?" I asked, angling my head down into the trench.

He looked down in and said, "When it dries a little. That's why I left the dozer."

He set his end of the board down and told me to do the same. It was a foot wide, nearly two inches thick, and maybe sixteen feet long. He positioned it in the corner of the foundation and by the time it got to me, the entire end was hanging off the inside of the wall.

"Just," Jessica said, reaching down and pulling the board onto the line of the wall.

Dino looked at me and said, "Help me here."

"They can put it straight on this part, honey," I said, pointing, "but then they won't have a ninety degree angle going in at the other end. See that?"

"So it's off a little," she said. "No one's going to see this corner. We'll plant a tree or something."

"Honey," I said. "You can't. He's right."

Her face crumpled up and she looked toward the end of the lake.

"This is our house," she said, turning on me. "You're just standing there smiling like this is fine?"

"It's not fine. Come on," I said, moving toward her, holding out my hand. "We'll have to fix it, but we can't frame on this. You'll have gaps everywhere. Even if you could hide it on the outside, the inside would be a mess."

"That roof doesn't go on and we lose the whole goddamn winter," she said. Lines extended out from the corners of her eyes.

"We're okay," I said, taking her hand.

Dino jammed his hands in his pockets and looked up at the sky.

"Gonna rain," he said. "You guys let me know when they can get back and redo this foundation."

He walked off with his head down and got into his truck.

Jessica slipped free and headed for the house. I followed and tried to put my arm around her as we crossed the lawn. The wind kicked up, blowing grit in my eyes.

"Want me to grill some steaks before this rain?" I said when we were inside.

"Not hungry," she said. "I thought you had a dinner at the lodge. I'll heat up that pasta for you and Tommy."

I took her shoulders.

"Come on, we've got everything we always wanted. Don't do this. We'll fix it and move on. This house is fine for now."

"You ever notice how everything's fine for you?" she asked, baring her teeth with a fake smile.

"What's wrong with that?"

"It's average," she said. She turned and marched

through the room and up the stairs, speaking over her shoulder as she went. "The average IQ is one hundred. The average income is thirty-five thousand a year. The average married couple has sex once a week. Sound good to you? Ten million dollars we're giving him and that son-of-a-bitch gave us a crooked house."

She walked into the kitchen and took down a bottle of Riesling.

"You talking about Johnny G?" I asked, stomach tight.

"Are we planning on giving ten million dollars to any other crooked sons-of-bitches?"

"Morris sent that hundred-million-dollar overage check to Con Trac today."

She took a glass from the cupboard, opened the wine, and filled it. She raised it to me and said, "Then the glass is half full, isn't it?"

"You think we could just leave? Run? What about Tommy?"

She took a big swallow and looked out at the lake. In a distant voice she said, "If we have to."

Then she looked at me and said, "Australia. France. Italy. They all have private schools that speak English. With money you can do anything. New names. All that."

"Jesus."

"But we'll be fine," she said, looking away again. "Things like this happen all the time. Always have, always will. Joe Kennedy was a bootlegger. Look at Martha Stewart. Back on TV. People forget what you did if you have money and now we've got it."

"What happened to the money?"
"What do you mean?"

"She really got ninety million?"

I shrug my shoulders. "I guess. Sure."

"That was okay? You going to jail while she was out there with all that?"

I look at the small window in the door, then back at his face and say, "Who cares, right?"

"I don't know, man. Did you?"

My chest tightens and the air seems thin.

He leans toward me and in a whisper says, "What really happened with her. Admit it. To yourself . . . It's time."

My sinuses swell.

"She ripped the bones from my back and chucked me down like a bag of jelly," I say.

"She was bad," he says.

"I told you she was."

"You never said how bad."

My brain grows so hot that it begins to melt, and the truth oozes out.

54

Bucky led the two women agents out to the small lodge. He'd seen the doubt in their eyes when he first began telling them the story, but had convinced them, especially the redhead, Agent Lee, at least to take a look. He checked the rearview mirror and saw their car churning through his cloud of dust as they went up the driveway.

Tim McCarthy, the investigator from the state police office, was already there along with a white Onondaga County coroner's van. The agents talked about McCarthy with him sitting in their office as if he were deaf. He knew from their discussion that for political reasons, the sheriff had given the FBI control of the investigation. If they did find a body though, that had to be handled by the coroner. According to Agent Rooks, the frizzy-haired one, McCarthy was using the new situation to worm his way back in. The redhead said she didn't blame McCarthy, that any good detective would do the same.

Bucky got out, shook hands with McCarthy, and watched him do the same with the agents before he introduced the man from the coroner's office. The assistant coroner had already unloaded a handcart with big bicycle tires that carried the GPR unit, ground-penetrating radar, used to detect buried bodies and graves. Down the hill, Bucky could hear the drone of the motorboat. Its long dark shape moved through the trees and along the glassy black water.

"I'm thinking he took his first shot from there," Bucky said, pointing to the tree stand. "Otherwise, why would Ben run down the bank in dress shoes?"

"Presuming it was Ben Evans wearing the shoes," Agent Rooks said.

Bucky looked at her, sizing her up the way he would a mule.

"The casing is under the stand," he said, pointing. "Right over here."

He led them to the tree stand. Agent Lee crouched down and slipped the shell into a plastic bag, then stood up and looked around.

"*Presuming* the gun was fired at Ben," he said, glancing at Rooks, "I'll show you where he was and the path he took."

It was a cloudy, chilly day and the leaves crunched under their feet as the agents followed him across the driveway and down through the woods. He showed them the muddy spot in the path, explaining the footprints he'd seen, but felt stupid doing it since the only thing left were small puddles. Agent Rooks had her hands jammed deep into the pockets of her blue windbreaker, and her lips worked sideways when Bucky described how he figured it all went down.

"Here's where the blood started to get thick, a chest wound, lung, liver, good blood," he said, walking toward the heavy brush. "The real blood was in that thicket over there. I can show someone later. Even with the rain, there should be something. There was a lot."

Bucky kept going down, until they came to the wider

path along the water's edge. He went left, back toward the road where Russel was waiting with the boat. The propeller shaft extended a good eight feet off the back.

"Swamp boat," Bucky told them. "It can take us in there deep. This is Russel, my son. He'll stay here and someone else will have to, too. There's only room for four."

Russel touched the bill of his cap and made way so they could get into the boat. Rooks scrambled aboard. Agent Lee paused and looked at McCarthy. He waved her on with a smile.

"I'll save you an argument," McCarthy said. "Just keep me in the game, here, okay?"

"I will," she said. "Thank you."

The coroner unloaded the equipment off his cart and into the front seat of the boat. On the end of a three-foot wand was a red box the size of a car battery. Next to him on the seat was a laptop that was wired to another box the size of a small suitcase, which in turn was connected to the wand.

The agents sat in the middle seat. Bucky squeezed past them both and restarted the motor. Russel lifted the bow and shoved them off. When the water became shallow, the long prop sprayed flecks of black mud into the air like an egg beater. The flat-bottomed boat eased through the dark water and the dead grass.

"I'll take you to the end of the soft spot," Bucky said, addressing the assistant coroner, "then work you back and forth across it a foot at a time."

"Perfect," the coroner said, focusing his attention on the screen in front of him.

"It won't be an exact grid," Bucky said. "But it'll be close."

"Close enough to find a body," the coroner said, looking up briefly, the tone of his voice indicating he was enjoying himself.

"What do we do?" Rooks asked.

"Just sit," Bucky said.

Bucky stood and peered over the coroner's shoulder at the screen. It didn't look like much, just a grainy kind of depth meter.

"See that?" the coroner said, looking back at them all.

"What?" Rooks said, jumping up and rocking the flat-bottomed boat.

Bucky grabbed the gunnels and held on. When the boat steadied, he eased up again so he could see. The coroner pointed at a shady, upside-down V.

"What is it?" Agent Lee asked.

"Probably just a log," the coroner said. "But that's how it works. That's fifteen feet underneath us. I've never done this over water or mud, but we'll get an even clearer picture because of the density."

"Less density, right?" Agent Lee said.

"Of course."

For the next forty minutes, Bucky pulled the boat along the rope line, back and forth, up and down, while the coroner sat hunched over the screen. The agents were restless and shivering, when the coroner barked out.

"Ho," he said.

"What?" Rooks said, rocking the boat again.

"Maybe something," the coroner said, glancing back at them. "It doesn't happen all at once, but if I'm right we can narrow the grid."

"What do you think it is?" Agent Lee asked.

"Well," he said, looking back and pointing at another broader upside-down V on his screen. "It's either a big rock . . . or a human head."

55

WITHIN TEN MINUTES, the four of them were staring at the shape of what looked like a sheet being pulled tight over a human face.

"He's down there," the coroner said. "Three point two meters. About a meter of that is water."

Bucky felt light-headed.

"How do we get him out?" Agent Lee asked.

"Swamp machine," Bucky said. "An excavator we use to dredge the ponds. I could get it in here, or someone could. It's got tracks and pontoons."

"How long will it take?" Rooks asked.

"A couple hours anyway. Probably half a day," Bucky said. "They'll have to dig around it pretty good to keep it from just caving back in. This stuff's like wet concrete."

Bucky unhooked the ropes and motored them back toward the road and the bank where McCarthy stood watching Russel smoke a cigarette. Bucky caught his son's eye and shook his head. Russel flicked the butt into the swamp. The coroner showed McCarthy the computer screen. Agent Lee asked him if he could get a forensics team there to test for blood in the dirt and to be available for when they got the body out.

"Don't forget the casing," Bucky said. "It'll match his gun."

"Which is where?" Agent Lee asked.

Bucky said, "The lodge, I'll bet. He took James's hunting locker. It'll be right in there."

"Would anyone else have access to it?" Rooks asked.

"Maybe Adam," Bucky said. "But that's about it."

"So it'll have his prints on it," Rooks said.

"What about a warrant?" Agent Lee said, turning to McCarthy.

"The judge teaches Sunday school at my church," he said.

Rooks clasped her hands and said, "Do we pick him up?"

"Once we take him in," Agent Lee said, "it's over. Everybody runs for cover."

"Once he finds out we confiscated his gun, it's over anyway."

"Seventeen years they've been working on this union," Agent Lee said. "Maybe we should make a hundred and ten percent sure."

"But goddamn," Rooks said, "it feels like Christmas is coming, doesn't it?"

"So," Bucky said, sensing the tension, his eyes shifting between the two of them before landing on Agent Lee. "What about Scott?"

"What about him?" Agent Lee asked, turning to him.

"He could help."

"You know where he is?" Rooks said.

"You know who did it," Bucky said. "Now the footprint I saw in the snow makes sense. It all does. If Thane finds out you know, he might run. I'd sure like to get those jets out of his hands."

"What's that got to do with Scott?" Agent Lee asked.

"If we could find him, *if*," Bucky said, smiling wryly at them both, "and he was cleared by you, then they might make him the CEO. Mike Allen was the one who put Thane in. Thane had him fooled. Him and everyone."

"Not everyone," Rooks said.

"Allen used to be with the UAW," Agent Lee said.

"Mike Allen's a good man," Bucky said. "Clean as you can get. James used to say that, and he knew. Mike's got money already. Lots. He wouldn't get involved in something like this. And, if we had Scott, Mike could clip Thane's wings."

"Unless it really was Scott," Rooks said, crossing her arms. "And all this is something other than what you're trying to make it seem."

"I'm a hunting guide," Bucky said, looking steadily at her. "I read the signs. I don't make 'em. Believe me."

"Bring him back," Agent Lee said.

"And he's clear?" Bucky asked. "From everyone?"

"It's our investigation," Agent Lee said. "Our call. As long as nothing new turns up, we'll let it play out. I think you're right. We've got our guy."

She looked at her partner, who shrugged and nodded.

"Okay with the county?" Agent Lee asked McCarthy.

"I met Scott," McCarthy said. "I knew his dad. From the beginning, I couldn't believe it was him."

They started up the hill toward their vehicles.

"Who's going to follow Thane?" Bucky asked.

"Let's get the gun first," Agent Lee said, looking at him over her shoulder. "Dorothy and I have a team meeting tomorrow in the city. If we've got a twelve gauge slug in the body and his prints on the gun, I think a surveillance team within the next couple of days won't be hard to do.

"Do you?" she said, putting a hand on Rooks's shoulder.

Rooks didn't think it would be hard either. When they reached the road, Agent Lee turned toward Bucky and was surprised by the look on his face.

"What's wrong?" she asked.

"A couple days is a long ways away," he said.

"Not when you think about seventeen years," Agent Lee said. She held out her hand and Bucky shook it. The agents got into their car. So did McCarthy. The coroner was on his phone calling for more men. Bucky told him he'd get the machine and be right back. Russel followed him to his truck.

Bucky turned to his son when they were alone. Russel was one of four boys, but the most like him by far. Quiet. Smart, not in a book way, but with things. Tough. Reliable.

"I'll take care of the swamp machine," Bucky said. "I want you to find him and follow him. Don't let him see you. Just call me and let me know."

"Thane?" Russel asked.

Bucky smashed his lips together and nodded. A red-tailed hawk screeched above. He looked up, through the infinite fingers of the barren trees, and caught the bird's shape moving just out of their reach.

He looked back at his son. Russel's eyes were big enough and dark enough so that he could see himself in their reflection.

"Be careful."

56

EVEN THE THIN MOON was burning bright enough to keep me awake. I moved closer to Jessica, her body curled in a warm ball on her side of the bed. I draped an arm over her and sighed, wiggling free from the covers. I looked at the clock. Two a.m.

I sat up and turned on the light, nudging her.

She rolled over, blinking, then threw her arm over her face.

"What?" she said, groggy, impatient.

"I keep thinking about those papers," I said. "In Morris's office. The overages. I saw Darlene on my computer the other day."

"Darlene?"

"Those two witches talked like they had people everywhere," I said.

"You said that already," she said, pulling a pillow over her head.

"If someone's down on the job," I said, scooting up higher in the bed, "why wouldn't they have someone in the office?"

She took the pillow off her face. "Jesus, it's two a.m."

"Half those guys at Enron got off because they shredded everything," I said. "Why the hell didn't we think of that?"

Jessica snapped the covers off her and swung her legs out of bed. She stamped out, and I heard her open the bathroom cupboard. I slipped out too and on an impulse went to the side window, peeking out from behind the curtains, scanning the lawn. Then I followed her into the bathroom and got there in time to see her tilting her head back with her hand cupped to her mouth. She bent over the faucet and swallowed some water. My old shaving kit was on the counter. I asked her what she was doing.

She ignored me and zipped up the shaving kit, stuffing it back under the sink. I reached for the knob and she slapped my hand away.

"Can I take something for a headache without you following me?" she said.

I grabbed the handle, yanked open the cupboard, and snatched the kit. She grabbed for it, cursing me. I turned my back and she pounded on it with her fists, but I had the kit open and I took out the empty pill bottles and one with only a few left. I rattled it at her.

She slapped at my hand and knocked the bottle to the floor. She jumped on it and clutched them to her chest, snarling up at me.

"Go shred your papers," she said.

"Headache," I said, shaking my head. "Christ."

"Some men don't need their wives to tell them when and where they can take a pee," she said.

"Right," I said. "You've got it tough."

She stormed past me and shot back into the bed, turning her back and pulling the covers tight. I stood there for a minute, trembling, and wanting to yank her out of there by the hair, knowing I never would. I felt like I couldn't breathe and instead of stewing anymore, I got dressed and hopped into the H2.

It was a forty-minute drive to the office and I did it in thirty. The downtown streets were empty. I pulled down into the parking garage beneath the building and got out, listening for any sound past my own breathing. There was an Eye Pass system like the one at the lodge, and I used it to get into the elevator lobby. When the doors opened on the third floor, I stepped out and looked around. The main stairway was lit, but the hallways were mostly dark.

James's office was off to the right and my eyes were drawn there the way you can't help looking at a horrible car accident. My heart jack-hammered in my chest. I wanted to run, but forced myself to take slow deliberate steps. Being inside Jim's office wasn't much better. Even though it was three in the morning, I had the feeling of being watched. I turned off the lights and went to the window, scanning the street.

A shadow moved on the fringe of a streetlight halfway down the block. The branch of a tree in the breeze or a person? I pressed my face to the glass, angling my head and straining to see. Whoever it was, if it was anybody, they were out of sight. It wasn't the first window I'd pressed my face to in the last few days. The feeling seemed to have taken root.

"Stupid," I said out loud.

I flicked on the light and attacked the file cabinets, looking for the Garden State invoices. It took me fifteen minutes, but there it was, signed by Jim, countersigned by me. I yanked the whole file free and slammed the cabinet shut. Without it, for all anyone knew, Jim could have paid the overage on his own. Or under the direction of Ben.

A giddy chuckle erupted in the stillness, and I had to force myself to slow down and check the office for signs of my work. One cabinet was ajar and I carefully closed it, then backed out and shut the light. The radio kept me company and the thrill of having the only document that could prove I'd taken the money carried me along without a thought. So, it wasn't until I was halfway down Route 321, the country highway between Syracuse and Skaneateles, that I noticed a set of headlights in the distance behind me.

Around the next bend, I pulled off to the side and quickly killed the engine. It was a dark truck that sped past me, and I sat with my heart pounding and my hands clenched. When it disappeared up ahead, I started the H2 and took off after it. The moonlight and my familiarity with the road were enough for me to follow without my headlights. It was moving fast. Chasing.

I was able to stay back, just keeping the set of red taillights in sight until we got to the village. I was coming down the hill in the center of town when I saw a police car nosing out of a side street. I pumped my brakes. The light changed and the dark pickup turned right. The cop pulled out and I crept along behind it, hands gripping the wheel, the file next to me taking on the importance of a dead body. The cop turned right. I put on my headlights and did the same. He pulled off in the middle of town and I kept going, scanning my rearview mirror and also in front of me for signs of the dark truck.

By the time I got home, I was edgy and in a sweat. I opened a beer and tossed the file into the fireplace, lighting it with a match and sitting back on the couch to watch the flames. I finished the beer, wondering why I didn't feel as good as I should have, my mind wandering to the pickup on the road.

I needed sleep. I went upstairs and checked on Tommy. He was lying facedown, his head turned to the side, and a glimmer of drool seeping from the corner of his mouth. I touched his face with the back of my fingers and felt ready to cry. I slipped out and down the hall to my bathroom. The shaving kit was under the sink. She'd put the pills back. I took one out and turned it over in my fingers, a smooth white lozenge. Sleep.

I didn't take it though. I was counting on the weariness that hung from my neck like a stone. I went into the bedroom. Jessica lay with her mouth wide, breathing deep. It was stuffy and I opened the window, letting the chill air spill in before lying down next to her.

That's when I smelled smoke.

57

I WENT RIGID. The truck, the shadows, the sense of being watched flooded my mind, twisting it into knots. I sprang to the window. The smell was gone, but soon I got another whiff. Cigarette smoke. The wind was from the west.

I left our room and slipped into the empty bedroom in the front corner of the house, keeping tight to the curtains. I didn't see anyone or anything. I went back to the bedroom and put on a shirt and some jeans, slipped downstairs, and found my boots and a jacket. I let myself out through the garage, grabbing a shovel off the wall. I skirted the trees and bushes, keeping to the shadows and working my way up to the top of our property with my nostrils wide.

When I got to the gates, I climbed up over the brick wall and dropped down outside. If someone was watching, it was more likely they'd have been on the outside of the fence rather than inside. I moved carefully, darting from tree to tree and scanning the area in front of me. When I got to the corner of the fence, I peeked my head around and saw him in the moonlight.

A bulky figure three quarters of the way down the fence line, leaning against it with his back to me, his face turned toward the house. I saw the orange glow of his cigarette. The tightness in my throat, the pounding in my chest, boiled into an instant rage. At the same time, I was horrified, the way you are when you take off your pants and see a tick fat with blood, buried in the soft meat of your flank.

In that moment, I believed that they knew about everything. That my meeting with the FBI witches was a sick game. They were toying with me. They knew about Ben, just as they would know about my stealing into King Corp to destroy the files. Everything I did was exposed because of this tick. I walked toward him with the shovel held tight to my leg.

I was ten feet away before he spun and gasped, dropping the cigarette. In the crook of his arm was a twelve gauge.

"Russel? What the fuck?"

The gun was at his waist, his finger fumbling for the safety. Without thinking, I swung the shovel and the blade clanged into the side of his skull, numbing my hands. He dropped and the shotgun's barrel rang against the steel fence. The split in his head met the corner of his eye, filling it with dark blood. His chest heaved in short rapid spasms and his arms and legs shivered until they stopped. He took one deep final gasp, shuddered, then his chest deflated, the air slowly hissing past his lips.

"Oh, fuck."

I was trembling, but the surge of panic made it easy for me to drag him by the heels toward the empty foundation. I pulled him to the edge of the trench, took the keys from his pocket, then rolled him in. The thump of his body was muted by the damp earth. I ran back and got his shotgun and the shovel, then doubled back again to pick up the cigarette butt. I pinched it between my fingers, cursed, and dropped it, cooling my fingers in my mouth, then flicking them in the night air. I picked up the butt more carefully this time, holding it by the filter, my nostrils filling with the stink of burning tobacco.

Into the trench they went, shovel, gun, and his smoke. I looked up at our bedroom. No sign of life. Then I climbed up onto Dino's bulldozer and fired it up. Pungent diesel filled the air as the dozer sputtered and came to life. Everyone in King Corp had spent at least two weeks on a machine. It was part of James's training from the start. He always said he wanted his executives to know what it felt like to move the dirt.

I backed up the dozer and attacked the corner of the bigger pile, pushing it toward the dark gash in the earth just this side of the crooked concrete wall. It took less than an hour to fill it, all the way around. Not a perfect job, but effective, and I ran the inside track of the dozer along the edge of the foundation to pack it tight.

By the time I was finished, the sky was brightening in the east, but the half-moon had disappeared behind a thick stack of clouds pushing toward us on that west wind. When I cut the engine, my ringing ears were filled with the hiss of the trees. I knew his truck would be up on the main road. I would find it and dump it in the Wal-Mart parking lot in Auburn. I shivered and pulled my coat tight around my shoulders, walking the perimeter of the foundation, sick from the smell of diesel and from what I had done, but at the same time light-headed over how perfectly I had covered it up.

58

Bucky's eyes shot open. It was pitch dark. Scott's snoring shook the rafters and the wall between their two rooms. Bucky's feet were on the floor. He blew into his hands, pacing the bare wood floor, the eagerness to get back making his skin crawl.

He started a fire in the stove, then filled the sink with hot water to do the dishes later before filling the pot to make coffee. After dressing, he put on both coat and boots and fumbled around outside in the dark, draining the water lines, shuttering the windows against the coming winter. That done, he took some fish from last night's dinner and put it into a pan with some potatoes and onions.

Scott appeared, bleary-eyed and scratching his stomach between the button holes of his one-piece underwear.

"Never thought I'd be sick of that smell," he said, pouring two cups of coffee and sitting down at the table.

"Too much of a good thing," Bucky said, emptying the frying pan onto two plates and setting them down.

"You'd think it was you who was stir-crazy to get out

of this place," Scott said. "Banging around underneath the floor in the dark."

"You're the one who wanted to leave last night," Bucky said.

"I think in your younger days you weren't afraid of the dark," Scott said, grinning.

Bucky chewed carefully, staring at his plate. He took a swig of coffee and winced.

"What's wrong?" Scott asked.

"Little strong."

"Not the coffee."

"Just a feeling," Bucky said, swallowing his last bite. "Maybe we should have gone back across in the dark. I've got that GPS."

"I was kidding you, Buck. It's not about Mike Allen?"

"No," Bucky said, wiping up the grease with a folded piece of bread. "He'll be fine. Relieved, I bet."

"It's bad?"

"Like I said, lots of stealing," Bucky said. "Everything's behind."

He looked up. Scott stared out the window at the pale light, his lip curled.

"Ready?" Scott asked.

"Put your stuff in the boat," Bucky said. "Let me rinse these and close up."

In minutes they were out on the water, cresting the foamy rollers, knit caps pulled tight on their heads, engines drumming steadily for home in the light of dawn. Scott kept his boat in the smooth water of Bucky's wake. By the time they got back, even the harbor was in a chop. The sky was angry and gray and the wind howled through the leafless trees, rocking the few boats that remained at dock and casting a spray across the water's surface. Bucky tied off both boats and climbed into his truck, dialing Russel's number before the door was shut. Scott got in on the other side.

Bucky started the engine while Russel's phone rang. He hung up when he got voice mail, then listened to his own messages. Russel left one at three a.m. telling how he'd followed Thane to the offices, saying he could show someone the window where the lights had gone on and that that might give them a clue to what he was doing.

"Can't be anything good," Russel said with a yawn before hanging up.

Bucky flipped his phone shut, comforted by the recent message. It would explain why Russel hadn't answered his phone. After being up so late, he probably turned it off to get some sleep. And it was quite possible that Russel's late-night observation would give them a leg up on the enemy.

Their plan now was to drive to New York to see Mike Allen in person. Scott insisted that they stop on the way so he could see his fiancée, Emily, and also his mom. Bucky couldn't argue, and it wasn't long anyway before they were racing down the interstate for Manhattan, Scott on the phone, setting up a meeting with the King Corp board chairman.

Mike Allen's personal office was a corner of glass overlooking Central Park. Mike sat facing them in a dimpled crimson leather chair. His gray suit, as always, was crisply pressed. The bright green handkerchief in his pocket matched the fashionable tie. Mike was dressed for business. He even had his lawyer.

Bucky had a low regard for lawyers. On their own they weren't always bad, but they tended to talk too much and he'd never seen anyone bring a lawyer to a meeting with good intentions. Like the lawyer and Mike, Scott also wore a suit. Bucky was comfortable, though, even in the fancy office, wearing boots, jeans, and a short camo jacket that matched his cap.

"I spoke with the woman agent in charge of the investigation," Mike said. "She said she wouldn't confirm or deny that Thane is a suspect."

"But she cleared me?" Scott said.

"I knew it wasn't you from the start," Mike said. "Come on."

"So, you'll help us?" Scott asked.

Bucky heard the lawyer clear his throat and say, "We've talked with the SEC. We have to be careful. This is a public company. Our allegiance in all this has to be to the shareholders."

"Mike?" Scott said. Bucky heard the pinching sound of Scott's fingers digging into the leather armrests.

"You know how I feel," Mike said. "Your dad and I went way back. But we don't want to jump to conclusions. Look, people were saying you were the one. I said nothing. We need to make sure, that's all. You guys were friends."

"Yeah? Ben was our friend," Scott said. "And my dad treated him like a son. Bucky saw his footprint that night, and the FBI is testing the slugs they took out of Ben to see if they came from *his* gun."

"But the FBI says they'll neither confirm nor deny," Mike said, holding his hands up. "That's how they said it. What am I supposed to do? If it's him, why won't they say?"

"They don't care if you leave Thane in charge, bleeding this company. They're worried about headlines. They want to take down the union, organized crime, not some corporate executive. You think they care what happens to this company?"

"So," Mike said, with a sigh, "you want me to call a meeting?"

"Right away."

"And if I do, and they want to stay with Thane?"

"How long will it take to get them together?"

"At least three days," Mike said. "I need a quorum."

"Do you think any of the old partners will help me?" Scott said.

"A lot of them are gone," Mike said. "But the ones who are there? Morris and Snyder you can probably count on."

"Good," Scott said, his jaw set. "In three days, Bucky and I will have enough to make it easy for them."

59

"And you didn't know?" he asks.

"I was like one of those bubbles in the market," I say. I see his confusion.

"The stock market," I say. "A bubble. Everything's hot, racing along. It's all good. You can't lose."

"Okay."

"Then it bursts."

Jessica dropped Tommy at school, then picked me up at the Wal-Mart. A fat guy with a long beard and thick glasses looked at me funny when I got out of Russel's truck, but he climbed into an old Chrysler station wagon, sagging and rusty. He was no federal agent.

I got into the H2 and Jessica slid over. She wore a leather coat and sunglasses, even though the sky was gray and windy.

"I saw how red your eyes are in the bathroom," I said, glancing over.

"We've all got issues," she said, staring straight ahead.

"I didn't mean it like that," I said. "I'm worried, that's all."

"Me too," she said, looking over at me. "You just buried Bucky's son in our foundation."

"You're the one who says pretend like it didn't happen."

"Only now how are we going to have them fix it? Just don't dig here, fellas. That Jimmy Hoffa thing. You know. Christ."

"So, we'll build it a little crooked like you wanted to in the first place."

"But *Dino* won't."

"I'll find someone."

She turned facing the road again and we drove in silence. She puffed her cheeks and let some air out and seemed to relax.

"Let's take a vacation," she said.

"Sure."

"I'm serious."

"Why not?" I said, still sarcastic.

"Yeah," she said, not getting it. "Remember when they found out about the Iran-Contra scandal? Reagan was at his ranch, and they asked him about it and he just smiled and got on his horse and rode off waving to everyone? That's how you do it."

I shook my head, but knew better than to argue, so I smiled and asked her where she wanted to go. She decided Barbados was the place. Sandy Lane. Five grand a night for a luxury suite. I figured, what the hell. We told Amy we needed her to watch Tommy for three days straight. I called the pilots and told them to saddle up. The Citation X had us there by teatime.

We watched the sun melt into the ocean from two

lounge chairs on the beach. Next to me in the sand I'd buried six empty bottles of Banks beer. Jessica climbed over on top of me, rum on her breath.

"God it's beautiful," she said.

I took her to the room and you would have thought we were back in that first summer we met. After, I lay spread-eagle on that big bed, the paddle fan slowly spinning, the tiny waves gurgling against the sand beyond our terrace. I shut my eyes. Everything seemed okay.

Then we went to dinner. The Ledges. A table on the water's edge, looking down at the sheer stone and the turquoise water sloshing below. We were drinking and laughing at the stuffy British foursome two tables down. One of the men had a bad rug and the tight-faced women were bleached-blond with crooked teeth and saggy necks.

The fun brought tears to our eyes and I wiped mine on a napkin. Jessica got up to use the ladies' room. I watched her go, her narrow hips and waist swaying slightly off key from her high heels and the wine. I sighed when she disappeared up the steps, then signaled the waiter and ordered another bottle of Dom.

I waited until my head began to nod, then I shook myself and stood up. My blood was instantly hot with panic and something more. I went upstairs, gripping the handrail to keep my balance. I scanned the bar. Men in blue blazers and women in white and floral dresses, made up for the night with fancy purses and matching shoes. Jessica wasn't there. The bathrooms were just beyond. I eyed the hostess, then ducked into the little hallway and rapped on the bathroom door, calling her name.

A fifty-something woman with fake boobs and a face-lift opened the door and glared. I told her I was looking for my wife and she told me she was the only one in there. I turned to the hostess.

"My wife," I said.

"I think she may have stepped out for some air," the hostess said in a heavy Dutch accent.

I pushed through a country-club-looking foursome who had just arrived and stood glaring around from the top of the steps. There was a doorman there in a uniform and hat, the guy who flagged cabs off the street. In his eye was something I didn't like.

"Where is she?" I asked.

He tried to pretend ignorance.

"Little," I said, holding my hand at her height. "Pretty. Dark hair. My wife."

His eyes got wide and flickered to my right. I jumped down the steps and started down the curve of the drive where three small cabs were queued up. They were empty. There was a plank fence that ran along the drive and when I reached the corner of it, I saw a little gathering. Three cabbies and my wife. She had a pipe in her mouth, drawing from a blue flame one of them provided from an upside-down Butane lighter. She looked at me with those glassy eyes, giggling, smoke curling from her nose. The cabbies laughed with her. Their teeth glowing in the dark.

One of the cabbies casually slid his hand off of her ass.

"And?"

I sigh and say, "I knocked one down, but he wouldn't fight. I was shouting. They were scared shitless. She told me to calm down."

"Did you?"

"I shoved her a little too," I say, looking him in the eye. "I'm not proud of it. We made up.

"Anger and sex," I say, smiling stupidly at the shrink. "It's a wild brew."

"Did she have a problem?" he asks.

"Looking back, I probably did too."

"You used drugs?"

"I was drinking like a fish. That's a drug, right?"

"The painkillers, though? Cocaine? That's what she was smoking?"

"Not me. She said she needed something. We were on vacation. The next day she got ahold of two bottles of Vicodin. Not that I couldn't have used it. I was crawling out of my skin. My hands shaking like an old lady's. The sun burning through the veins in my eyelids. Hungover. Cotton mouth. Tired. Sleeping like shit. Yeah, it was a hell of a vacation. On paper."

"And then you went back?"

"Yeah. What we deserved, I guess. Out of the pan, and into the fire."

60

WE WENT HOME and had a nice family dinner. Since we'd been gone, Jessica stayed straight long enough to put together a stir-fry with chicken and vegetables. Good food. Good for you. She grilled Tommy about school and how late Amy let him stay up. The caring mom.

I listened and worked on a bottle of Heron Hill Riesling, reminding Tommy that nothing came easy and getting a two on his math homework wouldn't get him much more than a job pumping gas. His eyes filled up, the lower lip came out, and he asked to be excused. Jessica gave me a frown, and I told her I wished my old man cared enough to encourage me to do my homework.

We went to bed like everything was normal. Except she was higher than a kite and I was smashed so bad I couldn't properly enunciate "good night."

The next morning, I took four Advils and left without waking anyone. I stopped at Johnny Angel's for a bacon, egg, and cheese sandwich and a coffee, forgetting to wipe the crumbs off my suit until I was walking into the office.

It was weird going in, thinking that the last time I'd been there was the middle of the night to steal some files.

Darlene wore this scared face that put a lump in my throat. She told me she was sorry and I looked into my office and saw Scott sitting there, waiting. I waved her off, telling her no problem, walked in, and shut the door behind me.

"Welcome back," I said, extending my hand.

He sat looking at it. I shrugged and sat down behind my desk, firing up my computer.

"What can I do for you?" I asked, my eyes on the screen like I was unconcerned.

"It's over," he said. "I want you to know that."

I laughed and looked at him.

"That it?" I said.

He leaned toward me, his ears flattening against his head.

"The board is meeting tomorrow in New York," he said. "You'll be finished. I thought I'd let you know. For old times' sake."

"To make up for the time I covered your back outside Sutter's Mill when those three guys jumped you?" I said.

"My family made you a lot of money since then," he said. "The chance you got here, most people would cut their arm off for. The top one half of one percent."

"You guys didn't do too bad off of me, either," I said.

His face turned a deeper shade of red.

"The FBI is on you."

"Funny," I said. "I've been working with them for a month now and no one said anything about me being on the wrong side."

"Don't they say the husband is always the last to know?" he said.

The remark hit home and my mind spun this way and that, Johnny G came to mind. Did Scott really know something or was he just trying to fluster me?

"I got work to do," I said, punching in my password and logging on.

"Payoffs?"

"Whatever it takes to get this baby done," I said, typing. "Building downstate is something your dad never did. It takes a special understanding."

"Fuck you," he said, getting up from his chair and reaching for the door. "Enjoy your last day."

61

THE CALL FROM MIKE ALLEN came within a half hour. I was rereading an e-mail update from Con Trac for the tenth time, trying to focus, but I pretended like Mike's call was just part of another busy day and something that I'd been expecting. He was nice, but there was enough distance in his voice to tell me I was now on my own with the board. I called Jessica and asked her if she needed anything on Madison Avenue.

"They called an emergency board meeting," I said. "It'd be good to have you with me. For luck."

My tone of voice was what I thought she would have wanted. What she would respect. Confident. Bold. At that moment, I was actually feeling that way. This wasn't about murder, I knew. I hadn't been arrested. This was about business.

My mind rang with the success stories she'd reminded me of. Enron. Martha Stewart. There was no reason not to be confident. For every executive punished for robbing a company blind, twenty others floated to earth with their golden parachutes. I'd seen deals get done just on one guy's nerve. There was no reason mine couldn't fend off this attack.

We got a suite at the Waldorf because the best rooms

at the Palace were all filled up. We had dinner at Fresco by Scotto and drank three bottles of Opus One with dinner. Afterward, I had a fifty-year-old port while Jessica sipped a Sauterne. Back at the hotel, we were both too drunk to do anything and she didn't even try to hide the three pills she popped down. The bed spun me to sleep, but it was like some kind of crash landing.

I kept waking up. Sweating. Delirious. Dreaming about Ben and Russel, Johnny G and Jessica. I groped for her somewhere in the night and she shoved me off. Sometime before daylight, my head started to pound. My mouth was dry. I stumbled to the bathroom and pulled the towel down off the mirror. My eyes were red, my skin pale and green, and my hair—where it wasn't plastered to my temples—stuck out all over the place. I threw up, then took four Advils again and lay back down, wishing away the minutes until the medicine could silence the drumbeat.

Somehow, I fell back asleep and when I woke, sun streamed bright through the gap in the curtains. I looked at the clock. I was late for the meeting.

The sheets were twisted and damp and Jessica slept with her back to me, snoring softly, her long dark hair a tangle. My mind wandered back over the dreams I'd had. I put my hand on Jessica's shoulder and jostled her to wake up and wish me luck. She swatted at me and moaned to go away.

I put on a suit and got some coffee downstairs. By the time I stepped into the waiting limousine my headache was muted. Mike Allen's secretary, a middle-aged woman who always had a pleasant smile, looked down and clutched at her papers when I walked by. I said good morning and if she replied, I didn't hear it. When I walked into the boardroom, Scott's face was the first one I saw.

62

J ESSICA HEARD A KNOCK at the door. She pulled the pillow tight, but she kept hearing it.

"I'm sleeping," she said.

It kept coming. She threw off the covers, and yanked open the door.

Pete grinned at her and licked the perpetual sore on his lower lip. He was dressed in the same jeans jacket she'd first seen him in at Johnny's mountain cabin and his hair was still slicked back.

"You called Johnny's cell?" he said. His eyes ran up and down the front of her silk teddy and he grinned. "Don't."

"What do you mean?"

He leaned toward her, looked around the hall, and softly said, "It's over. The feds. Found your husband's pal buried in the mud. Got his gun. Prints. Ballistics. All that shit looks like it's going to add up. Don't call no more."

"Where's Johnny?"

Pete looked at his watch and said, "Right about now, he's pullin' the sheet off a nude statue at the Met. He's a classy guy, you know. You? You're more my speed. I don't know, maybe you and me could pick up where you and him left off."

"You're shit," she said, slamming the door.

She heard his creepy laughter through the door and waited until it was gone before she went into the bathroom and took two pills. She took a shower, dressed, and put on perfume. The medicine started to work. She took a car to the Met, stopping only at an office supply store on the way to buy a small Dictaphone. As she ran back to the waiting car, she let the wrapper fall to the street, and tucked the Dictaphone into her purse.

The massive columns reminded her of a giant courthouse. Inside the lobby, there was a special velvet-roped entrance hung with a sign announcing the special VIP opening of the United Workers Union Donatello Exhibit. Jessica floated past the attendant who asked if he could please see her invitation.

She pretended not to hear. When he caught up to her and put his hand on her arm, she said, "I'm supposed to find John Garret, Johnny G. With the union."

The attendant's eyes went quickly up and down her figure. He swallowed and tried to smile, nodding his head. Jessica kept going, down the stairs into the sculpture courtyard, where curtains and a stage provided the backdrop to a huge sculpture in the center of the stone floor.

About a hundred people in suits and dresses tilted their heads up at Johnny's massive form. The slabs of his hands were planted on either side of a small wooden podium. He wore a tuxedo with a red tie and cummerbund and a red rose in his lapel.

Jessica descended the steps and stood at the back. The

room was abuzz around her, dreamlike because of her pills. The minute Johnny unveiled the statue to the sound of gentle applause, she eased her way through the crowd. She got to him before he was off the small stage and she stepped up. The woman she recognized as his bleached-blond wife was talking with another woman just behind him.

Johnny was listening to the mayor with an empty expression on his face.

She hooked her arm in his and tugged him away.

"Johnny," she said, beginning to walk him across the stage toward three short steps.

Johnny whipped his arm free. His face snarled, but his words were soft. "Are you fucking kidding me?"

"Don't call?" she said, twisting her mouth and tilting her head.

Johnny spun this way and that, then glanced back at his wife, who was still gabbing. He locked his fingers on to her upper arm and dragged her off toward the pearl curtains that hung immediately behind the stage. Jessica let out a small yelp, but she kept her feet moving and managed to somehow stay upright on her high heels.

"Jesus," she said.

"You don't just come here."

"You don't want to see me, Johnny?" she said, lowering her voice. She touched his cheek.

"You crazy slit," he said, but his tone had changed. "What are you, high? I knew you were crazy. Fuck."

"Crazy 'cause of you," she said, her voice husky.

"Fucking crazy," he said.

"Remember the Essex House? It's right down the street."

He looked over her shoulder, then grabbed her bottom

and pushed his hips against her and she felt him through the suit and smiled.

They went up the back stairs and took a cab down Fifth Avenue, their hands already groping each other through their clothes. Johnny got the room while Jessica fumbled with the Dictaphone inside her purse, clicking it on. In the elevator, she lightly kissed his ear and pushed his grabbing hands off her bottom, telling him to wait.

In the room, she put her purse on the night table and took off everything but her black lace underwear and bra, straddling him on the bed.

63

Afterward, jessica ran a nail through the thick fur on Johnny's chest. He puffed a Marlboro and stared at the ceiling. Jessica twirled her finger until it was wrapped in the graying hair. She gave a little tug.

"Did you ever kill a man?"

"Who?"

"Anyone," she said, softening her voice. "Could you do that?"

"What's it to you, huh?"

"Something about a man that can do that. That power," she said. "Like Thane."

Johnny snorted.

"The rookie?" he said, wincing with pity.

"You did?"

"Milo was mine," he said, dragging on his smoke.

"Among others," he added, exhaling two plumes out his nose. "That James King thing your husband did? That was like a mugger. A ghetto stabbing or something. Three bullets in the brain. That's how you do it."

She grinned at him, shaking her head.

"What?" he said, his eyes shifting to her.

"I want a little help with something."

His laugh came out like a bark. "Sure you do. You think I didn't know that? But your problems, I can't fix."

"I guess you'd call it a fix," she said, gently tugging his chest hair again.

"Dope?"

"Vicodin. Vicodin," she said. "Something for the edge."

"You look high."

"It's not high. Give me a break."

Johnny scowled and said, "Oh? And you think I owe you a fucking favor? Huh?"

He rolled away, nodding his head, mumbling about favors, and reached for the purse on the nightstand.

Her heart froze.

But he pushed her purse aside, took the notepad, and wrote down a New Jersey phone number. He tore off the paper and handed it to her. "Anton. You tell him I said it's okay."

"I'd like a decent supply," she said, letting go of his chest hair and tracing her finger up the hill of his belly. "I'm thinking about a trip."

"You do that again," he said, his voice husky. "You won't have to worry."

He put his hand on the back of her head and slowly pushed her down.

64

I LOOKED AWAY FROM SCOTT and walked in.

"Thane," Mike Allen said, rising from his seat, "I've been calling your cell phone."

"They're running the fiber optics today," I said, showing my somber face around the table. "We had a non-union crew and the UWU was trying to shut it down. It's all set now."

I sat down in an empty leather chair and sighed, giving them a feel for how difficult things were.

"I thought you were in Barbados," Scott said.

"I had a vacation scheduled that I cut short," I said, looking impassively at him. "Is that what this is about? My vacation schedule?"

"Thane," Mike said, sitting down himself, "this project is in trouble. The stock is half of what it was a month ago. We have a fiduciary duty as a board."

"You got to make a call," I said, nodding and looking around. "I know that. I know the problems, believe me. I'm living it. It's damn easy to come in halfway into this thing with a bunch of unions that this company has never done business with that we're trying to get along with to get this thing done and say, this is wrong and that's wrong. I know it's wrong. I'm working to make it right."

"The purpose of this meeting—" Mike Allen began.

"No," I said, cutting him off, "we all know the purpose. There's a reason people don't like to build downstate. There's a reason King Corp has never done it. News flash. The decision to do Garden State was James's, not mine. I like the Miami Beach deal. We just hit a home run in Toronto with the same kind of project. Hotel. Shops. A parking garage.

"We weren't ready for this, but there it was. You needed someone to take over. Everyone knows the whole thing with James was a tragedy. It's unbelievable. And it's a tragedy the FBI thought his own son did it. But it all happened and you and I were left to deal with it.

"You people want to jump ship midstream?" I said, opening my arms. "Be my guest. Let Scott deal with the unions. Let him work through his father's mess with Con Trac."

"My father never wanted Con Trac to do this job," Scott said.

I looked at him for a moment and said, "Oh, you knew what he wanted, right? He told you everything, because what he really intended to do when he took this company public was turn it over to you. I forgot."

I snorted, looked down, and shook my head in pity.

"What about the FBI now?" Scott said, pointing at me. "They say you're in with the union."

"Yeah, last week it was you," I said. "You know what the FBI stands for? Famous But Incompetent. They're media hounds. I've been working with them as an informant for the past month. They wired me up and sent me to a meeting with Johnny G. He tried to push this deal *away* from Con Trac to OBG. Ask them. Let's get the tape.

"The FBI," I said, snorting again. "They don't know what they want. Believe me, their business has nothing to do with getting that mall built. They've been trying to break this union for years. Where are they? They don't know who to point their finger at next."

"You've seen the financials," Scott said, ignoring me and looking around the room. He tapped his palm on a stack of papers in front of him. "Money going out totally out of sync with what's being done on-site. This project is a disaster. The only people making money are these nebulous contractors. Three thousand dollars a day for a Porta Potti? A hundred thousand dollars a week for twenty floodlight generators but there's only two on-site and the plumbers can't work after dark?

"You heard Agent Lee," he said, nodding at the speakerphone in the middle of the long table. "They know I'm not involved in what's happening. Thane? Maybe he's right. Maybe he's just drunk with power and he got sloppy, forgetting everything he ever knew and spending money like water. But if he's really in on this? If what the FBI thinks is going on really is? I hope everyone here has real good indemnification policies."

I smiled at that remark.

Mike Allen shook his head, and said, "There's no need for that."

"There is a need for it," Scott said, standing up and thumping his stack of documents again. "I'm not fucking around and I'm not worried about anyone's feelings. This is in black and white. My lawyers are making a record of it."

Mike Allen said something about threats not being necessary. Tension was high, and he walked Scott out of the boardroom. When Mike came back, I expected we'd talk some more. Scott had obviously hurt his case. But instead, Mike gave me the same "thanks for coming" treatment and escorted me out as well. The board had to take everything into consideration.

He said they'd call me.

My limo crawled in the brutal morning traffic. I tried Jessica's cell phone and got voice mail. There was no answer in the room. Maybe she was in the shower. But when I got to the Waldorf, our room was empty.

My cell phone rang. It was Mike Allen.

The board was going to take the company in another direction.

My stomach took a nosedive.

65

IN THE CORNER OF THE ROOM off the tiny kitchen, there was a musty old La-Z-Boy. Bucky sat there with his boots and jacket on. There was an old movie on TV. James Cagney, ranting to his dead ma. Bucky nodded off.

Judy shook his arm and asked him if he could come to bed. He could use some real sleep. He looked at her, trying to place just where they were, then shook his head and got up. He paced the cramped room a few times, then told her he was going out.

"Where?" she asked.

"I gotta keep looking," he said.

"Where?"

He stared at her with his hand on the doorknob. Her eyes welled up behind her glasses and she twisted the belt of her robe between her fingers.

"I gotta go," Bucky said, choking.

He drove to Russel's house, knowing he'd feel that sick knot in his stomach when he didn't see the truck and feeling it even more powerfully than he remembered. He went in, checked the answering machine, called his son's name as he dashed through the narrow hall, up the stairs, through the bedrooms.

He drove to King Corp's offices, his teeth clenched so tight that his jaw hurt by the time he got there. He circled the building, covering the same ground he'd gone over ten times in the past few days. This was the last spot he knew Russel had been. The trail was here. There was always a trail. But he couldn't find it.

His limbs were heavy from lack of sleep. His eyes burned. He stifled a yawn and circled the office building again, then changed direction and walked to the FBI offices. He sat on a low stone wall outside the glass doors. People started to show up for work. When Bucky saw the two women, he stood and greeted them. They asked if he had word from his son and their faces turned somber at the news he hadn't.

"We've been on him from the minute he touched down," Agent Lee said, her face long at the news that his son hadn't turned up.

"Did you bug him?" Bucky asked.

"The house and the cell," Agent Rooks said.

"The surveillance team knows about your son," Agent Lee said. "If they hear anything, we'll know about it right away and we'll call you first thing."

Bucky looked at them for a minute. Agent Lee glanced at the door and said, "Well."

"Are you going to get him?"

"The prints on the gun," Agent Lee said, "they're his. We're waiting for ballistics. It's coming together."

"We'll get him," Rooks said.

Bucky nodded and turned away. His truck took him to Skaneateles. Thane's house. He drove down the private road and into the driveway, stopping outside the gates.

Through the bars he could see the yellow house. Beyond the fence in the empty lot were two mountains of dirt, one with a sizable chunk carved out.

Bucky sat staring at it.

He put his hand to his face and stroked his mustache, making an O with his mouth, then he slammed the Suburban in reverse and backed out with tires squealing. He drove up to the main road, went past a set of barns to the construction road leading to the dirt piles. The truck slid to a sideways stop. Bucky got out and coughed in the cloud of dust, sweeping it aside with his hands, swimming toward the broken dirt pile.

An unfinished job.

The rusted yellow dozer was parked at an angle in front of the foundation. Its tracks covered most of the perimeter. Bucky circled, following them. At the far corner of the foundation, there was an open pit that exposed the concrete corner. The tracks swerved around it. Whoever did the work missed a spot. Sloppy. Someone who didn't know his business. An unfinished job. Like a track in the mud.

Bucky's hand went to his mustache again. He looked around. Thane's house loomed beyond the fence. Bucky walked toward it, breaking the clotted dozer treads under his boots. He stopped at the fence, running his fingers along the edge of a black steel bar, letting a small burr knick his skin. He looked at his finger and the tiny drop of blood, then walked away from the lake with his eyes on the other side of the fence. Tall trees obstructed his view of the house. When he came to an opening, he anchored his feet and studied the ground.

Trampled grass. A cigarette butt in the blades beyond the fence. Bucky knelt and reached through, taking the tan filter in his fingers. He held it at arm's length, squinting until he could make out the word "Marlboro." Russel's brand. Bucky stood and stepped carefully back, thinking about the weather since Russel's message. Some rain the day he got the message, the day he brought Scott back. But dry since.

He looked at the spot where Russel must have stood, making a ten-foot circle around it in his mind. He got down on his hands and knees and started through it, blade by blade, breaking them as he went to mark his own progress.

After a time, his back and knees began to ache. He looked up at the field, five acres. A sea of faded grass surrounding the empty foundation. He knew he'd look at every one of them before he went back to that little room.

An hour later, he found the russet patch of dried blood.

66

I PACED THE ROOM. I took a walk, through the streets to Central Park. Down the Literary Walk. The place I saw her first. I stopped at Bethesda Fountain and sat down, listening to the water's hiss, watching a bum trundle under the bridge with his shopping cart. I must have tried her cell phone a hundred times before I gave up and just walked back to the hotel in a daze.

The room was empty.

I tried her cell phone some more. When the phone rang, I snatched it so hard the base crashed to the floor. It was Amy, asking what time we'd be back because her mother had had a small stroke. I was flustered enough to ask her to stay anyway. Thinking of the cash we'd gotten from the job site, I offered her a thousand dollars. I offered her five thousand. Ten.

"Mr. Coder," she said, beginning to cry. "I can't for anything. It's my mom."

I left a note on the bed that read, "CALL ME!!!" then took a car to Teterboro, dialing her cell phone continuously. When I saw the stony look on Frank's face, I knew I wasn't flying the Citation X back. I called the office to have Darlene get me a flight from Newark. All I got was voice mail. The receptionist told me that Darlene was gone. She no longer worked there.

I got my own flight, paid with a credit card, and took a cab to the house. When we rolled through the gates, I saw a big orange excavator in the empty lot, its bucket swinging and dumping dirt. I felt a pain in my chest, a tight stabbing that stole my breath. Bucky's Suburban was there too. And a state police cruiser.

Amy was waiting at the door and she walked past me and got into her car without speaking. I went to the window and watched them working, not paying attention to the house or me, knowing they hadn't seen the cab. I called for Tommy, my voice shaking, but got no answer. He was downstairs, playing Xbox. I tousled his hair and asked if his mom had called. He said no without looking up. I pulled the plug on the TV and told him to come on. Now.

He helped me stuff a suitcase with his clothes. While I zipped it up, he went to the window.

"Cool," he said. "What are they doing?"

I looked out. The machine was clawing at the foundation.

"Come on," I said, grabbing Tommy by the arm.

"Can I bring the Xbox?" he asked.

"You got two seconds," I said.

He dashed for the stairs and I went into our bedroom and grabbed the bag of money. Our payoff from the project. Most of the half million in cash was still there.

We piled into the H2 and I burned up the driveway, half expecting to see police lights in my rearview. I drove Tommy to my mom's house. I was like a man with a tick, dialing her number on my cell phone, getting no answer, and snapping it shut, only to open it again a minute later. As I pulled down the street, I realized it had been nearly a year since I'd been there to see her. Last Christmas.

It hadn't changed. It never would. A single-story, white aluminum box squeezed into a row of houses whose only difference was the make of the car in their tiny driveway.

She was in there, her hair gray, bent over, TV too loud, waiting for the end. There was the recliner I bought her in the corner. Still stacked with books. The plant long dead. I finally got the volume turned down on the TV. She sat scowling up at me from the musty couch.

"I need you to take Tommy for a while, Mom," I said.

"Where's the mother?" she asked, her eyes unwavering and cold.

"Ma, I need you."

Her chin trembled a bit and her eyes moistened.

"He can stay in your room," she said. "Come here, Tommy. Give Grandma a kiss. That's it. Take that to your father's old room.

"Now put that on," she said to me.

I put the TV on and took Tommy by the hand and down the hall. My old room was smaller than my closet at home. I moved some dusty trophies off the bureau and set down his suitcase. The bed still had that old blue NY Giants cover on it, although it seemed to sag even more in the middle. Tommy clutched a gym bag to his chest. Inside was the Xbox.

"It's not for long," I said, squeezing his shoulder.

He looked up at me, shaking his head.

"No, Dad," he said.

"Don't 'no' me, son. I don't want to do this, but I have to," I said.

"Where's Mom?" he said, looking at his sneakers and starting to cry.

"Now look it," I said, kneeling down, pulling him to me, and squeezing him. "Don't you do this. You're my man. You're my little man, right?"

When he stopped, I sat him on the edge of the bed and went out into the hall. I crossed through the living room and into my parents' room, taking the dusty TV off the bureau and carrying it back past my mother with the cord dragging between my feet.

"That's your father's TV," she said, glowering.

"Oh, he needs it?" I said, glaring right back at her. "You be nice to Tommy, Mom. God damn it, I need this. Please."

"Where *is* the mother?" she said, softer this time, her eyes darting toward the door.

"I'll call you, Ma," I said.

I set up the TV in my old room and helped Tommy hook up his Xbox. He asked me to play *Ghost Recon*. Just one game. I told him I was sorry, kissed his head, messed up his hair, and left him. I got two grocery bags out of the kitchen, took them to the car, and filled them with half the money. A lot. More than two hundred grand. That's what I handed to my mom when I asked her again to be nice.

"Buy him some things, Mom," I said. "For that game if he wants it. Some clothes."

"Are you in *trouble*?" she asked, glancing at the money and raising her voice above Judge Judy.

I looked down the hall and softly said, "I don't know, Ma. Maybe."

67

ANTON REACHED DOWN and took the last of Jessica's cash. It was a small pharmacy on the hill in downtown Secaucus. The seams between the faded linoleum floor tiles were black with dirt and it smelled like formaldehyde and rubbing alcohol. In her hand was the bag containing six vials of Vicodin. That would last her a while.

Before Anton could give back her change, the phone behind the counter rang. He picked it up, answering in his thick Italian accent.

"For you," he said, handing her the phone.

She raised her eyebrows and put the receiver to her ear.

"That was nice," Johnny said in a rough voice. "Real nice. So I thought I'd do you a favor."

"I thought we couldn't talk on the phone," she said.

"Not on yours, or his," Johnny said. "The two of you are red-hot. That's my favor. Don't go home, and be careful what you say on your phone. The phones are tapped and they got transponders on the cars. I told your husband it's not smart to run off to the sunshine when there's work to be done. Watch your credit cards too, they can be on you in a couple of minutes."

"Where am I supposed to go?" she asked.

"What am I, a fucking guidance counselor?" he said. "I'm you, Switzerland looks good. You got some money there."

The bell on the door in the front of the pharmacy tinkled and Jessica spun around. It was just two teenagers.

"I need some to get there," she said, her voice small.

"Yeah," he said. "You do."

"Will you help?"

"I'm no fucking bank."

"I need a car," she said.

"It'll cost you," he said. "Everything will, and I don't need another blow job right now, so you better think. I gave you a bagful of Franklins a couple weeks ago."

"Thane," she said.

"There you go."

"Can you get me a car right away?"

"For a hundred grand, sure."

She thought and then said, "Give me five hours, say, eight o'clock. Can you have someone take it into Central Park? Go in on Sixth Avenue, take two rights, and pull over at the light at the beginning of the Literary Walk."

"The fuck is that?" he asked.

"There's some statues," she said. "Shakespeare in that circle of flowers. For a hundred thousand dollars your guy can buy a map."

"You're a pain in my ass."

"What kind of car?" she asked, staring at Anton until he looked away.

"I'll see what I can come up with."

"So I can look for it."

"Hang on."

He covered the phone and she heard him talking to someone.

"I got a 1986 El Camino. Kind of a gold. It'll make it to Canada, no problem."

"Eight o'clock. Thanks, Johnny."

"You owe me," he said, and hung up.

68

Pete watched Johnny while he stared at the phone, then looked over at him and said, "Kill them both."

"For a hundred grand?"

"Not for the fucking money," he said, a look of disgust on his face. "Get the money if you can, but I don't want these two yokels trying to outrun the feds. They get snatched, they'll turn. This thing is a fucking mess."

"Women always fuck things up," Pete said.

"What's that supposed to mean?" Johnny said, his eyes blazing.

"I didn't mean nothing," Pete said. "Just women in general."

"Well, this one's smart," Johnny said, "so don't fuck it up."

Johnny picked up the phone and poised his finger over the buttons without dialing.

"Well," he said. "Go."

Pete heard him punching in a number as he closed the door. Out on the street, the day was turning cold. Pete pulled his leather coat close and patted the .357 under his arm. He'd need a throwaway and he knew where to get it. His green Excursion was parked on the sidewalk and he climbed in. The El Camino was out back of a garage in Paterson. Two stupid Guatemalans drove it up from Atlanta with some stolen slot machines they intended to put in the back room of a truck stop off of I-95.

Pete waited for the garage guy to move a couple cars blocking the El Camino, then he got in and headed for the G.W. Bridge. There was another guy with a pawnshop on 117th Street who owed him a favor. In his rearview mirror the sun melted into a blood-red pool beneath the horizon of dark clouds. Pete stared at it and almost swerved into a tractor-trailer.

The guy at the pawnshop had three guns to choose from. One had a homemade silencer, a can of hair mousse, packed with glass and painted black. It had been welded onto a .380 and he broke it down so he could hold the barrel up to the light and check the seam. It looked good, so he snapped it back together and put it in a bag with a box of hollow-point shells.

Retail was two grand. The guy took five hundred for it. Not a bad investment. He knew that for a job like this, Johnny would give him half the cash.

He looked at his watch and knew he had time for a rack of ribs. There was a place a couple blocks away near the Columbia campus. Dinosaur Bar-B-Que. Pete licked his sore, weighing the pain of the spices for the taste of meat that fell off the bone. He decided to take the pain and he headed uptown a few blocks, parking on the street and sitting down in a small booth by himself with a napkin tucked into the collar of his shirt.

The idea of killing that bitch and her stupid husband made him hungry as hell. He ordered a pint of beer and the Big House Special with a full rack of ribs.

"Hungry, aren't you?" the waitress said.

"Goddamn right."

69

One of the cops had ahold of an arm. He pulled the body out of the dirt pile and it rolled over, face up. Clods of earth spilled down the cheeks and out of the ears and the wide vacant eyes.

Bucky cleared his throat and swallowed.

"That's him," he said.

After a minute of standing there, he felt something warm trickle down his chin. He'd bitten right through his lip.

He turned away from his son and watched the dark blue Crown Vic racing its way down the construction road, trailing a cloud of dust. The women agents got out and stopped in front of him.

"Is it?" Agent Lee said, nodding toward the dirt pile.

Bucky nodded.

"I'm sorry," she said, and her cell phone rang.

Bucky turned away. He opened the door to his truck and stopped before climbing in. Agent Lee was talking loud enough for him to hear. She was telling her people she thought they had another one and to stay right with him. She snapped the phone shut and started toward the Crown Vic.

"He's taking the back roads, heading to New York," she said to her partner across the hood. "She called him from someplace in Secaucus. I guess he's got a bag of money and she's got a plan. She told him to meet her at their special place in Central Park, whatever that is."

"We'll give them something special," Agent Rooks said.

"It's a big place."

"Only about a thousand acres of woods, tunnels, and ponds."

The car doors slammed and the two of them drove off. Bucky waited until they were out on the road before he started his engine. Before he put the Suburban in gear, he reached into the backseat, gripping his deer gun with its red laser sight and rattling the box next to it. It was full of twelve gauge slugs. One stop he wouldn't have to make.

He drove out to the road and made a left on Route 41A, heading toward New York.

He knew the story of how they met.

70

I KNEW THEY WERE BEHIND ME. It was a feeling more than anything else. I never really caught them in something stupid, just headlights that always seemed to be about a quarter mile back, no matter how fast or slow I went. The notion of a transponder someplace on the H2 hit me and I considered whether or not I could stop and find it. Where would it be? Under the chassis? Behind the bumper?

Anywhere.

I needed a different plan. They could have pulled me over at any time, but they didn't. They wanted something more. Her? Whatever it was, I had the sense that I didn't have much time. I pulled over and rechecked my map, finding the fastest way to I-84. There was no sense in crawling along like this if they knew where I was anyway.

I needed to get to her. I had the money. She had the plan. If I couldn't lose them between here and there, I didn't deserve to get away. I took the G.W. Bridge, marveling at the universe of lights. A universe of possibilities. The perfect place to get lost. I shot down the Henry

Hudson Parkway and got off at Seventy-ninth Street. It was on Amsterdam I made a quick left on a yellow light. I shot north three blocks until the lights turned on me, then pulled over and ran out of the Hummer. It was still running.

I took off, through the smell of hot food and people walking to and from the spate of streetside restaurants, then checked behind me quick and ducked down Eighty-fifth Street. I sprinted full-out until I crossed Central Park West and disappeared into the black shadows of the trees. I crouched down behind a big maple and watched, my hands clinging to the rough bark, catching my breath while I scanned the street corner.

People in long coats came and went. Cabs. Limos. A few cars. No one running. No one following. After fifteen minutes, a black Town Car with two men in suits drove slowly down the street, their heads searching the sidewalk. Agents. They had no idea and I felt giddy with my success.

I turned toward the heart of the darkness and headed toward where I knew she was waiting.

71

THERE WAS AN ARMY–NAVY STORE in Binghamton and a Home Depot just down the street. Bucky stopped to buy a long green overcoat, an officer's coat stripped of its rank. Thick wool that could hide a firearm. At Home Depot he purchased a hacksaw and a ten-inch half-round file. In his truck, he sawed off the black synthetic stock of his shotgun at the grip, then used the file to smooth the edges. The barrel of the gun was short enough, a slug barrel specially made for deer hunting, short and easy to maneuver.

With his knife, he cut through the pocket of the coat so he could grip the gun beneath it without looking the least suspicious. He got back out onto the highway and called Judy, telling her he wouldn't be home.

"Did you find him?" she asked, crying since she'd picked up the phone.

Bucky didn't answer.

"Oh, God," she said.

"We'll talk when I get back," he said.

"Bucky, what're you gonna do?"

"Just what I can," he said. "I'm hanging up now."

And he did.

He stroked his mustache and rode in silence, cracking the window for some fresh air, keeping pace with the faster traffic, but not wanting to get pulled over with the gun.

When he got to the big city, he found a parking place on the street toward the north end on the west side of Central Park. Leaving the gun on the floor of the backseat, he found a drugstore with a tourist map. He bought a bottle of water and a package of beef jerky that almost made him throw up. He wasn't sure if it was the beef or the stink that came up at him from a subway grate.

Back in the truck, under the dome light, he cursed at the map. The Literary Walk was a big damn place. Maybe a tenth of a mile. Maybe two. There were statues all up and down it. He knew Thane said something about a statue, but never which one.

There was nothing for it. He pulled on the big green coat, slid five shells into the shotgun's magazine, and tucked it under the flap of the coat. He packed another five rounds into the good pocket and slid out onto the sidewalk. Under the streetlamp, he held the map up to get his bearings, then looked around before hopping a low stone wall. He wanted to stick to the woods where he could take a leak like a man.

It was eerie, the smell of the trees and the leaves and the night rustlings of raccoons with the artificial glow of lights and the concrete buildings towering over the tops of the leafless trees. He heard a waterfall and headed toward it, marveling at the clear flow of water in the middle of a rancid city. He checked his watch. It was just past seven, and he allowed himself a minute to stand there on the edge of the stream and say a prayer regarding his son.

He approached the long colonnade of elms, four deep they were, from the west. It was there he came upon a statue that made him stop again.

Eagles and Prey, it was called.

He looked up at the bronze birds. Two of them, their awful talons ripping at the half-dead body of a goat. He said a second prayer then, asking God for him to shoot well and take the eyetooth from the man who took his.

To his figuring, the walk stretched from the edge of a pond, past a massive fountain and through a brick tunnel beneath the road, then up some steps and down the long colonnade, forty feet wide, that ended at another, smaller circle where the statue of Shakespeare looked down on the lesser human souls.

Bucky walked its length entirely, then positioned himself in what he determined to be the middle. He marched there, back and forth, occasionally going most of the way down its length, one way or the other, according to the instincts that rarely failed him.

72

Of course i thought about the fact that we had come full circle, meeting there like that. But from the dark of the trees, I saw that the bench where I'd first seen her was empty except for the shadows of the twisted branches above. I crossed the path and saw a dark figure to the north, heading away. Still, I hurried and kept low and to the shadows.

I found her well off the path, sitting on the crest of a spine of black rocks. She was clutching herself and swaying in a slow uneven manner. As I got closer, my eyes scanning the darkness for danger, I heard her singing softly to herself.

I traveled the length of the rocky spine, climbing to her, and saw why she was clutching herself. Under her thin coat she was wearing a dress and already there was a layer of white frost on the grass.

I called her name and she rose and, weaving her way toward me, opened her arms. I hugged her tight and we kissed each other. I felt the icy chill of her hands on my face as she separated from me.

"The money?" she said. "You have it?"

I slung the bag off my back, letting it thud down on the rock. My eyes were adjusting and I could see that hers were puffy, but moist, almost gleaming in the pale glow of the city sky.

She was stoned.

I saw the bulge in her coat pocket and reached for it. She slapped my hand away, but it hit her package and I heard the rattle of pills.

"How the hell can you think straight with that stuff?" I asked.

"I'm fine," she said, crouching to the bag. The angry look that flashed across her face made me think that maybe she was.

"I've got a car coming, but we have to pay for it," she said, counting out the bundles of money until she had ten thick wads of it. "We'll go to Canada. Buy passports. Try to get Tommy. Where is Tommy?"

"My mother."

"Good. You did good. They might watch him. Yeah, but we'll get him. We'll have the money.

"Okay," she said, rising and handing me the bundle of money. "You take this."

I did and she bent down, zipped up the bag, and put it over her shoulder. Then she stepped past me, heading for the place we met, and asked, "What time is it?"

"Eight."

"Time," she said.

My heart was pounding good. There was a charge in the air I couldn't explain. Maybe because we were going to make it, together.

We kept close to a thick oak tree. I wrapped her in my leather coat and hugged her from behind, warming my nose in her soft hair, still able to smell the hint of shampoo. She continued to softly sing. Something I couldn't make out. We kept our eyes on the road and it wasn't two minutes before we saw a set of headlights and a gold El Camino pulled over next to Shakespeare's circle.

We saw a man get out and march past us, to the middle of the path at the head of the walk. He stood there with his feet apart, his hands jammed into the pockets of his coat, glaring down the walkway as if daring someone to approach him. We eased out behind him.

"Hey," Jessica said, weaving only a little.

The man spun. It was Pete. He wore an evil grin and his eyes darted all around us.

"Where's the money?" he asked, holding out his left hand.

I nodded and held out the bundles.

"Where's the keys?" she asked.

"Set the money down," Pete said.

"Set the keys down," she said.

"You don't trust me?" Pete was grinning and I didn't like the way he kept one hand in the pocket of his coat, but he took the keys out with his free hand and jingled them in the gloom.

I set the money down and backed away.

"Toss them over," she said.

Everything happened fast. Pete tossed the keys into the air and bent like he was going for the money, but when he was halfway over, he straightened up quick, the long ugly pistol in his hand, coming our way.

I had the sense of motion in the distance behind him, but it only registered like a shadow, shifting in the dark corner of a wood. I heard the shotgun at the same time Pete's face exploded. I spun and dove, rolling and scrambling up in a crouch, moving for the trees. In the corner of my eye, I saw

Jessica sprinting for the car. Coming down the walkway at a full run was the dark figure of a man with a sawed-off shotgun—the man who blew Pete's head apart had been aiming for me. I stayed low, dodging between the trees, working my way toward the road so I could cut Jessica off.

I heard the car start and the engine rev. A shot sounded behind me. I dove to the ground as the slug whizzed past my head, thudding into a tree above me. I rolled again and came up out of it on the move. I sensed the car moving my way fast, I was almost there. I bolted from the trees into the light. Jessica swerved and slowed just a bit. I grabbed for the door handle, but she kept going. I held on, my feet dragging on the pavement until it burned right through my shoes. I was screaming at the top of my lungs.

The car was swerving, but accelerating fast. She veered, and my legs swung wide and nicked a lamppost. I thought I'd been shot and the shock made me lose my grip. I skipped across the pavement on my back and rolled to a stop. Slowly I got up, feeling for broken bones.

The pain in my knee was excruciating, my pants and the flesh were torn and I thought the white gleam in the midst of the blood was the bone of my kneecap. But, it seemed like I could walk. I moved slowly after the car, then began to limp, then hobble. Finally, I regained enough control over my legs to jog. I was almost to the bend in the road when I heard another gunshot. This time it came from far away up the road and the slug ricocheted off the pavement with a twang. I didn't look back.

Whoever it was, they were still coming after me. I bolted into the trees and wove my way back across the Literary Walk, across another road, and into some thick stuff. I felt safe there. In the dark. I knew that park and I knew there were plenty of places to hide.

73

Bucky knelt beside the lamppost and passed the beam of his pocket flashlight over the metal. He saw the fresh scrape, the white flesh, the blood. He allowed himself a small smile.

The roadside was full of grit and he could actually follow the man tracks out and up along the road, even seeing where they went back into the trees. By that time, there was blood enough for him to follow. Nothing more than a pinprick every six or seven feet, but it was fresh and it gleamed bright red under the beam of light.

He stopped to reload the shotgun and tuck it back into his coat. He didn't know where people might be in this maze of paths and woods and open grass, and it wouldn't surprise him if the shots had raised some excitement. He wasn't upset with himself. A gun of this ilk couldn't be counted on to shoot too well, and he would have had him but for the other man popping up like an arcade target.

He had reached a wide swath of open field by the time the sirens got close to where the dead man was. Too distant for him to waver in his quest.

The helicopter was another problem.

Bucky heard its chopping grunt before he could locate it. It swept out over the park from over the buildings to the west and kept going past him, he presumed for the crime scene. Nothing to worry about at the moment, so he refocused his attention to the grass. The faint white frost left clear man tracks, and Bucky jogged its length aware that Thane was beginning to drag his right leg, and picking up the pinpricks of blood on a far path. They took him over a wood bridge, smooth and bowed up in the middle.

A mallard quacked at him from the water, angry at being disturbed. It sounded right. He kept going until he could actually hear the waterfall again. It lifted his spirits. Up ahead in the darkness, he heard voices. He waved the coat aside and gripped the gun with both hands, letting the laser play along the winding path up ahead.

Someone was coming. He crouched into a shadow and let his shoulder rest against the smooth bark of a beech. He could smell the distinctly sweet scent of its decomposing leaves all around him. He could hear the footsteps now. Close. He took a breath and held it.

The man rounded the bend, and Bucky laid the red dot on his nose. The man swatted at it and reared back. Bucky relaxed his finger. Not his man.

Whoever it was, he had his cell phone out, crashing down through the woods like an idiot, yelling into the phone.

Not good. Not with a helicopter about.

Bucky set his mouth and kept on up the path without bothering looking for blood. The man had been ruffled before the laser sight. Probably at the sight of Thane, dragging his bloody leg. Bucky jogged with his mouth open, stepping softly, the better to hear. Something loomed up ahead. There were lights. Not many. A stone building.

Bucky remembered the map. Belvedere Castle it was called. The high point in the park. He recollected there were stairs going down, but only on one side, past a garden and some kind of theater.

Bucky stopped going up. He turned to the left and slipped through the woods, keeping what lights the castle showed to his right, circling the hill, cutting off the escape.

He circled the castle, past the theater and through the garden and up the rough-hewn stone steps. Up the rock cliff, the castle sat, waiting. Bucky crouched over the path and scanned it hard for a sign in case he'd already come down this side. Nothing.

He started slowly up the steps, quiet. He knew he had him, it was a matter of time. But the helicopter was coming his way. It was back there, buzzing like a chainsaw on a fall day when you wanted to listen for the step of a hoof. It couldn't be helped.

Neither could the sound of car engines, moving fast through the park, brakes screeching and tires squealing.

"Sumbitch," Bucky said, allowing himself that luxury in all this noise.

He began to hurry. He heard shouting on the far side. The copter was above him, piercing the night with its brilliant beam, adding to the light of the iron lampposts on the rampart. And in it, Bucky saw the dots of blood. They led across the stone courtyard, and he saw to where. A dark, hidden corner of the rampart. Crouched down, his hands over his head, was Thane.

Bucky stood straight and swept aside the long coat, raising the gun. His chest heaved with the effort of his run, and he paused an instant to gain his composure for a certain kill shot.

The red dot fell on Thane's center. It was an instant too long. The figure of a woman stepped between him and his mark. She was pointing a pistol at him, double-clutched.

"Drop it!" she yelled.

The red dot from his shotgun's sight settled just above her Adam's apple. The shot would punch through her neck and smash her brainstem, killing her instantly. She'd never pull the trigger. He could put her down and then kill Thane. Bucky took a deep breath, then let it out, his shoulders sagging.

"Hello, Agent Lee," he said.

His finger came off the trigger and he let the gun drop.

74

But they got her?" he asks.

I nod and say, "They picked her up getting on a bus in Massena and busted her for the drugs. Ten years, they told her she'd get that for sure, taking that much across the border. Half the time in New York, you do more time for drugs than killing someone. Like Bucky. Five years' probation he got for killing that guy."

"She turned on you too?"

I smile at him and say, "You think because of what she did that she didn't care?"

He shrugs.

"She didn't know I had ahold of the door handle," I say. "I believe that. I also know that she was always one step ahead. Her stop for a Dictaphone before she found Johnny G at the Met? She had what they wanted. Johnny G on tape, taking credit for Milo."

"But you're here," he says.

"Not for the three life sentences they wanted," I say, watching his face. "She lawyered up the minute they put the cuffs on her. Total immunity, for giving them Johnny G.

I cut my own deal. Pled guilty to manslaughter one. Twelve years. That meant six."

"But she never testified," he says.

I look away, squeezing the ducts in the corners of my eyes.

"She kind of left that to me, right?" I say.

"The money?"

"I think she figured they'd blame me since I was the man."

"Who?"

"The union."

"But they didn't?"

"Apparently not."

75

THE MAN RUBBED HIS EYES and shook the sleep from his head. He put his seat up, pushed off the thin airline blanket, and looked out the window. The misty clouds gave way to the lush green hills outside Milan. It reminded him of the Catskills.

Inside the airport, he looked for a sign. The guy was a kid, practically. Long dark hair pushed behind his ears, a dark leather coat with a lime green button-down shirt underneath. He spoke English and as they traveled north toward Como, the two of them smoked up a storm and the kid told him what he knew.

"She buy Apuzzi Palace two year. Seven million," he said. "Call it Black Hole now. Old palace. One day, very nice."

"The fuck is that?" the man asked.

The kid rumpled his brow.

"Why?" the man said, speaking slowly. "Why Black Hole?"

"Like a spider," he said, nodding to make the man understand. "Everything go in. Nothing out."

"Spider?"

"Spider hole. Black hole," the kid said, shrugging and lighting up another cigarette. "Many packages. Many deliveries. Food. Furniture. Clothes. Jewelry. Even cars. Much much money. But nothing come out. No people. No garbage. Nothing."

"The *fuck*?"

The kid shrugged. "Big. Very big palace. You'll see."

When the road from Milan split at the south end of the lake, they went right, into the town of Como. The sun came out. Narrow streets. Old stone buildings. Churches. Shops. Men in suits riding Vespas. Kids wearing colorful sneakers. Dogs hunched down and hurrying between cars. They twisted and turned, finally catching sight of the lake nestled between the ancient mountains. The piers of the town extended out into the glittering water, welcoming tour boats, classic wooden Chris-Crafts, an occasional Scarab.

There was only one road on the east side of the lake, a winding course that followed the curve of the precipitous hillside. Below, between the road and the water, nestled in ancient trees, were the stone mansions from another age. The Apuzzi Palace was surrounded by a white stone wall. Like the palace itself, the wall was chipped and worn, black at the seams, gray on its face. Impressive, but only from a distance. Grand.

When they pulled in through the great iron gates, the man saw the damp weeds, the rotted window sashes, the cracked panes, the missing roof tiles, and the dark green mold that crept up out of the earth to stain the crooked shutters. They came to a stop in the cobblestone circle and mounted the sweeping steps. The doors were bound in rusted iron, rotted timbers with cracks big enough to look through.

They got out and the man nudged the kid, holding out his hand.

"Oh," the kid said, digging into his pocket and producing a small switchblade. "Here."

The man opened it and shaved some of the hairs off his arm, then closed it and put it in his own pocket, keeping his hand there. On the way around back, the man stopped to peer through the dirty windows of a ten-bay detached garage. Inside, the cars were three-deep and coated in dust. Mercedeses. Volvos. Porsches. One was a Bentley. He pursed his lips into a silent whistle.

Out back, there was a series of terraces that descended to the water's edge. Rotted poles, painted with fading barber stripes, suspended the skeleton of a dock. The hedges were overgrown and the pool was empty except for a few inches of green slime in the very bottom. They looked up at the palace. Two three-story wings extended off to either side of the main structure. The only sign of habitation was the boxes and furniture crowded against many of the windows.

The kid led him to a locked door, but when the man pushed his hand against it, it bowed inward.

"Shit," he said, and kicked it in.

Inside, he twitched his nose.

"You smell that?"

The kid pinched his nose and rolled his eyes.

"Like a fucking dead animal or something," the man said, putting his hand over his face.

The room was filled with boxes stacked halfway to the sixteen-foot ceilings.

"Look," the kid said, running his hand along the edge of one of the bigger boxes, "Subzero is good, no?"

The man gawked at the boxes. Lamode china. Lalique

figurines. Stuff that was like gold if you could get it off the docks in Newark.

There was electronics, cookware, furniture, luggage, clothes. All new, in unopened boxes. They wove their way through the maze of narrow lanes that reminded the man of the streets they'd come through in Como. One smaller room was completely filled with shoes and purses. Prada. Gucci. Louis Vuitton. Even the man knew about that shit. Another room was filled to the top with boxes of food, most of it canned, some spilled open. Peaches. Spaghetti. Soup. Pudding.

"The fuck?" the man said.

The deeper they went into the palace, the more it smelled. The man put his sleeve to his face, pressing his arm tight to his nose.

One doorway had a set of stairs that descended into a basement. The smell wafting up out of it was excruciating. The man poked his head through the doorway and started to retch, backing up and bumping the kid.

They staggered away and rounded a corner where they found a grand curving staircase that led to the upper floors. There was a dirty track up the middle of the faded green carpet and they followed it. There were fewer boxes upstairs, but the rooms were uninviting, each one crammed with dusty furniture the way the man remembered his grandmother's attic in Howard Beach.

Toward the end of the hall, the bedrooms on either side were overflowing with catalogues and newspapers. It looked like a recycling center with stacks that spilled out into the hallway and only the narrow track that cut through the center to what was obviously the master suite.

The smell got stronger there, but it was a different

smell than the basement. It was the ripe smell of a human being, sour, pungent, but not like the sewage smell from below. The man thought he heard someone babbling, and he flicked out his knife. His heart pounded. It sounded like a monster movie in there.

He pushed the kid aside and gripped the ornate door handle.

It was locked.

The mewling noise from behind the door rose and fell, then went silent.

He stepped back and kicked it in. The door sprang open, then bounced back at them, giving him just a glimpse of ragged hair and a dirty white bed canopy.

Jessica lay face up on the bed, her skin white and pasty. Glassy-eyed. Her lips quivering in rapture. Her hair was matted and dirty. Her emaciated arms were webbed with pale green veins and spotted with tiny bruise marks. A heroin needle hung limp from her flesh. Bony fingers pawed feebly at the dirty bedspread.

The man breathed through his mouth and stepped up to the bed. He put one palm on her forehead and slit through the side of her throat. The carotid artery spewed blood. Her eyes rolled up into her head and she smiled. Something about it made the man look around for something heavy to smash her face in with, but by the time he had wrenched a marble lamp free from the desk, she was dead.

76

I look away, letting him know that I'm finished, thinking back to the winter day in the yard when I first heard the story told to me by a guy in here for armed robbery whose cousin was connected to the union.

"I'm sorry," the shrink says.

"Yeah, well."

"Does that worry you?"

"Them?"

"For your son? You?"

"They don't bother with people's kids. And they never got anyone in a Witness Protection Program before. It's a hundred percent."

"I've heard that," he says. He takes a deep breath, pats the tabletop, and stands up. "Well."

"Cured, huh?"

"You've come to grips with what happened," he says. "Most people never get that far."

He holds out his hand. I take it, and we smile.

My cell is emptied out. Already waiting for the next sucker. Two federal agents from Witness Protection arrive in the afternoon. They look at me like I'm something stuck to their shoe and give me a dossier on who I am. I have a history. An uncle with a glass eye. A mom with parents from Dublin. A collie I grew up with. An odd little story that all adds up.

They put me on a small private plane and we take off heading west. They've lined up a job at a metal shop on the edge of town in Bozeman, Montana. I did some metal-work in middle school and it's the best I can do among the choices they're giving me. Everything is very low-key. A brown two-bedroom ranch down a gravel road. A small green four-door Chevy. I'm not to go to the same store more than once a month. I will keep a log.

The big agent with the crew cut, Karp, he's staying with me for a time. A real treat, seeing his bland pasty face staring at the TV every afternoon when I get home. The way he breathes through his nose with a little whistling noise while we assault our frozen dinners across a little round Formica table in the kitchen.

The night before he's to leave, I find him on the front stoop, watching the lightning flashes, the wind whipping at his flannel shirt, hands stuffed deep in his pockets.

"So this shit works?" I say.

He looks at me and offers a smile that quickly fades before he nods.

"They never got one of your guys?"

"It's impossible," he says. "Sometimes I'm sorry to say that."

"'Cause that's what we deserve?"

He stares into my eyes for a moment, then shrugs and says, "A deal's a deal. And we always keep our part. That's the difference."

He pushes past me and in through the front door.

"Nice knowing you too," I say in a voice he can't hear.

When he does leave, though, I actually miss the company. I have been warned about relationships. Friends are a no-no. A woman is okay, just not a married one. I keep my eyes open for the single type, but Bozeman is no big city and I'm not allowed to join any organizations where you might meet one.

There are woods at the end of my lane, though. Woods that stretch up into the hills. Woods where deer and bear battle to live.

I go to Wal-Mart and look at the guns, intend to heft one, but change my mind. I buy a compound bow instead and listen to the kid behind the counter tell me about the elk. My blood heats up a bit and I buy a target to set up in back of my house, and some field points for the arrows to practice with.

The mindless work in the metal shop doesn't kill me. I buy a cookbook and do a little of that. Do I think of her? Of course. But it's him I think about mostly, hoping that he's thinking about college now, knowing he'll have the money to get there, wondering if he has any fond memories of me at all and will I ever see him again.

By the time the nights get cold, I'm good enough with the bow to take it out into the woods. I put up several tree stands along a high ridge where the game move at dawn and dusk. My farthest outpost is in the crook of a tall beech beside a narrow hissing brook. I leave work early one day and hike in.

I fall asleep there, just listening. When I wake I know it's too dark to hunt. The flying squirrel I sometimes see chitters and takes off into the dark space, flapping his mammal wings and wavering through the darkness.

When a branch snaps, my heart stops.

"Hello?" I say. My mouth dries up and a shiver runs

through me. I scurry down and creep along the bank of the stream. I am totally aware of the world around me. The mossy smell of the air and the trees. The sound of the water. The blackness of night. And I know I'm not alone. I freeze and stare hard at the vague shapes in the darkness behind me, my stomach sick, fear coursing through my blood. I sense a bit of movement, and hear the faintest metallic click.

Orange flame lights up the trees, and my chest burns for a moment before I lose my breath and grow numb. My fingers dig into the soft moss and I scuff up dead leaves with the heels of my boots. Something warm fills my mouth and trickles from the corner down my cheek while the rest of me goes cold.

The black shadow of a man leaps the stream and looms over me. He snaps on a light, blinding me, and scans the steaming wound in my chest before he clears his throat. The light drops down beside his leg. In the glow I see the long drooping mustache. The sad dark eyes. Empty eyes that remind me of my own when I'm shaving and thinking of the son I'll never see.

The batteries in the flashlight rattle as he clasps it alongside the barrel of the big gun. When he raises it, I lose sight of the face.

All I see now is that cold blinding light, and everywhere around it ... darkness.

About the Author

TIM GREEN is the bestselling author of ten previous thrillers, as well as two works of nonfiction, including the *New York Times* bestseller *The Dark Side of the Game*. After playing eight years in the NFL and becoming a member of the New York State Bar, he worked as a featured commentator on *Good Morning America*, National Public Radio, and FOX Sports. Tim lives with his wife and four children in upstate New York, where he's writing his next book and practicing law.

1

Sam's head was back against the wall, his eyes painfully closed—the look of a refugee. Crusted blood caked the edges of his nostrils and sloppy crimson smears marked the trail that must have run down either side of his mouth and off his chin. His white Yankees T-shirt, oversized to hide a stomach that spilled over his belt, was stained and spotted and rumpled.

Jake's jaw tightened and he drew deep breaths of air through his nose. He flung open the door and Sam looked at him, blinking back fresh, seventh-grade tears. The principal, Ms. Dean, burst out of her office, shooting her glare at Jake, then Sam, then back to Jake. Ms. Dean wore a frumpy blue dress. She had a small grandmotherly face with curly white hair and petite round glasses. Hers was the sort of face you might expect to see on a can of baked beans. She tapped the backs of her fingers against the open door of a conference room and said, "In here, please."

Jake put a hand on Sam's husky shoulder, giving it a squeeze before following the principal's orders. She snapped her fingers at Sam. Jake cleared his throat, felt his cheeks go warm, and sat down at the far end of the table after folding his raincoat and laying it over the back of the chair to drip. Ms. Dean pointed to a chair and Sam sat down at the opposite end of the table. The principal put a piece of paper in front of Jake, and handed him a pen.

"An order of suspension," she said. "This is three. One more and he'll be expelled, Mr. Carlson. We can't have this fighting."

"Ms. Dean," Jake said, offering her the same smile that he used to open the hearts of total strangers.

"No, Mr. Carlson," she said, showing him her trembling palm. "I know it's been hard for Sam, losing a parent. But this school is supposed to be a safe zone for my students."

"Are you sure about what happened?"

Ms. Dean frowned, the little crescent wrinkles at the corners of her mouth rippling outward and down toward the tuft of fuzz on her chin.

"He bit them," she said.

Jake flashed a look at Sam, who only hung his head.

"I saw the teeth marks," she said, "and there was blood on his braces."

Sam tightened his lips and winced.

Jake scrawled his signature below the principal's.

"Come on, Sam," Jake said. He got up and grabbed his coat, walking past his son and letting himself out into the office.

"I think he should see Dr. Stoddard," the principal said, raising her voice. "Obviously, whatever you're doing privately isn't working."

Sam followed close behind, filling the entryway with his large presence. Jake wasn't a big man, but at just thirteen, Sam was nearly as tall and weighed about the same. It wasn't unusual for people to overestimate his age by three or four years.

Outside, Jake held the umbrella for Sam, giving him all the protection it could offer against the teeming rain. He saw Sam into the passenger side, slamming the door before collapsing the umbrella and tossing it into the trunk. He climbed into the seat of his BMW coupe and wiped away the courses of water running down his face.

"You bit them? Are you kidding me?"

Sam slumped further into the seat and deepened his scowl. He folded his thick arms across his chest and angled his head away so that Jake could see nothing of his features except the ends of those long dark lashes and the tip of his pug nose. Jake slapped the steering wheel, whipping droplets of rain from the stringy ends of his hair across the burled wood dashboard. He cursed, slammed the car into gear, and raced off into the downpour toward home. The wipers pounded out their beat, fighting off the hissing buckets of rain as they crossed the bridge to Atlantic Beach.

"My father would have kicked my ass," Jake said. "Is that what you want? Is that what this is about? I'm too easy on you? I'm your buddy and you want some goddamn assurances that I'm in charge?"

Jake pulled up short at a light, stomping on the brake so that Sam bumped his head against the dash.

"Where's your goddamned seat belt?" Jake said. "Can you follow at least one rule?"

Jake just stared at Sam until Sam popped open the door and ran out into the rain.

All Jake could do was watch as he ran across the parking lot, a husky, hunched over shape in tennis shoes whose bear-gait sent him into the misty gray rain coming in off the ocean until it swallowed him completely.

"I don't belong," Sam said, his face contorting as if someone had pinched his skin, then let go.

"I'm sorry, Sam," Jake said. He knelt down and touched Sam's shoulder.

Jake hadn't bothered with the umbrella when he went after him. His suit clung tightly to his body and dark blue dye stained the backs of his hands. Sam sat balled up underneath the boardwalk with his head between his knees, trembling. Heavy drops from the boardwalk above plunked into the lake of water surrounding them and the rain hissed as it struck the dunes beyond.

"They say you're not my dad," Sam said, his head back in his knees, his shoulders shuddering. "Everyone sees you on TV and they say you're not my dad. I tell them to shut up, but I don't look like you, and if someone hits you, you always said to hit them back."

"Sure," Jake said, moving his hand from Sam's shoulder to his dripping head, "but you don't bite people, son. You just don't."

Sam's head jerked up and his big dark eyes had that red cast.

"There was three of them. Mike Petroccelli was choking me from behind and I put my head down. I didn't bite him. He was pulling my head off and my braces cut his arm. There was three of them. I didn't bite. I swear to God."

"Is that what all these fights are about?" Jake asked. "You being adopted?"

Sam nodded his head and dropped it back between his

knees. When he spoke, his words were muffled. "I want you to find my mom."

Jake lost the feeling in his arms and legs and his head felt light.

"Your mom's gone, Sam," Jake heard himself say.

"No," Sam said, his voice barely audible above the shattering rain on the boardwalk above, "not Mom, my real mom. I want you to find her."

Jake felt his lunch pushing up into his throat and he swallowed it back down.

"The records are gone. That was part of how we got you. We wanted you so badly, your mom and I. You have to know how bad we wanted you, Sam."

"Someone knows."

"What do you mean?"

"I mean, someone out there knows. There are things on the Internet about everyone."

Jake shook his head. "You're talking about finding a person. You don't just go Yahoo it."

He studied Sam for a moment then looked at his watch. "I know you don't want to hear this, but I've got to get you home and get to the city. I got the nanny Angelina Jolie just fired."

Sam rolled his eyes.

"I know," Jake said. "Who gives a shit, right? But we get to live in a house on the beach and eat Häagen-Daz by the gallon."

"You find everyone else," Sam said, looking up at him, his eyes looking into Jake's. "That's what you do. You find people. They talk to you. That's your job. I want you to do that for me. I want to find her."

Before the crap he was doing now, Jake had spent time in the streets of Kabul and Baghdad. He'd seen the mobs, the fighting, smelled the gunpowder, the burnt and rotting flesh. That didn't scare him the way this did because this wasn't someone else's problem that Jake was there to give an account of. This was his problem, and he knew it was a problem. His instincts, the same ones that had launched his career as a journalist, had told him back when they got Sam that something was wrong. It wasn't anything on the surface; all the documents were there. The lawyers had signed off. There were assurances.

But Karen had gone through the first of many operations back then, and she was desperate for a baby, desperate because she knew that no matter how it turned out she could no longer have children of her own. And, back then, when they were praying that maybe she'd been cured, Jake wanted to give her that baby more than he'd ever wanted anything. To make her a mother. To make her life complete. And as hungry as Jake was for his own success, it paled next to the yearning he felt for Karen to have what she wanted and for her to be happy.

So he had pushed it.

Jake realized Sam was still looking into his eyes and it made him start. Sam's eyes usually shifted, his head tilting down, his face disappearing beneath that dark thatch of unruly hair. This time though, Sam held his gaze. Maybe it was because Jake had seen that same desperate look in the faces of so many strangers that, despite the fact he was scared, he said yes.

"Okay, Sam," he said. "I'll find her. I'll try."